PRAIS[
*THE SECRET (*

'*The Secret of Elephants* is a novel о.  .
Prepare to fall in love with Vasundra Tailor's writing, I know I
did . . .'

—Amanda Prowse

'Tailor's debut is both evocative and intriguing.'

—Booklist

'A beautiful and thought-provoking tale which looks at the themes
of family, class, tragedy, secrets, betrayal and forgiveness.'

—Jen Med's Book Reviews

'A lush, intriguing, absorbing debut by Tailor that does a lovely
job of blending historical events, intense emotion, and thought-
provoking fiction.'

—What's Better Than Books

# The
# PROMISE
## of
# RAIN

ALSO BY VASUNDRA TAILOR

The Secret of Elephants

# The PROMISE of RAIN

## VASUNDRA TAILOR

LAKE UNION
PUBLISHING

Text copyright © 2024 by Vasundra Tailor
All rights reserved.

Published by Lake Union Publishing, Seattle

www.apub.com

Amazon, the Amazon logo, and Lake Union Publishing are trademarks of Amazon.com, Inc., or its affiliates.

ISBN-13: 9781542039413
eISBN: 9781542039406

Cover design by Emma Ewbank
Cover image: © Andreas M / Unsplash; © RooM the Agency
© Westend61 GmbH © mauritius images GmbH / Alamy Stock Photo

Printed in the United States of America

*For my two precious angels – Maya and Amelie*

'All things must come to the soul from its roots, from where it is planted.'

*St Teresa of Ávila 1515–82*

# PART 1

# Chapter 1

## *North London, July 2018*

He didn't want to discuss it. He didn't even want to contemplate it. Her mother had given her strict instructions not to ask him any questions. But Anna needed to know. Now, more than ever.

As she parked her car outside the surgery, Anna pondered over the best time to raise the subject again. The previous day, she had found something in her parents' cupboard that she'd never seen before. She'd been stunned by the explanation her mother had given her. But it had only heightened her curiosity.

She turned off the engine and sat for a moment clutching the object she'd discovered. It was a gold chain with a freely hanging pendant. Anna wore it round her neck. She gazed at the gold disc, the size of a penny coin, shiny and bright, freshly polished the night before. Her middle name 'INDIRA' was engraved on it in capital letters.

She'd been searching for something else when she stumbled upon it. Her mother had asked her to check if her passport was still valid for their upcoming trip abroad. Nestled beneath the folder that held all their important documents, she noticed a brown envelope with her name inscribed on it. The necklace had slipped out when she turned the envelope over.

'I'm guessing this is my thirtieth birthday present,' she'd playfully remarked to her mother with a cheeky grin.

Anna had been startled by her mother's reaction. With a horrified and enraged expression, her mother had leapt out of her chair and snatched the necklace from Anna's hand.

'That doesn't belong to you!' she'd hissed, glancing anxiously over her shoulder.

'But it has my name on it,' Anna had responded, perplexed, seeking an explanation.

Her mother had hesitated and dodged all her questions. However, once she had composed herself and considered how much she would disclose, she revealed that the necklace belonged to another Indira, someone connected to Anna's father from the time before his adoption.

Anna had always been aware of her father's adoption, but she knew nothing about his life before it.

'I don't understand,' she'd declared. 'Why have I never seen this before? And how come it's got my name engraved on it?'

With a sigh, her mother had returned to her seat and stared hard at the necklace in her hand. After a long minute of silence, she'd said wearily: 'This is your father's only possession from the time of his birth. He has no clue about this other Indira, but I persuaded him that we should name you after her. It seemed the right thing to do.'

Anna had gaped in disbelief. Her parents had told her they'd chosen her middle name because they wanted to acknowledge her father's Indian heritage. Now, however, she was hearing a different story.

'Look, Anna,' her mother had said firmly. 'Your father is very sensitive about his past. You are well aware of that. So don't go asking him any questions, okay? All he can tell you is that he's had this necklace since he was born. Nothing more. Just accept that and move on.' She paused, deep in thought, her eyebrows furrowing in concentration. Then, with a brisk nod, she returned the necklace to Anna. 'You might as well keep this now. I will speak to your father later to explain.'

Anna had left her parents' house with more questions than answers. Shaking her head in frustration, she gazed out of her car window, contemplating whether she would ever learn the truth about her father's birth. She took a deep breath and readied herself to step out. A sudden tap on the window made her jump. Peering in with a smile was Tom, the senior partner at their surgery. He opened the door and stepped aside while she climbed out.

'How's my favourite doctor?' he asked with a twinkle in his eye.

'Fine,' said Anna, her heart fluttering under the warmth of his gaze. They had been together for nearly two years yet his charm never failed to make her feel like an infatuated schoolgirl.

'You seemed lost in thought. What's up?'

'Erm . . . I'll tell you later. There's something I need to sort out with my parents.'

'Okay.' He gestured towards the entrance of the surgery. 'Ready for the onslaught?'

Anna nodded, walking alongside him into the building. She knew there'd be a long list of patients to see before the day was over. They parted ways at the reception desk, with Tom wishing her a good day. Anna watched him disappear through the swinging doors, before shifting her gaze to the waiting area. It was eight thirty in the morning, and the room was already filled with people. Anna put her personal concerns aside and focused her attention on the needs of her patients.

'Good morning, Anna,' the senior receptionist greeted. Lowering her voice, she discreetly pointed towards a patient seated in the back row. 'You should see Mrs Thakur first. She's in a bad way.'

Anna turned her attention towards the back and saw a young woman in a *salwar kameez*, her head partially covered by a scarf concealing half of her face. Her gaze was lowered, and she seemed huddled into a ball, as if wishing to be invisible.

Anna frowned. 'Give me two minutes, then send her in.'

In her office, Anna logged on to the computer system and signed in. She was scanning through Gita Thakur's medical records when there was a gentle tap on the door.

'Come in.' She watched her patient enter the room slowly and take a seat gingerly on the chair beside her desk. 'Hello, Gita.'

'Hello,' Gita croaked. Trembling, she slowly pulled back the *odhani* that covered her head. Keeping her gaze lowered, she lifted her chin to reveal what she'd been concealing.

Anna fought back a gasp. Gita's face was covered in bruises, a patchwork of purple, black, and blue, marring her otherwise smooth, dark skin. Fresh cuts, still unhealed, were visible beneath her red and swollen eyes.

'My God! What has he done to you?' Anna exclaimed, shock and concern evident in her voice.

Gita raised her eyes, and Anna could see the despair in them. With slumped shoulders, Gita clasped her hands together tightly.

'He's gone too far this time,' said Anna as she reached for Gita's hand to see the bruises on her lower arms. 'Where else did he hurt you?' she asked gently.

Gita gestured towards her thighs and back. Silent tears trickled down the wounds on her cheeks. Anna squeezed her hand but quickly released it when Gita winced. She had clearly endured a severe beating.

As Anna watched the woman weeping piteously, her heart went out to her. She had confided in Anna about the circumstances that had brought her from India to the UK. Gita had arrived as an eighteen-year-old bride, following a husband she barely knew. She'd married him to please her parents. He was twelve years her senior and a perfect stranger. She'd discovered only after the wedding that her husband had a learning disorder that affected his ability to understand and think things through.

Five years previously, his mother had brought him to their village in Gujarat, seeking a suitable wife. Gita's parents had viewed it as an opportunity for their daughter to have a better life abroad. Little did they anticipate the cruelty she would endure.

Anger rose up Anna's throat. Gita was her third domestic violence patient in just as many months. Each time a victim of abuse walked through her door, Anna's outrage bubbled over. Their plight had prompted her to join a charity dedicated to supporting victims of domestic abuse. She regularly volunteered for the organisation as a medical advocate.

During her three years at the medical practice, Anna had witnessed far too many women brutally assaulted by their husbands or partners. However, in Gita's case, it was not her husband who was attacking her; it was her husband's younger brother.

'You need to move away, Gita; both you and your husband.'

Gita shook her head. 'My husband will never leave. You know how it is in Indian families.'

'I'm afraid I don't know what that's like. I'm not from an Indian family,' Anna clarified.

People often made that mistake because of her South Asian features and having Indira as her middle name. But Anna was only half Indian. The other half of her heritage was Black Zimbabwean. Anna knew a lot about her African heritage but sadly, nothing at all about her Indian ancestry.

Reflecting on her dual heritage always depressed Anna. Being mixed race was not a problem; it was the lack of knowledge about her full history. This gap in her understanding of herself loomed like a dark cloud, casting shadows over many aspects of her life.

'Please listen, Gita. One day you will end up in hospital or worse. I hope that this time, you will consider going to the police. There's enough evidence to have him arrested.'

Terrified of the potential repercussions, Gita refused to report the abuse or seek refuge in a shelter for victims. Frustrated, Anna had suggested she return to her parents in India. But Gita insisted that such a decision would bring shame upon her family.

It made no sense to Anna. Shaking her head, she picked up the phone and called the practice nurse to tend to Gita's injuries. As the nurse attended to Gita, Anna typed up a prescription for painkillers and electronically sent it to Gita's nominated pharmacy to be picked up when she was ready.

Once they were alone again, Anna tried to persuade Gita to move away from the constant danger within her home. 'The beatings are not going to stop, you know.'

Gita's voice barely rose above a whisper as she responded, 'I know.' She paused, then spoke with a little more conviction. 'So . . . can I still go to the shelter?'

'Of course!' Anna was surprised and relieved. Finally, her patient was taking her advice. 'I'll contact the safeguarding team. They always take prompt action. Do you want to go today?'

Gita nodded, her gaze shifting to the carrier bag she had brought along. 'I put some clothes and things in there.'

'That was good thinking. I'm really glad you've made this decision. Come with me. I'll take you to our practice manager who will make all the necessary arrangements. Someone will come here to pick you up and take you to a shelter where you will finally be safe.'

Gita pulled her *odhani* over her head once again, looking agitated. 'My brother-in-law will come looking for me.' Her face was creased with fear.

Anna assured her that the practice staff knew how to handle such situations. Hoping to calm her nerves, she promised to visit her at the shelter as soon as possible. Gita took a deep breath and followed Anna, her eyes cast downward.

Leaving Gita in the capable hands of their practice manager, Anna returned to her office, feeling a vague sense of dissatisfaction with herself. She hadn't managed to persuade Gita to involve the police. Another perpetrator of domestic abuse was getting away with his criminal behaviour. There were far too many women like Gita suffering in silence. Anna wished there was more help out there for them to have their voices heard.

The receptionist popped her head round the door. 'You look like you could do with a nice cup of tea. Shall I bring one over before your next patient?'

Anna smiled gratefully. A lot of people were waiting to see her, and she needed to regain her focus. She worked diligently throughout the rest of the day, taking only a brief break for a sandwich at her desk. But all day long, she couldn't shake off the despondency that sat on her shoulders, weighing her down.

Finally, when it was time to go home, Anna logged out and switched off her computer. She looked forward to a quiet evening in her flat with Tom. Although he didn't live with her, he stayed over whenever he could. Anna made her way to his office and stood outside his door, listening for the sound of voices from within. Hearing nothing, she knocked and entered.

Tom looked up from his computer and smiled.

'Still working?' she asked, taking a seat across from him with a heavy sigh.

'No. Just logging off.' He frowned. 'Why the sad face?'

Anna sighed again. 'I had another domestic abuse patient today. I find those cases really tough.'

'I know you do. But don't beat yourself up. I'm sure you did your best,' Tom reassured her.

'I wonder,' said Anna, looking depressed.

Tom studied her for a moment before leaning forward. 'You're a good doctor, Anna. Never doubt yourself.'

Anna lifted her shoulders and inhaled noisily. Tom shook his head, making a tsk sound. Then he smiled and turned to his in-tray. He pulled out an envelope and handed it to her. 'I'm sure this will cheer you up. Have a look.'

The envelope was white, adorned with foreign stamps and marked with various postmarks. It was addressed to Dr Anna Indira Kotze MBChB MRCGP c/o Dr Thomas Ingles.

Intrigued, Anna carefully opened it and retrieved a one-page letter. It was from India. As she read the contents, astonishment swept over her. It was an invitation from a pharmaceutical company to attend a medical conference in Delhi. She'd never been invited to an event outside the UK before.

Anna looked at the dates for the event. It was for five days in January 2019, in six months' time. She stared at the letter for a moment, thinking that there had to be some mistake. If it wasn't a mistake, it was a welcome surprise.

She'd always wanted to visit India. Her dream was to go there with her father, who had a connection with India. The problem was, he had no interest whatsoever in making that trip. Anna was keen to get a sense of the country and to meet people with whom they both shared a heritage. But he was resolute in his opposition to visiting India.

Bringing her eyebrows together, she questioned Tom. 'Why am I receiving this? I don't understand.'

'It's because I asked the pharma company to invite you. I conducted some research for them and they want me to present my findings at this conference. They also need me to be the chair for the entire week. I agreed on the condition that they extended the invitation to my esteemed colleague, Dr Anna Indira Kotze.'

'Is that allowed?'

'Of course, it is. You assisted me with the research. Have you forgotten?'

Anna recollected. 'Was it that survey I carried out when I first joined the practice?'

Tom confirmed with a nod. Double-checking the dates, Anna realised that if she attended the conference, it would be immediately after a three-week holiday she had already booked.

'You know I'm on annual leave in December,' she reminded Tom. 'I'm going to Zimbabwe with my parents.'

Tom shrugged. 'That's no problem. We have ample time to find locum cover.' Giving her a winsome smile, he lowered his voice. 'Think about it, Anna. The two of us travelling together to India. You told me you always wanted to go. And Delhi is not far from the Taj Mahal. Wouldn't it be great to go there together?'

Anna smiled. This was a good opportunity for her. But she couldn't help thinking of her father. Despite his reluctance to visit India, she still held on to the hope that one day, he would change his mind.

Tom was watching her keenly. 'This is about your father, isn't it? About his mysterious past.'

Anna gave a slow nod. 'I told you how funny he is about India. He was born in Zimbabwe, but India is where his roots are. So I don't understand why he refuses to go there. And I know he loved his adoptive parents, but he's very strange about his biological family. He's not the slightest bit curious about them. He says he doesn't need to know. But I do, and I can't let it rest.'

Tom was curious. 'Why does it matter so much? And why now?'

'It's always mattered, Tom. I just don't like to go on about it. But yesterday, I found this at my parents' house.' Anna pulled out her gold chain from around her neck. She held up the pendant so he could see the name engraved on one side of the shiny disc.

'This was once owned by someone else called Indira. My dad has had it with him ever since he was a baby. But he's never shown it to me and yesterday was the first I heard of it. My parents kept this hidden from me all this time. It clearly meant something to them because they named me Anna Indira. This necklace is the only thing my father has from his birth family, yet he's never made any attempt to trace it back to them. Don't you think that's odd?'

Tom conceded that it was. 'Have you asked him why he hasn't?'

'I have. He says he's not interested in his past. I've asked him many times to tell me what he knows, but he just clams up. He hates talking about it. My mum says I should leave it alone because he has nothing to tell me. But he must know something!'

'Is there anyone else you can ask? Another family member, maybe?'

'No. My father has no family of his own. You know, growing up, I always wished there was someone who could teach me something about the Indian culture. Without that, I've always felt incomplete.'

'But you do know about your mother's culture, don't you?'

'Yes. I know all about my mother's Black Zimbabwean background. I've met my mother's siblings and all her cousins. But on my dad's side, there's just nothing.'

Tom looked thoughtful. 'If your father has never spoken about it, he must have a good reason for keeping silent. Maybe you should let it go, Anna, for *his* sake.'

'That's just it! I can't let it go.' Anna furrowed her eyebrows in frustration. 'I have no information about one side of my family. Wouldn't you want to know who your grandparents were, or what happened to them? There's a part of my history missing and I need to find it. And now that I've discovered this necklace, I'm even more eager to uncover the mystery surrounding my dad's birth.'

Tom sat back and regarded her with narrowed eyes. 'Well, how do you hope to do that?'

Anna chewed on her lower lip. She was certain that the first step was to ask her father to disclose all that he knew, even if it distressed him. She'd have to make him understand why it was important to her and how it was affecting her. The second step was to make enquiries when she visited Zimbabwe at the end of the year. That was where her father's story had begun, and it made sense to trace his history back to the place of his birth.

# Chapter 2

It was a cloudy Sunday morning when Anna drove to her parents' house, a week after she'd found the necklace. They lived in a semi-detached house on a street off the main road in Harrow in north-west London. Her dad's car was in the driveway, so Anna parked several houses down and walked back up. She rang the doorbell and waited a few moments before her father opened the door, giving her a weak smile.

'Hi Dad.' Anna kissed him on the cheek. His skin felt warm, and she detected the comforting leathery scent of his aftershave, the brand he always used and never changed. Taking a few steps inside the hall, the herby smells of cumin, coriander, ginger and garlic enveloped her.

'What's cooking?' she asked her mother who was stirring something on the cooker. A delicious aroma filled the air. Her mother turned around to let Anna kiss her cheek. The two of them were of similar height and and both had curly jet-black hair. Anna's tight curls were shoulder length while her mother combed back her Afro-textured hair in a bun at the back of her head. Their facial features were also different. Anna's mother had a round face, wide nose and full lips. Like her father, Anna had an oval-shaped face, straight nose and thin lips. She'd also inherited his bushy eyebrows, something she could have done without.

'Chicken curry, the way you like it without too much spice,' answered her mother. Seeing her husband slipping past them to go out to the back, she asked him to stop. 'Mathew, can you pick a few green apples for me? I want to make some pickle.'

Moving away to let her mother finish cooking lunch, Anna followed her father through the double glass doors into the long, narrow garden. He went straight to the middle right of the neat, tidy lawn to one of their two leafy apple trees. They were both laden with firm, green cooking apples. He picked five or six from the low branches and took them back to the kitchen.

'These okay, Theresa?'

'Perfect.'

Anna went to sit on their old garden swing on the lawn just off the patio. The sun was peeping out of the clouds, dropping hints that it would soon be a bright, sunny day. Stretching out her legs, Anna made herself comfortable and looked around at all the flowery plants and bushes. The garden was Mathew's pride and joy. He took great pleasure in making it look healthy and colourful. Joining her on the swing, they sat in silence, each with their own thoughts, rocking gently back and forth.

After a while, Mathew asked: 'Is your passport in date?'

'It is. So all three of us are good to go.' She smiled.

Mathew did not return the smile. Anna knew he was thinking about the necklace she'd found and was probably worried about being pressed for an explanation. She also knew that he was pleased she was going with them to Zimbabwe. They went 'home', as they called it, every few years without Anna because she was usually too busy with work or studies: five years of medical school followed by two years as a junior doctor, and finally as a qualified GP.

She watched her father sit back and survey his garden. While her mother was busy in the kitchen, Anna decided that this was a good moment to raise the topic that was foremost on their minds.

'Dad, I'm sorry to bring this up, but I have to ask you.' With a furrowed brow, he turned to face her. 'Why did you never tell me about the necklace?' She spoke softly.

His body tensed. He blinked a few times then looked away, hands clasped on his lap. She placed her hand on his and squeezed. 'Please don't get upset. I just need to know.'

'I don't want to discuss it, Anna.' His voice was quiet but firm.

'But why? Why can't we discuss it? You kept this necklace safe all your life and you named me Indira after the person who once owned it. It must mean something to you. Who gave it to you? Was it your adoptive parents?'

Staring into the distance, he was silent for a long minute, then he nodded, once.

'Were you very young when they gave it to you?'

Again, he nodded.

'What did they tell you about it?'

This time, he shook his head and spoke with force. 'No! The past is the past. You must leave it alone.'

'I can't leave it alone! Believe me, I've tried.' He continued to stare at something in the distance. 'Please look at me, Dad. I want to explain.'

She waited until he finally turned his face. 'When I was little, it didn't matter to me that I knew nothing about your life before you were adopted. I accepted what you told me: that Grandma and Grandpa Kotze gave you a happy childhood. I never met them, but you said they were good people and loving parents. I wish they were still with us.' She paused, hoping Mathew would say something about them. But he sat quietly, looking at her with a sad expression on his face. Anna paused, then willed herself to continue.

'The older I get, the more I want to know about your *real* parents because they were my grandparents. Now that I've seen the necklace, I can't stop thinking about them. I want to know who Indira was.'

Mathew swallowed hard, and his eyes turned misty.

Anna gave him a beseeching look. 'I'm sorry, Dad, but don't you see how important it is to find out who they were? They were a part of you and therefore a part of me. I know nothing about that side of my roots. I only know about my African side.'

'Is the African side not enough for you?' Startled, Anna turned to face her mother leaning against the back door, listening to their conversation. With arms folded, she fixed angry eyes on her daughter.

Anna clicked her tongue in annoyance. 'It's not about that, Mum. I'm proud of my African side. You know that. The point I'm making is that there is a part of my history missing, and I deserve to know about that part.'

Theresa began to walk towards them. Anna felt a shiver of apprehension as she watched her mother approach. She hoped the discussion would not morph into an argument. Anna's relationship with her mother was complicated, damaged by her forceful parenting style and demanding nature. Growing up, Anna had always been a little afraid of her. Even now, she knew it was best to stay on her good side.

On the flip side, Anna knew that her mother loved her, and if the need arose, she would be protective of her. But she seemed far more protective of her husband. Mathew was a gentle soul: quiet and mild mannered. Because of that, Theresa always felt the need to shield him from any hurt he might be feeling. The minute she thought someone was upsetting or being unfair to him, she would jump to defend him. It irritated Anna because she knew that in his own understated way, Mathew was quite capable of speaking up for himself. He had an inner strength and steely determination that Anna wished she had inherited.

Arms on hips, Theresa stood across from them, a fiery anger etched on her face. Before she could pounce, Anna put her hand to her neck and pulled out her necklace.

'You must have known I would be curious about this. It has my name on it. You chose that name for me because of this inscription. You both hid this from me for all my life. Why? What do you know about it that you haven't told me?' Anna swung round to face Mathew. 'Dad? You must know something. Please tell me.'

Theresa took a step forward and spoke with urgency. 'Listen, child. Don't go upsetting your father.'

'Mum, please. I'm entitled to know everything that you both know. Unless you tell me, I will keep asking you the same questions. I'll never stop.' Anna heard the break in her own voice. With an exasperated sigh, she sat back on the swing and fixed her eyes on the garden. Her parents' lack of understanding was hard to fathom. Why couldn't they see how deeply this was affecting her? Many times, over the years she had tried to articulate her need for information about her Indian roots and heritage. But they were never willing to discuss it.

For a while, there was silence. Anna was aware of her parents looking at one another, communicating without words. They often did this, sharing their thoughts telepathically. It was the strangest thing. They could have a long conversation just by exchanging their thoughts through the ether. The only sound was that of two red-breasted robins chirping while pecking seeds from a bird feeder on the lawn. Letting go of the pendant, Anna studied the birds, admiring their large heads, big eyes and striking orange-red bibs.

Eventually, Theresa broke the silence. 'Okay, child. Let's go inside, and we can talk over lunch.'

She didn't sound happy, and Mathew looked troubled. But clearly, they both realised that a full discussion was unavoidable. Relieved, Anna followed them in, a bubble of anticipation and anxiety fluttering in her stomach.

The cloth over the circular dining table was a typical Zimbabwean print fabric with images of elephants and African drums in alternating squares. As a child, Anna had loved the bright orange and green colours. But over the years her tastes had changed and she now found the colours too vivid and rich. Looking around the room, all the soft furnishings were brightly coloured, leaving no one in any doubt as to the origins of this family. Her parents had been in the UK for nearly forty years, but their home was still little Zimbabwe.

Mathew set the table for three, and Theresa handed over to Anna a variety of hot dishes to place around the centre. As always, it was a veritable feast with chicken curry, roasted corn on the cob, and green vegetables with herbs. Instead of rice, Theresa had made sadza, the traditional Zimbabwean staple made with cornmeal and water. Slices of buttered bread were heaped on a plate with a green salad on one side and fresh apple pickle on the other.

Anna waited for her mother to say grace. Religion was a strong driving force for Theresa. She attended the local Pentecostal church every Sunday morning. Much of her free time was given up for church events, whereas Mathew and Anna were lapsed Christians. A huge disappointment for Theresa. Over the years, Anna had noticed that her mother had given up on trying to bring them back to the faith, which brought her a sense of relief.

After the small talk and a few bites of food, Theresa gave Mathew an encouraging look. Mathew took a sip of water and cleared his throat, his gaze fixed on his plate. He began to speak, his voice shaky and filled with emotion. 'I was two months old when I was adopted. My parents told me what they knew about my birth when I was about seven years old. They told me that I was . . . that I was a . . .'

His voice faltered and he cleared his throat once more. Theresa reached out to pat his hand. They stared at one another for a moment. Anna watched her mother give Mathew a look of profound sympathy.

'It's okay, love. I can tell her if you like?' offered Theresa, raising her eyebrows. Mathew threw her a grateful look before taking another sip of water. Picking up his knife and fork, he busied himself with the food on his plate.

'Your father finds it very difficult to talk about this. That's why we never mention it. But since you feel so strongly, I will tell you everything we know. But it's going to be a shock. Be prepared.'

Anna's heart started racing, and she felt herself holding her breath.

'Your father is trying to tell you that he was a foundling.' She paused, giving Anna time to consider this. Confusion clouded Anna's face as she simply stared at her mother. Theresa continued. 'Yes. He was a foundling, left as a newborn baby outside a church door. A nun from the school attached to the church found him in the morning and took him inside.'

Anna's mind reeled, trying to make sense of it all. 'That can't be right!' she blurted out, feeling as though she had misheard. 'You told me he was an orphan living in a children's home.'

Theresa shook her head. 'We never said that. You put that thought into your head and it was easier just to let you believe that.'

Anna turned her gaze toward Mathew, hoping for some clarity or confirmation. But he kept his eyes averted, unable to meet her gaze. Turning back to her mother, Anna gathered her thoughts and spoke slowly, trying to process the information she had just received. 'Okay,' she said, her voice tinged with disbelief. 'So, Dad was found outside a church.' She allowed that image to settle in her mind. Her heartbeat pounded in her ears, and she made a conscious effort to calm herself. With a deep breath, she continued, her voice steadier this time. 'What happened after he was found?'

Theresa took another moment to chew her food before continuing the story. Anna followed suit, taking another bite, her mind racing with questions and a mixture of emotions.

When she was ready, Theresa spoke again. 'I'll start at the beginning. This is what your father's adoptive parents told him. He was born in 1954 in Zimbabwe somewhere near the city of Fort Victoria. Just newborn, he was left in a woven wicker basket with a handle. In the morning, the nun found him sleeping soundly on a soft cushion, swaddled in a white sheet and wrapped in a red shawl with Indian motifs. He had a white woolly hat on his head and a soft white baby blanket covered him to keep him warm. Under the blanket was the necklace you are wearing.'

She paused to look at Mathew, giving him a chance to comment. He said nothing, so Theresa continued. 'The church was a Christian Mission station which had a covered porch area, and the basket was inside that porch.'

Anna nodded. 'Right. The basket was not out in the open. Dad was under shelter, well covered and warm.' Hoping to bring Mathew into the conversation, she turned to him and spoke in a gentle tone. 'So, whoever left you wanted you to be safe. Wouldn't you say so?'

Still Mathew said nothing. Theresa pressed on.

'It was early morning, and the nun who opened the door looked around but saw no one nearby who might have left the basket. She took it inside and raised the alarm. There was a small school behind the church where several nuns and a priest taught the local children. They looked after your father and kept him with them for a few days.'

Again, she paused and looked at Mathew. This time he commented. 'Not a few days. They kept me for two months.'

Theresa gave him a tender smile. 'Right. It was two months. The day they found you, they called the police who searched everywhere, didn't they? They sent people out to all the surrounding areas and towns to see if anyone knew about you or saw anything that might lead to your parents.'

Anna leaned forward. 'How did they know Dad was Indian?'

'Because of his appearance; his facial features. Also the Indian shawl and the necklace with the engraving of a female Indian name.'

Anna turned to Mathew. 'What happened to the shawl and other things, Dad? Do you know?' Mathew shook his head.

Theresa answered for him. 'They must have been removed, then lost or forgotten somewhere. Unlike the gold necklace, they probably weren't considered important enough to save.'

'Pity,' said Anna.

Theresa agreed. 'The police used all the items when they carried out their search. They checked with Indian families in all the towns around the church. They drew a blank everywhere they went.'

'Do you think they did a thorough search?' Anna asked her father.

Mathew shrugged his shoulders. 'Who knows.'

Anna blew out her cheeks. It was a lot to take in and she felt quite shaky. 'I'm sorry, Dad. It must have been so hard for you when you found out.'

Mathew shrugged again, looking down, moving food around his plate.

'So, you were never in an orphanage?'

'There were no orphanages for people like me.' Mathew kept his voice flat.

'What do you mean?'

He clammed up again. Theresa explained. 'It was the time of the colour bar in Zimbabwe. Very bad for non-white people. The segregation laws meant that there were separate children's homes for white kids and black kids, but none for Indians and Coloureds. That's what mixed-race people were called: Coloureds. I know we don't use that term any more, but that was what we used to say. There weren't many Coloured and Indian people at that time so there were no orphanages for them. And because of the racist laws, none of the other homes could give your father a place.'

'So what happened?'

Theresa looked at Mathew, but he was still unwilling to take up the story. Pressing her lips together, she took a breath and continued. 'The nuns couldn't keep your father either because they were there to run a school for local black children. There was a mixed-race teacher called Mrs Kotze at the mission school. It was she and her husband who adopted your father. We know it was all done legally because we have the birth and adoption certificates.'

Once again there was silence round the table. Anna was trying to keep up with the information overload. Her brain was struggling to process it all at once. Eventually she asked: 'So Grandma Kotze was a teacher at the school?'

Mathew nodded. 'She drove in from the nearest town a few days a week.'

'What happened after the adoption?'

Mathew raised his head and looked directly at Anna. He seemed a little more confident now. Clearly, he was comfortable talking about this part of his life. 'She stopped working so she could take care of me, and we moved to the capital city where there were better job prospects for my father. I went to an Indian and mixed-race school in Salisbury. Later, I went to a secondary school called Mountford High. We lived in a suburb called Arcadia. I came to the UK in 1981 after Zimbabwe declared its independence.'

Theresa gave a short laugh. 'You left me out of the story, Mathew! Tell Anna how we met.'

Anna gave a little smile. She'd heard that narrative many times about how she had seen him at a church where choir groups from different communities were invited to sing. During the event, they had struck up a friendship. After a two-year courtship, they were married, and the rest was history, as she loved to say.

Mathew coughed. 'We don't have to go over that again.'

Theresa gave him an indulgent smile and continued the story. 'The Kotzes were good, church-going people. They had your father baptised at the church where he was found. I forget the name. What was it, Mathew?'

'Rukuvoko Church. It's on my birth certificate. Under the parents' section, it says "unknown".' His voice quivered when he uttered the last word.

Anna chewed her lip. She hated to see him distressed. Leaning towards him, she pulled forward her chain and said in a gentle tone: 'Your biological parents may be unknown, but they left you something that belonged to them: this necklace. It's a clue, Dad. Don't you want to know who Indira was?'

Mathew turned away, but not before she saw the broken expression on his face. Theresa reached out to pat his hand again.

Anna hesitated before continuing. 'I think this necklace was deliberately left by your parents so that you might follow up and find them. Why, Dad? Why have you never gone looking for them?'

Mathew shook his head. When she'd asked him before, he had shrugged his shoulders and said he didn't feel the need. He was happy without that knowledge. Anna had always found that odd.

Mathew looked at Theresa and they spoke again with their eyes. She watched her mother give Mathew a small smile of encouragement. Eventually, he looked at Anna intently and said: 'If my birth parents didn't want me, why would I want them?'

And there it was. Anna saw the hurt behind his eyes. He had been abandoned. How could anyone not be traumatised by that? Her father coped by blocking it out of his mind. He didn't want to know, and he didn't want to discuss it. But what *did* happen that day? Anna pictured a young couple leaving a newborn baby in a basket outside a church door. Surely parents would only do that if they had no other options? She didn't believe that Mathew's parents had forsaken him through choice. Something terrible must have happened for them to do such a thing, and she had to find out what that was. Seeing the pain in Mathew's face, she was even more convinced that searching for the truth was the right thing to do, not just for herself, but for her father too.

# Chapter 3

From the small balcony of her third-floor apartment, Anna watched Tom parking his car. The shiny black BMW sparkled in the evening sun as its rays slanted on to the bonnet and roof. He got out and flicked the locks before looking up. Shading his eyes with one hand, he waved with the other.

Anna smiled and went to buzz him into the building. She opened her front door and waited, listening to him quick-tapping his way up the stairs. As soon as he reached her, he lifted her off her feet and stepped into the flat. Kicking the door shut behind him, he walked into the living room with her body pressed against his.

'You're in a good mood today!' Anna laughed as he playfully showered her with kisses. At six foot two inches, he was a giant of a man: tall, broad shouldered, and starting to show a little middle-age spread. Next to him, she felt tiny. A foot shorter than him, she felt the strain on her neck as she smiled up at him.

'Why shouldn't I be? I'm with you, aren't I?' Putting her down, he settled himself on the sofa and pulled her towards him.

'How was the symposium?' she asked.

'Terrible! Everything that could go wrong did go wrong.'

'What happened?'

He exhaled noisily. 'The chair of the conference phoned in sick, and they asked me to take his place. Halfway through, the mic system broke down. The final straw was when they gave me a live survey to conduct on the screen, with two hundred international delegates sending comments through their mobile phones. It was total chaos. I mean! Why ask me to do that?'

'They obviously didn't know what a Luddite you are.' Anna patted his cheek in mock sympathy. 'Never mind, Dr Ingles. They'll know better than to ask you next time.'

'Too right they will.' Looking into her face, his eyes softened into a smile. 'Did you miss me today? How were things at the practice?'

Anna thought about Gita, her patient in the shelter for women suffering domestic abuse. They had called the practice to say Gita was asking to see her. She'd been there for over a week now but was struggling to settle in.

'I'm worried about her, Tom. Do you think I did the right thing in sending her there?'

Tom looked surprised. 'Of course, you did. She was in danger, and you found her a safe place to go. Why do you doubt yourself so much?'

Anna pursed her lips. She hated being reminded of her need for reassurance. She considered it a weakness and tried hard to hide it, especially in her workplace. Shrugging her shoulders, she gave him a weak smile. 'I do try.'

Tom tutted. 'I know you do. You did show a lot of guts when you confronted your parents last Sunday. How do you feel now that you know so much more?'

Anna considered. 'Better, I guess. But it was a huge shock to learn that Dad was a foundling. I understand now why he wants to block it from his mind. He grew up feeling that his parents rejected him. And he doesn't want to be in the position of being rejected again. That's why he has never gone looking for them. But it's different for me. I want to investigate further. I'm going to try to find my father's biological parents or at least, see if I can find out what happened to them. I'll be doing a lot of detective work when I get to Zimbabwe in December.'

Tom puckered his brows. 'That reminds me: we need to find locum cover for you. How long did you say you would be away?'

'Three weeks.'

'That's three weeks for Zimbabwe then two weeks for Delhi, right?'

Anna puckered her brows. 'I can't go to Delhi, Tom.'

'What? I thought you agreed!'

'No, Tom, I didn't agree. I just said it would be a good opportunity. But I've been thinking about it and don't feel this is the right time for me.'

Tom screwed up his eyes. Anna knew he was annoyed. He stared at her for a moment, then shook his head.

'This is what frustrates me about you,' he said with deep wrinkles on his forehead. 'You can never make up your mind.'

Anna breathed in, looking away. She didn't want to admit that she hoped to visit India with her dad, not him. After her discussion with her parents, she was even more convinced of that.

Tom watched her for a moment then gave a loud sigh. 'Why do you do this? Why do you go quiet on me?'

When Anna remained silent, he blew out his cheeks. 'Speak to me, Anna, for God's sake! I never know what's going on in that head of yours. You're so emotionally unavailable sometimes. I wish you would let me in.'

Anna watched him wrestling with his annoyance, trying to curb his impatience with her. He'd complained to her before about her unwillingness to share her feelings with him. She was aware there was some truth in that. She found it difficult to open up to him. Then again, she found this difficult with everyone, even with her parents. Something deep inside her always prevented her from speaking up, letting people in.

Anna had often wondered if this was a result of her not knowing her roots. She didn't know where she came from; not fully. She felt different from other people. She had tried to explain this to Tom, just as she did to her parents. But it was a struggle to articulate her emotions. No one seemed to understand that deep down, she felt like she was not in the driving seat of her own life.

'I'm sorry,' she said, giving Tom a weak smile.

'Fine,' he replied, in a voice filled with reproach. 'I'll explain to the conference organisers that I'll be going on my own.'

Anna sat up and kissed him lightly on the lips. 'Thanks,' she murmured. 'We'll go together another time. I *do* want to see the Taj Mahal with you.'

Tom grunted but said nothing.

Anna took his hand in hers. 'You haven't forgotten our trip to Brighton this weekend, have you?' At his request, she had booked a two-day trip to the seaside resort to get away from their busy lives in London. 'Our hotel is right next to the Royal Pavilion.'

'The Royal Pavilion is not the Taj Mahal,' he said drily.

Anna gave a short laugh. 'Maybe not. But we can pretend it is, can't we? You have to admit, it does look like an Indian palace.'

Tom rolled his eyes. He was clearly still disgruntled. But Anna knew he would be in better spirits when they were away on their own. She looked forward to the weekend.

~

On the evening before they were to set off for Brighton, Anna came home from work with a spring in her step. The weather was warm and sunny even at 7 p.m., and sunshine was predicted for Brighton throughout the weekend.

Tom had agreed to pick her up early on Saturday morning for the 50-mile drive from London. Anna was packing a few clothes into an overnight bag when her doorbell rang. Looking through the peephole, she was surprised to see Tom on the other side.

'This is a nice surprise,' she said. 'How did you get in?'

'I followed when someone else was buzzed in.'

'Oh. I didn't know you were coming tonight.'

'I came straight from the practice.' Giving her a kiss, he followed her into the lounge. 'I've got some bad news.' Running his fingers through his hair, he took a seat and stared up at her with a frown. He reached for her hand.

Anna felt a twinge in her stomach. She had a sense of what he was going to say.

'It's about tomorrow . . .'

Anna narrowed her eyes. She stared at him for a moment, then took back her hand.

'We're not going to Brighton, are we?' She pouted, and even to her own ears she sounded like a grumpy teenager.

His answer was an anxious, beseeching look. With a slow shake of her head, Anna stepped back and walked away to the balcony, disappointed and furious with him for letting her down. The trip was meant to be a celebration of their second anniversary together.

Her mood took a sudden dip and her happiness evaporated like water in dry air. Struggling to hide her emotions, she stared mindlessly beyond the perimeter hedge at the cars driving past. It wasn't the first occasion Tom had let her down. Their plans had been scuppered many times at the last minute. Closing her eyes, Anna gripped the metal bar on the balustrade.

Tom came to stand behind her. Wrapping his arms around her waist, he brought his lips to her ear. 'I'm sorry. The kids are coming to me tomorrow. She has to go away this weekend.'

Anna frowned. It was forever thus. *She.* His high-powered IT consultant ex-wife. Constantly making him change his plans, she had too much power over him even though they were divorced. It didn't seem right. Unfolding herself from his arms, Anna went back inside. She took a seat, picked up her remote control and started to flick through the television channels.

Tom filled the glass doorway of the balcony. 'Don't give me the silent treatment, Anna. Say something.'

She continued to flick, refusing to look at him.

'Anna. Please try to understand.'

Anna turned off the television and sighed. 'It's too hard, Tom,' she said in a small, tired voice. 'I never seem to be a priority for you.'

He took a step towards her, but she held up both hands. 'Don't!' She paused for a moment then tutted. 'I think you should go home.'

With a grimace, he moved towards her.

'No, Tom!' Her sharp tone stopped him in his tracks. 'Just go home.'

It was unusual for Anna to be so forceful. She usually accepted any change of plans with stoic resignation. But this time she couldn't hide her anger and disappointment. Tom's face puckered into creases. For a long minute, he stood where he was, breathing hard, as if he was struggling to come to a decision. Eventually, he said: 'All right, I'll go. But please don't shut me out. I'll call you tomorrow. Okay?' There was now an edge to his voice, one that told her he was displeased. This only served to antagonise her further.

Without a smile, she gave him a curt nod, looking only at the blank television screen. He waited a few moments, saying nothing. Eventually, she heard him take noisy, heavy steps past her. The front door opened and shut with a sharp click.

Anna breathed out slowly and cursed herself for making her life so complicated. The two of them were different in so many ways. She was a thirty-year-old mixed-race woman, single, and fifteen years younger than Tom. He was white, divorced with two young children, and still dancing to the tune of his ex-wife. Anna had known right from the start that she and Tom were an unsuitable match. So why did she allow herself to get tangled up in his tricky, thorny life? She'd fallen for the wrong man, and she had no one else to blame.

It wasn't the first time she'd chosen the wrong man. Anna thought about her last boyfriend, David. She had adored him. But after a year he had ended the relationship, saying it wasn't working for him. Looking back, Anna couldn't help thinking that perhaps she had been too needy and inflexible with him.

With Tom, she always tried to fit in with his commitments. From the start, she had accepted that, being a father, he would sometimes need to be with his children. But this trip to Brighton had been booked well in advance. Anna was angry with Tom for cancelling it; but deep down, she was furious with herself.

Thinking about the children, a girl of eight and a boy of six, she felt the familiar tug of guilt and self-doubt. They hadn't met yet, but Tom had promised her an outing with them before the end of summer. How would they react when they saw her with their dad? Would they like her?

Anna's dream was to marry Tom in the not-so-distant future and have children soon after. He'd told her that he shared the same dream. She could see them living happily in a detached house with a garden not too far away from the practice. She would welcome his children to their home. But would they accept her as their stepmother? Anna wasn't sure.

Disappointed and depressed, Anna went to her bijou kitchen to get herself a drink. She spotted a half-finished bottle of Chardonnay on the side shelf of the fridge. Reaching for that, Anna walked back to her lounge, intending to drown her sorrows by emptying the bottle.

Hours later, lying on her sofa watching a long, emotional film on Netflix, Anna realised that she had not only finished the Chardonnay, but was on her way to half-emptying a second bottle. When she tried to get up, the room began to spin. Falling back on the sofa, she curled up and closed her eyes. It was not until the early hours of the morning that she was finally able to climb into her bed.

～

On Saturday morning, Anna woke up to the sound of her mobile phone vibrating on her bedside table. She reached over and picked it up. Bleary-eyed, she noted that it was from her friend Fiona.

'Ah. You're still there,' she chirped. 'Glad I caught you before your drive to Brighton.'

Anna took a moment before replying. 'No Brighton. It's been cancelled.'

'What? Why?'

Anna let out a tired sigh and updated her friend on the latest state of affairs. Fiona was the only person she'd spoken to about Tom. Anna had introduced her to him over dinner one evening when they had first started dating. Fiona had taken an instant dislike to him. Tom had been charming, but Fiona had come away unimpressed. She thought that Anna should leave him and regularly tried to persuade her to walk away. It wasn't just that she had Anna's best interests at heart; she simply did not like Tom. She believed he was untrustworthy.

'The bastard!' she hissed.

'Please, Fiona. Don't start.'

There was silence for a moment. Then Fiona tutted. 'Fine. I'll just say that it's high time you woke up and smelled the coffee. Okay. The reason I rang was to say I'll be away next week. I'm taking Callum to Glasgow to see his grandparents.'

'Okay, cool,' Anna said in a small voice.

'What are you going to do today?' asked Fiona in a no-nonsense tone. 'Please don't stay in your flat feeling sorry for yourself.'

When Anna didn't reply, she tutted again. 'Come on, Anna. Come join me and Callum for a swim at the Lido. It will cheer you up. We can have a chat over hot chocolate and muffins. What do you say?'

Still, Anna stayed silent. 'Listen. I'm not taking no for an answer. I'll be waiting outside the entrance at a quarter to two. Callum's class starts at two p.m. sharp, so make sure you're on time.'

~

Anna cursed as she swung her VW Polo into the Finchley Lido car park at 1.55 p.m. She was in no mood for swimming, but she knew her friend was right to get her out of the flat. Wallowing in self-pity was not going to get her anywhere. Grabbing her mesh bag that held her swimsuit and towel, she joined Fiona and her son.

'You're late,' grumbled Fiona.

'Sorry.' Anna bent forward to speak to the seven-year-old boy. 'How's my champion swimmer?'

Callum grinned. 'I can do a whole length now.'

Anna raised her eyebrows in mock disbelief. 'That's impossible.'

'I can! I'll show you.' Callum swelled his chest with pride.

Before long, they were in their swimsuits, sitting on the edge of the pool, dangling their feet in the water. Callum was with a group of boys at the other end of the pool. Their instructor was a middle-aged South Asian man with a shock of grey hair. He reminded Anna of her father, who had also been a swimming instructor in his youth. When she was little, he used to take her swimming every weekend.

The Finchley Lido was a big, bright indoor pool close to Fiona's terraced house. Anna enjoyed swimming and tried to go with her friend as often as she could. A strong smell of chlorine pervaded the air around them, offending their nostrils until they got used to it. Through the glass roof, the early afternoon sun poured down golden beams of light, making the water shimmer and sparkle. Anna kicked her legs in and out, creating foamy waves, making loud splashing sounds. The cool sensation on her skin was refreshing and energising.

'What was Tom's excuse this time?' Fiona's disparaging tone was as clear as the pool water.

'Don't rub it in, Fiona! I'm not in the mood.'

Pre-empting another lecture from her friend, Anna began to tell her about her upcoming trip to Zimbabwe. She'd already mentioned that she would not be going to the conference in India.

'Thank God you're not going with Tom,' she said. 'It would have been a mistake. And I'm glad you're not going to Brighton with him.'

'Oh Fiona! Don't be like that.'

'Like what? You know I don't think Tom is right for you. And when your mother hears you're dating a divorced man with children, she's going to go nuts.'

'Stop it.'

'You haven't told her about him yet, have you?'

Anna sighed. Knowing how disapproving her mother would be, she had not said a word to either of her parents. Her father was more likely to accept Tom as a suitable partner for her, so she was planning to tell him first. But even after two years of being Tom's girlfriend, she hadn't found the right time to do that.

Fiona softened her tone. 'Don't stress, Anna. Just chill. Come on. Let's get in the water.'

Glad of the change in gear, Anna slipped into the water and bounced up and down to get acclimatised. Fiona jumped in and the two of them splashed about, having a bit of fun before swimming several lengths of the pool. When they'd had enough, they got out and towel-dried themselves. Fiona called out to Callum and pointed to the café so that he knew where to join them when his class ended.

Sipping hot chocolate and taking a bite of her muffin, Anna could feel Fiona's eyes on her. She hoped she was not going to mention Tom again, but it was a vain hope.

'Where is he today? In Brighton with his ex-wife?' Fiona asked.

'Of course not!' Anna scowled. They'd been best friends for over a decade, since their student days at Glasgow University. Despite her bullishness, Anna knew that Fiona was only trying to stop her from getting hurt.

'Don't torture yourself like this, Anna. You've got to walk away from him. You're setting yourself up for so much pain.'

Anna knitted her brow. 'You can't know that.'

But even as she said the words, Anna felt her usual doubts creeping in. If only she had Fiona's confidence. Fiona always seemed so sure of herself; clear on who she was and what she wanted. Anna was uncertain about so many things and indecisive at the best of times.

Pulling herself out of her introspection, Anna changed the subject to tell her friend about her plans for Zimbabwe. She had already given her a blow-by-blow account of the discussion over Sunday lunch with her parents.

'I have a cousin who works for the local newspaper in Harare. He will know where to look for official records. I've already seen the certificates my father holds, but there may be other files and records held somewhere. I need to find those.'

'How does your father feel about you digging into his past?'

Anna drew in a long breath. 'He's not happy at all. And Mum is still furious with me for bringing all this to the surface. So I haven't told them much about my plans. I'll go about investigating without getting them involved. I've already started doing background searches on the internet. You wouldn't believe how much information there is about orphans and foundlings across the globe.'

'I can imagine. But I hope you're not spending all your free time glued to your laptop. What are you doing tomorrow?'

'I'm not sure.'

'Want to come with me to a charity fundraising meeting? One of my colleagues runs these events, and he needs more volunteers.'

Anna considered for a moment. Usually, she was happy to be involved in any charity activities, and when she had time, she did extra sessions as a medical advocate. But she thought she would pass this time.

'I think I should go to see a patient of mine. She's not doing too well, and I promised to visit her.'

Anna was thinking of Gita. The shelter was an unfamiliar environment for her and she had been asking for Anna. As she was unexpectedly free the next day, she resolved to drive over to see her. Her thoughts shifted to the plight of women violently attacked in their own homes. She knew from her charity work that the number of women suffering domestic abuse was staggering. It was a comfort to know that she was able to help some of the victims. She hoped Gita was doing well.

# Chapter 4

The young woman behind the desk was busy on her phone. She sat in one section of the reception hall, surrounded by cabinets and shelving units. Nodding to Anna with a smile, she gestured towards a sitting area at the back of the room. Taking a seat, Anna looked around at the small rectangular hall with the solid oak front door facing her. On the wall near the door, a large cork notice board displayed posters, leaflets, and a host of information sheets all in a neat and tidy order.

On her right there was a staircase and adjacent to that, the hall opened into a corridor. Anna imagined that it led to shared areas for the residents, while the upper floors were for their private accommodation. She'd been expecting a building like the ones purpose-built for elderly residents in care homes. But this shelter was made up of two residential properties joined up to look like a large house for an extended family. From outside, no one would suspect it was a special place for victims of domestic violence.

Glancing down at the wooden coffee table, Anna noticed that it was aged with signs of wear and tear. There were light scratches and faded stains on the surface. But it was well-polished, giving off a faint scent of linseed oil. Stacked on one side of the table were some journals and women's magazines.

The receptionist was speaking in a low, polite voice. Her accent was not London-based and had a subtle twang that sounded strangely familiar. Anna thought she was strikingly beautiful with her dark skin tone and unblemished skin. Her high cheekbones and aquiline nose were accentuated by her long dark-brown hair tied back in a ponytail.

'Can I help you?' she called when her phone conversation was over.

Anna walked up to the desk. 'I'm Dr Kotze. Here to see Gita Thakur.'

The woman gave her a warm smile. 'Oh yes. Thank you for coming. And thank you for ringing earlier.' She began to tap at her computer. 'I just need to confirm a few details.' She asked for Anna's name, her surgery and the name of the referring safeguarding officer.

'Dr Anna *Indira* Kotze?' she asked, looking up, emphasising the middle name.

Anna nodded. People were always intrigued when they heard her full name. Sandwiched between Anna and Kotze, her Indian middle name seemed incongruous. She could see the woman was curious, but she refrained from asking any personal questions. Recording all the necessary information, she asked Anna to sign the visitors' register and gave her a lanyard labelled GP to wear around her neck.

'Mrs Thakur is rather anxious,' she said. 'She asked us to call you. We've tried to explain that she's safe here, but I don't think she believes us.'

'Yes. She's been through a lot. What terrifies her is the thought that her family will track her down. It will take a long time for her to recover, physically and mentally.'

'I'm sure.' The woman picked up the phone. 'If you wait a moment, I'll call someone to take you to her.'

Anna cast an eye over the office area behind the receptionist. On one cabinet, in a clear vase, a beautiful arrangement of pink, purple and yellow gladioli brought colour into the room, emitting a honey-sweet fragrance into the air. Anna breathed in appreciatively.

Brightening up the whole expanse of the room was sunlight filtering through a wide window overlooking the car park. On the window ledge, Anna could see a framed family photograph taken in a flower garden somewhere light and bright. But her eyes were drawn to the back wall where a photo calendar was hanging between two framed certificates. She stared at the image in surprise.

'That's Harare city, isn't it?'

'Yes, it is. Have you been there?'

Anna smiled. 'Yes, my parents are from Zimbabwe.'

It was the woman's turn to look surprised. 'So are mine! I mean, I'm from there too.' She was about to say more but was interrupted by a man who appeared behind Anna.

'You wanted to see me, Miss?'

Anna stepped aside. He was an older man with a wrinkled face and cheeks red with rosacea.

'Yes, Jack. Could you take Dr Kotze to see the new resident, Gita Thakur? You know who I mean?'

'I do. She's in the garden.' He nodded to Anna before turning round to lead the way.

Thanking the receptionist, Anna followed the man through the corridor, passing a row of framed prints of colourful flowers along the wall. They brightened up an otherwise dull and uninteresting passageway. They went past two closed doors, one on either side. The second set of doors were open, letting light into the corridor.

Jack turned into a large sitting room on the right. Several residents looked up from watching a programme on a television screen mounted on the wall. They sat on individual armchairs of all

41

different styles and colours. Like the coffee table in reception, the furniture looked dated and used, albeit clean and tidy.

Jack walked her straight through to the French doors which were open to the back of the building. They stepped on to a stone patio beyond which was a wide expanse of lawn. A few leafy trees and neatly trimmed bushes along the wooden fences surrounded the corner property.

Anna saw Gita straight away. She was sitting alone on a blue bench against the wall. It was a warm Sunday afternoon and other residents were outside chatting in low voices while they watched their children play. Gita looked so downcast that Anna felt a pang of pity for her. Walking over, she sat down beside her. Gita looked up in surprise.

'Dr Kotze! I didn't know you were coming today.'

'I wanted to see how you were doing. Sorry I couldn't come sooner.' More than two weeks had elapsed since Gita had been driven to the shelter many miles away from their practice.

Gita's face clouded over. 'Did they come looking for me, the day I left?' The fear in her voice was palpable. She began to push back the cuticles at the base of her fingernails.

'Your brother-in-law did come. But don't be scared. Our practice manager dealt with him. He came to the surgery straight after the safeguarding officer phoned your husband. He was told that you were assessed as a victim of repeated violent attacks, and for your protection, you'd been taken to a place of safety. He made a scene at reception, demanding to know where you were. He was informed that if he caused any trouble, the police would be called.'

Gita gave her an anxious look. 'Were they called, the police?'

'No. Your brother-in-law made a big fuss, but eventually he went away. You don't need to worry about him any more. But Gita, won't you reconsider? Why don't you report him?'

Gita took a breath. 'Because I know he will come for me. Even if he goes to jail, when he comes out, he will look for me and find me. Then he will kill me.'

'He won't find you. And even if he did, there'll be a restraining order put on him. As soon as he comes near you, he'll be back in prison.'

Closing her eyes, Gita simply shook her head.

'Everyone here is protected and completely safe. You can see how strong the security is. Even I had to go through hoops to get inside.' Gita continued to look worried. 'What's troubling you, Gita? Is there something else on your mind?'

Gita took a moment before responding. 'It's very strange living here.' She glanced around at the other families and added: 'There's no one like me.'

'They *are* like you. They may not be from India, but they are all victims of violence. It's early days, so it's bound to feel strange. You'll soon get to know them.' She leaned closer to inspect Gita's face. 'Let me have a look at your bruises.' The swellings had gone down but they still felt tender. 'How are your other injuries? Still painful?'

Gita brought her hand up to her right eye where a white discharge was visible at the corner. 'That looks infected. I'll write you a script for an antibiotic,' Anna said.

Gita scrunched up her eyes. 'I don't know if I've done the right thing coming here.'

Anna responded firmly, hoping to dispel her doubts. 'You definitely made the right choice. Give yourself some time to settle in. If you need anything, speak to the manager. Don't be afraid to ask for help.'

Anna sat with her for a while, trying to cheer her up. The sun was warm on their faces and Gita was wearing a short-sleeved cotton *salwar kameez*, with her *odhani* covering her hair. Anna had never seen her wear anything other than Indian outfits. She wondered if that was a rule imposed on her by her in-laws.

'I'm glad you were able to bring some clothes with you,' Anna remarked.

'Yes.' Gita paused for a moment and added: 'I also have my passport. Just in case . . .'

Anna raised her eyebrows. 'Just in case? In case of what?'

Gita looked at her hands, absently pushing back her cuticles. After a hesitation, she finally spoke, her voice trailing away. 'I was thinking that maybe I should go back to India . . .'

Anna was glad to hear this and curious as to why Gita had changed her mind. Previously, she'd said she couldn't go back because it would bring shame on her family.

'I'm sure your parents will be happy to have you back. They wouldn't want you to suffer.'

Gita looked at her with a pained expression on her face. 'You don't understand.'

'What don't I understand? Tell me, Gita. Maybe I can help you.'

Looking dejected, Gita shook her head. 'If I go back to my parents' village, people will talk. A failed marriage is a disgrace.'

Gita broke off and continued to push back her cuticles. Anna wished she could shake some sense into her. But as her GP, all she could do was suggest and advise.

'I'll be off now,' she said gently. 'If you need me, just ask the staff to phone the surgery and leave a message. I'll call you back.'

As she took her leave, Anna made a mental note to ask their senior receptionist to contact the shelter every few days to check up on Gita.

At the reception desk, the young woman asked: 'Is Mrs Thakur okay?'

'Not really. She's very fragile at the moment.'

'We'll keep an eye on her and let you know if there are any concerns.'

Anna smiled. She was curious to know more about this beautiful woman who looked about the same age as her. 'Are you here every day?' she asked.

'Almost every day. I'm one of the trained support staff.'

'So, you're not a receptionist?'

'No. Just helping out on the front desk this weekend. I'm a key worker.'

Curious about the role, Anna enquired: 'What exactly does a key worker do here?'

'We help the residents settle in and make sure they receive the support they need, like help and advice, access to welfare benefits, safety planning and so on. Gita Thakur has been assigned to me, along with four other residents. I'll be looking after her. My name is Roshni, by the way. Roshni Virani.'

'Nice to meet you. Sounds like our paths will be crossing a lot over the coming months,' Anna said warmly.

Roshni smiled back and her gaze fell upon the gold chain around Anna's neck. 'I like your necklace,' she commented.

Anna lifted the pendant and looked down. 'It belonged to my father, but it has my name on it, so it's mine now.'

Roshni leaned forward to read the name. 'Indira. That's a beautiful name.'

'Thank you.' Anna turned to the register on the desk. 'I've signed out. Do I need to do anything else?'

'No, that's all. But before you go, could I ask you something? You said your parents came from Harare. That's where I'm from. My whole family still lives there. It's not often I meet someone from my hometown. I might even know your family. I am Indian and our community is quite small in Harare.' Roshni's face was lit up in anticipation.

Anna smiled, realising why Roshni's accent had seemed familiar. She spoke with a similar twang to that of her parents.

'I don't think you would know them,' Anna replied. 'My father is Indian, but he was never part of the community there. And he moved to the UK with my mother nearly forty years ago.'

'Oh.' Roshni looked disappointed.

'When did you come over?' asked Anna.

'Five years ago. This is my first job since I qualified as a healthcare worker.'

'Well. I look forward to working with you while Gita Thakur is here. I'll drive up whenever I can. But please let me know if there are any problems.'

As Anna walked away, she could sense Roshni's curious gaze on her back. She had a feeling that they would have much to talk about in the months to come.

# Chapter 5

Three weeks later, Anna met her friend Fiona again at the Finchley
Lido. Her son Callum was telling her how much he had enjoyed
his half-term week in Scotland.

'Pops and Granny took us to the seaside.' His face lit up. 'And
then we went to a small island where we all rode bicycles. We even
went on a boat and sailed around a huge lake.'

'Largs, Millport and Loch Lomond,' explained Fiona.

'Cool. Are they well, your in-laws?'

'They are. And delighted to see Callum.'

Anna had a deep fondness for the Glaswegian couple who had
embraced her friend when she married their son. Unfortunately,
the marriage hadn't lasted. But that had made no difference to the
old couple's feelings for Fiona. Callum's father lived and worked in
Peru and only visited his son and parents every few years. Fiona had
filed for divorce when Callum was just two years old.

As usual, Callum went off for his swimming lesson, and the
two friends enjoyed a short spell in the water before stretching out
on the poolside chairs. Anna closed her eyes and reminisced about
her own swimming lessons.

Suddenly, a shriek caught her attention. Near the diving boards
on their left, a young man playfully wrestled in the water with an
Asian woman. The first thing Anna noticed was his platinum-blond

curls atop his head. The sides were shaved off to almost nothing. The blue of his eyes matched the crystal-clear water in the pool. She could tell he was tall and athletic as he bounced up and down, laughing as he rough-handled his companion.

The woman giggled and playfully splashed water at him. Anna thought they made a beautiful couple. As she continued watching, she realised the woman was Roshni Virani, the receptionist from the domestic abuse shelter. Just as she recognised her, Roshni looked in her direction and caught her eye. For a moment, they stared at one another. Then Anna smiled and gave a little wave. Roshni looked puzzled, until recognition lit up her face. She waved back and spoke to her friend, who turned to give Anna a cheeky grin.

Fiona was curious. 'Who's the Adonis?'

'No idea. But the woman is someone I met recently.'

Not wanting to stare, Anna turned away and explained how she'd met Roshni and how they discovered their connection to Zimbabwe through a calendar on the wall.

'She looks a bit like you,' said Fiona, taking a good look at Roshni. 'You could almost be sisters.'

'Don't be daft! I look nothing like her.'

'I think you do. Dark hair, dark skin, Indian facial features. The only difference is that your hair is short and curly while hers is long and straight.'

'That, and the fact that she looks like a Bollywood film star whereas I look like Miss Piggy with my horrible snout.'

Keeping a straight face, Fiona made an exaggerated point of staring at her friend's nose. Anna gave her a good-natured shove before they both burst out laughing at their own childishness.

Later, as they sat at a café enjoying their usual hot chocolate and muffins, Anna asked Fiona about the fundraising meeting she had missed.

'It went well. The guy who coordinates these events was really pleased because a lot of volunteers turned up. He's very smart this chap. When he's not at work, he's running fundraising events all over the country. He goes to India quite a lot too. I think he's got links to some charities there,' Fiona shared.

'What sort of charities?'

'I'm not sure. But he was interested in your medical advocacy work too. I told him about it and he wanted to know more. I thought about connecting you two.'

'If it helps with his charity, I don't mind talking to him,' Anna replied.

'Great. His name's Nick, by the way.'

Just then, Anna felt a tap on her shoulder. It was Roshni, wearing a pretty white beach dress over her swimsuit. Her wet hair was tied up in a ponytail and on her feet, white flip-flops matched her dress. Looking like a glamorous model, she smiled down at Anna.

'Nice to see you again,' she said. 'Is this your local pool?'

'Yes. I've not seen *you* here before.'

'It's my first time. My boyfriend lives nearby. How are you?'

'Fine.' Anna asked her to join them and made the introductions.

'I've been meaning to ring you about Mrs Thakur,' Roshni said. 'Will you be able to drop by sometime soon?'

Anna frowned. 'Is she okay?'

'Oh yes. She's okay. It's just . . . she often mentions you.'

Reading between the lines, Anna understood that Roshni did not want to say too much about a resident in front of Fiona. She nodded and agreed to pay them a visit as soon as she could.

After some small talk, Roshni got up to leave. 'If you let reception know when you're coming, I'll make sure I'm on duty that day. See you soon.'

⁓

By the time Anna made it to the shelter, Gita had already been there for six weeks. There was a young man at the reception desk who informed her that Gita could be found in the sitting room, and that Roshni would see her afterwards. Anna found her patient reading a magazine in one corner of the room.

Pulling up a chair next to her, Anna said a cheerful hello. Gita looked up and her lips curled into a small smile. 'How are you?'

'Fine.' Gita's smile belied her real feelings. Anna could sense her sadness.

'I've been keeping a check on your progress,' said Anna. 'I'm glad to see your eye infection has cleared up. Do you still have any pain?'

Gita shook her head. She began to push back the cuticles of her fingernails, a sure sign of her anxiety.

'What is it, Gita? Are you still worried your brother-in-law will find you here?'

Gita shook her head. 'No. It's just . . . I can't stay here any more.'

Clearly, Gita was not happy at the shelter. Anna hoped she wasn't going to put herself in danger again.

'You're not thinking of going back to your in-laws, are you?'

'No.' Gita was emphatic. 'Not there. But . . . I've decided to return to India.'

Anna smiled, delighted that Gita had changed her mind.

'I can't go to my parents' house,' she explained. 'But I think I could go to stay with my older brother. He lives in Mumbai. Sometimes, we email each other. Before I came to this shelter, I never told him about my problems. But now . . .'

Anna waited for her to continue. This was the first time she had mentioned her brother. Anna had assumed her whole family lived in the village.

Gita bit her lip, her eyebrows knitted with worry. 'Last week, I used the computer in the office. I emailed my brother and told him everything. He straight away said I should leave this country and go to stay with him.'

Anna thought this was the perfect solution. But Gita still seemed troubled. 'What's stopping you, Gita? You have no children so there's nothing preventing you from leaving the country. It makes sense for you to go back to India, stay with your brother, then make plans to leave your husband for good. I'm talking about divorce. Isn't that what you want?'

'I do. But my brother will have to pay for my flight. He's married and they have a child. I'm worried his wife will not be happy about him spending money on me and having me live with them.'

'Oh Gita,' tutted Anna. 'You mustn't stress like this. Look. You can't know what's in your sister-in-law's mind. She might be fine about it. Why don't you accept your brother's offer? Once you're there, you can see how things are and then move forward with your life. You're a smart girl. You'll find a way to make things right.'

'You really think so?' Gita's face was a mixture of hope and anxiety.

Anna gave her a fond and reassuring smile. 'I do think so. You can do it, Gita. You're stronger than you think. And Mumbai is a big city. Like London. You'll be fine there.'

Gita looked curious. 'Have you been to Mumbai?'

'No. I've never been to India. But someday I will.'

Gita nodded, looking pensive. Her face wore a glazed, faraway expression. After a while, she looked directly at Anna and said: 'If you come to Mumbai, will you visit me?'

Anna was taken aback by the earnestness and hope in her voice. It wasn't just a polite or casual throwaway line. She really wanted Anna to meet her in Mumbai.

'It will be my pleasure,' said Anna. 'Tell you what, let's keep in touch so if I do go there, I can drop in on you. I want to know how you get on anyway.'

Gita flashed her a grateful smile. She looked less anxious than before, and a small light of hope shone in her eyes. Changing direction, Anna asked how she was getting on with Roshni, her key worker. Gita spoke warmly about her, saying she was kind and helpful, providing lots of useful information.

'That's good. I'll go and have a word with her now to tell her you're thinking about returning to India.'

Standing up, she urged Gita to accept her brother's offer as soon as possible. She was pleased to see that Gita's shoulders were no longer slouched. After promising to be in touch soon, Anna took her leave.

~

The receptionist put a call out for Roshni and within minutes, she came through to welcome Anna. She led her to a large office overlooking the front garden.

'Thanks for coming,' she said. 'How did you find Gita?'

'Not good at first. She doesn't seem to have adjusted to living here at all.'

'No, she hasn't. I've introduced her to a few people, hoping she would make friends. But she's such a private person, people tend to leave her alone.'

'Has she told you about wanting to leave?'

Roshni uttered a sigh. 'She hasn't, but I suspected that. It's why I wanted you to speak to her. Unfortunately, from time to time, we do get residents who want to return to their abusers, believing that things will be different. They usually never are.'

Anna shook her head. She explained that Gita was considering leaving for India to stay with her brother in Mumbai.

'Oh, I didn't know that. She did tell me she'd emailed her brother and he was furious about how she'd been treated. He wants her brother-in-law arrested. But of course, Gita refuses to report him to the police.'

'I wish she would,' said Anna in frustration. 'These monsters never seem to get punished and it makes me so angry. Gita is frightened he'll go after her when he comes out of prison.'

Roshni agreed. 'There's another reason too. It's the whole going to court thing. The system is extremely distressing for victims. The hearings are often delayed and giving evidence is always a retraumatising experience. The suffering is relived all over again.'

'This is so wrong!' Anna blew out a breath. 'How long can she stay here?'

'We try to move them on as soon as they are ready. But this place relies on charitable funds so it's often difficult to keep things going. When people are referred to us, we give them a safe space to escape from their abusers. While they're here, we provide emotional and practical support to plan their lives going forward. We try to find accommodation for them, but it can take a long time, especially making all the financial arrangements.'

'Would she qualify for financial help?'

'She should do. We'll help her apply for housing benefit so that her rent is covered and see to it that she becomes self-reliant when she leaves.'

Anna was concerned. Gita had never had to live on her own and earn her own keep. Independent living was going to be a challenge for her. She was bright and astute, learning how to read, write and speak English by joining English language classes when she first arrived from India. But she was inexperienced in so many ways. Returning to India was the best option for Gita.

Roshni looked at her watch. 'It's five thirty already. And it's Friday. Do you have to go back to your surgery?'

'No. Why?' Anna replied.

'I'm finished for the day now. There's a lovely wine bar not far from here. Would you like to go for a drink?'

Anna smiled with pleasure. She felt an affinity towards this woman with whom she seemed to have a lot in common.

'That would be lovely. I don't often come to East London. Are we driving?'

'No. It's just a short walk away. You can leave your car here.'

# Chapter 6

The high street was only a five-minute walk away from the shelter. As they approached, Anna could hear the sound of the rush-hour traffic on the main road. When they got there, she saw vehicles streaming past in both directions. Cars, lorries, buses, cyclists, delivery vans and scooters all moved along, filling the air with noise and the smell of exhaust fumes.

They joined the throng of people walking briskly on the pavement, going about their business or making their way home after work. The sound of feet tapping and the odd horn buzzing resounded around them. Shops and offices were being closed while pubs and restaurants were ready and waiting to be filled with customers at the start of the weekend.

Roshni led the way to the pedestrian crossing at the traffic lights and waited for the green man to light up. Once across the street, they walked to the left then turned right on to a quieter road. Anna followed Roshni up to the entrance of a wine bar with wide double-fronted windows. Anna looked with interest at the hanging baskets and window boxes filled with colour-coordinated flowers. The blossoms were incredibly eye-catching with their contrasting shades of violet, glowing orange and deepest red. Anna recognised begonias, fuchsias and lobelias among the huge variety of rich scented English blooms.

By mutual consent, they took seats at a small table on the pavement outside the entrance. A beautiful butterfly flitted around the hanging baskets and the hum of a few bees was audible just behind Anna. When the waitress came round to ask for their drinks order, Anna was mindful of her drive back and chose orange and lemonade with ice, while Roshni asked for a glass of red wine. They ordered small plates of hummus, olives, bruschetta and pitta bread. Anna breathed in the sweet smell of the flowers behind her.

'Nice place,' she said.

'It is. I brought my mother here yesterday, and she couldn't get over the burst of flowers everywhere.'

'Does she live with you?'

'Only when she comes over for a visit. She lives in Harare with my dad and twin sister.'

'You have a twin?'

'Yes. She's in my mum's good books because she got married last year.' Roshni paused while the waitress placed their drinks on the table. 'Can you guess why my mum is here?' Taking a sip, she rolled her eyes and made a face. 'To introduce me to some suitable boys.' At the word suitable, she drew air quotes with her fingers.

Anna raised her eyebrows. 'What about the boyfriend we met at the pool?'

Roshni opened her eyes wide. 'Oh no! She doesn't know about him. My mother's idea of a suitable boy is one that is pukka Indian. She would not be happy if I married an Englishman.'

'Is that what you want to do? Marry your Englishman?'

Roshni shrugged and held up her palms. 'I don't know. Maybe one day. Trouble is Mum wants me to start meeting eligible Indian boys right now. She thinks I might miss the boat because I'm already thirty-four. That's ancient in her mind.' Again, she rolled her eyes. 'My auntie has lined up some guys for me to meet before Mum returns to Zim in three weeks. In fact, we're going to see one of them in Harrow tomorrow.'

Roshni was grinning and pulling faces as she spoke, making Anna laugh out loud. She'd heard about the introduction system in Asian communities, but she couldn't imagine going through such a meeting herself. It would be too embarrassing. But she thought her own mother would probably appreciate such a system, as it would allow her to introduce Anna to boys that *she* considered suitable. Anna had no doubt that Tom would be regarded as highly unsuitable.

At that moment, a mobile phone started to ring. It was a ring tone with bells, whistles and a happy uplifting melody on a loop. With a little gasp, Roshni bent down and began to rummage in her handbag.

'Sorry,' she said, accepting the call. 'Hello, Mum.'

Anna decided to give Roshni some privacy. Miming the word 'loo', she indicated she was going inside. The interior was like a Tardis, more spacious than she had expected. An enormous glass dome in the ceiling flooded the room with natural light and ventilation. With strategically placed greenery around the room, the place felt fresh and inviting.

When Anna returned to her seat, she found Roshni lost in thought, holding her phone and staring into the middle distance. Anna commented on the lovely decor inside, but Roshni just tapped her phone and frowned.

'I hope you don't mind but my mum is coming round to meet you,' she said.

'Really?' Anna thought she was joking.

'Yes. As soon as I told her that I was with someone whose parents are from Zimbabwe, she insisted on joining us.'

Anna gave her a sceptical, incredulous look. Roshni grinned. 'Sounds crazy, I know, but she's on her way. I live in a maisonette just ten minutes from here. She's been at home all day, so I suppose she's bored and wants to come out for a bit. Is that okay with you?'

Surprised but not put out in the least, Anna said she would be happy to meet Roshni's mum. There was no rush for her to get home and driving at this time of the day would be madness. Sipping her drink and relishing the tasty hummus on pitta bread, Anna sat back, anticipating the arrival of Roshni's mother. They didn't have to wait long.

Roshni, facing away from the street, caught her mother's reflection in the glass window before her. Jumping up, she pulled out the chair beside her.

Anna smiled at the woman who was an older version of her beautiful daughter. She was of medium height, bespectacled and elegantly dressed in straight black trousers with a light green silk blouse. Her straight dark-brown hair was cut in a sophisticated bob that fell neatly to her jawline. She could easily pass as Roshni's older sister.

'You must be Anna Indira,' she said with a slightly high-pitched nasal twang. She beamed across the table. 'I'm Savita. So nice to meet someone from Zimbabwe.'

'Lovely to meet you. Although it's my parents who are from Zimbabwe,' Anna clarified.

'Yah, that's what Roshni told me. How long have they been here?'

'Nearly forty years. They came in 1981.'

Savita nodded knowingly. 'So many people left around that time. Most of my friends, in fact. Did your parents live in Harare, or Salisbury as it used to be called?'

Roshni jumped in. 'Mum! Stop interrogating her.' She turned to Anna and apologised. 'My mum asks way too many questions.'

Anna chuckled. 'It's cool. I don't mind.'

'You see,' Savita said, giving her daughter a pointed look. Then, facing Anna again, she continued: 'Have you ever been to Zimbabwe?'

'Yes, a few times. Although my last trip was over ten years ago.'

Savita smiled. She ordered a glass of orange juice and began to describe the changes in her country over the past decade. She said she enjoyed living there despite its political and economic problems. Roshni joined in to describe some of the challenges facing young people like herself who wanted to further their studies and find work that was fulfilling and rewarding.

'I came here because there are so many more opportunities for me,' she said. 'And I love being in London because there is so much to do.'

Savita tutted. 'But you have to settle down and get married at some point.' She paused, then turned to Anna. 'What about you, Anna? Are you married?'

'Mum!' Roshni exploded, looking appalled.

Anna was taken aback by the direct question, but she recognised that Savita was not being intrusive. She was simply curious and interested.

'It's okay,' she laughed. 'I don't mind sharing. The answer is no, I'm not married. But hopefully, one day I will be.'

'Of course,' Savita replied, looking a little sheepish. 'Sorry if I embarrassed you.'

'Not at all. My mother would also like to see me married. But these things happen only when they're meant to.'

Roshni grinned. 'That's what I keep telling Mum. But she doesn't agree.'

'No harm in lending a helping hand to get things moving,' Savita said, giving her daughter another pointed look.

She went on to say that Roshni was going to meet a potential marriage partner the next day. While she stayed at her relative's house, Roshni would be meeting him on her own at a specific restaurant where they would get to know one another.

Anna observed mother and daughter talk openly about the whole set-up. They both had vibrant personalities, exuding confidence and self-assurance. Savita was in her sixties, but she had a youthful joy about her, brimming with mischief and delight.

'Would you like another drink?' Savita asked Anna, noticing her empty glass.

'No, thanks. I should actually be heading home.'

Savita looked dismayed. 'Oh no, don't go. I'm just getting to know you. You haven't told me about your parents yet. Are they from Harare?'

'Yes, they are. My mother's family still lives there,' Anna replied.

'Oh really?' Savita sounded delighted. 'I bet I know them. I know all the Indian families in Harare. There aren't that many.'

Anna explained her parents' situation, highlighting their lack of connection to the Indian community. Clearly intrigued, Savita probed further, and before she knew it, Anna found herself recounting her father's upbringing with his mixed-race adoptive parents, and how he met and married a black Zimbabwean woman in 1976. She described their move to London and eventual settlement in Harrow, where Anna herself was born in 1988.

'How amazing!' Savita exclaimed, genuinely fascinated. 'That really is an unusual story. In Salisbury, in the sixties and seventies, mixed-race people mostly lived in an area called Arcadia. If your father lived there, he must have gone to Mountford High, which was a school for mixed-race and Indian children. Because of the racial segregation laws, Mountford was the only high school in Salisbury for people like us. I was there from 1966 to 1972. Maybe your father and I were there at the same time.'

Anna pondered over Savita's questions for a moment. Arcadia and Mountford High were the exact names her father had mentioned when he spoke about his upbringing in Harare. It felt surreal to hear those names once again.

Savita continued, her curiosity piqued. 'If you tell me which year he was born, I can work out which year group he was in.'

'He was born in 1954,' Anna responded.

Savita sat up straight. Her face was a picture of disbelief. Shaking her head, she spoke with absolute certainty.

'I *do* know your father. He's Mathew Kotze, isn't he?'

Anna's jaw dropped in amazement.

Roshni seemed just as nonplussed. 'How could you know that?' she asked. 'I never told you Anna's surname.'

Fixing her gaze on Anna, Savita explained. 'There was only one high school in Salisbury for Indians and mixed-race kids. I was also born in 1954. Mathew and I were in the same class from our first year in high school until we took our O level exams. He was the only Indian boy with us who was adopted and living in Arcadia.'

Anna finally found her voice. 'Wow! That's . . . incredible.' She couldn't quite believe what she was hearing. Surely it wasn't possible?

Savita took a long sip from her glass, then slowly lowered it. 'The last time I saw Mathew was in 1970 when we were taking our O levels.' She hesitated before adding: 'It would be wonderful to see him again.'

Anna was still overwhelmed with disbelief. What were the chances of bumping into someone who'd been to school with her father so long ago? And in a country so far away? Anna was dumbfounded.

'Do you think your father would want to meet up?' Savita furrowed her eyebrows. 'I remember how private he was and maybe he would rather not.'

Taken aback by this turn of events, Anna was uncertain, but she said she would phone Mathew in the evening to check. Savita urged Roshni to exchange phone numbers with Anna so they could link up on WhatsApp straight away.

Savita went on to explain that although they'd not been close friends at school, she and Mathew had known each other well. He had left school after the exams, so they were not together in the sixth form. She'd heard he was working as a swimming instructor somewhere.

Anna blinked. Mathew had definitely been a swimming instructor. The story was beginning to sound more plausible. 'He *did* do that for a while, but then he was offered an engineering apprenticeship near his home, and he worked as a motor mechanic. He still does that part-time.'

Anna looked at Savita with fresh eyes. Her assertions were sounding increasingly credible. She began to imagine her father at school with her. Mathew was the polar opposite of Savita in nature. She seemed so bubbly while Mathew was a veritable introvert. Anna wondered if he had been different as a teenager, perhaps a bit more carefree.

As if she could read her mind, Savita began to talk about Mathew being quiet and thoughtful in class. 'He was different from other boys. Mathew was shy and liked to keep in the background. Is he still like that?'

'Yes, very much so,' said Anna. 'He doesn't like to draw attention to himself. I guess you could say he's the reflective sort, thinking before saying what he wants to say.'

Savita nodded, knowingly. 'That's how I remember him. He was a bit of a loner, preferring his own company. But that was understandable, I suppose. We knew he'd had a tough upbringing.'

Anna knitted her brows, startled to hear her say that. 'You mean, with his adoptive parents?'

'No, I mean before that. He was a foundling, wasn't he? His real parents left him as a baby outside a church. That's tough for anyone.'

Anna found herself holding her breath. Any doubts she had about the veracity of Savita's assertions were simply blown away. She really did know Mathew all those years ago. But it was astounding to hear her speak about Mathew's painful past in such a matter-of-fact way. To know that other people in Zimbabwe were aware of what had happened to her father was mind-blowing. Wondering what else Savita knew, she nodded with a tight smile, hoping she would say more.

'I always wanted to ask him about that,' continued Savita, looking pensive. 'But I could tell he didn't want it mentioned at all. He must have told you how some boys tried to make fun of him. They were bullies really, but Mathew just ignored them. I really admired him for the way he handled himself.'

'Yes.' Anna's smile was strained.

'And because he was so obviously Indian, there was a lot of gossip about who his real parents were.'

Maintaining a neutral expression on her face, Anna asked in a quiet voice: 'What sort of gossip?'

Roshni had been listening quietly to the conversation, but now she put her hand on her mother's arm and interrupted. 'No, Mum. Anna doesn't need to hear any gossip.'

Anna took a deep breath and focused her gaze on Roshni. 'Actually, I do. I'm very interested in what your mum has to say because my dad refuses to speak about his past. I would very much like to hear everything she can tell me.'

Savita seemed a little shaken up. She apologised and began to backtrack. 'It's all gossip and rumour. I shouldn't have said anything.'

'Please tell me what you know, even if it is only gossip and rumour,' Anna pleaded, her voice filled with emotion. 'It's very important to me.'

Savita exchanged a glance with her daughter, clearly uncomfortable and uncertain about how to proceed. Eventually, she spoke in a kind and gentle tone. 'People talk a lot of rubbish, so I wouldn't pay too much attention.'

Anna locked her gaze on to Savita. 'Please tell me what you heard.'

Savita's expression softened. She held Anna's gaze and nodded. 'All right. I'll tell you what I remember hearing at that time. There was talk about your father being left at the church because his mother was unmarried. Today, it's not unusual to hear about unmarried mothers, and people are less judgmental. However, over sixty years ago, it caused quite a scandal and led to a lot of gossip. There were whispers about who the baby's father could have been. Fingers were pointed at some well-known families in the community.'

Anna exhaled slowly. 'Do you know these families?'

'Some,' Savita replied in a hushed and sombre tone. 'There were many stories flying around, so I'm not sure people really knew what was true and what was false. One story was that his mother was a girl from a local family. However, another story suggested she was from India. The rumour was that she gave birth to the baby and then returned to India without him.'

Anna chewed her lower lip, thinking hard. If Savita knew so much about what was being said at the time, she wondered how many other people could tell her more. A glimmer of hope sparked within her, fuelling her determination to uncover the truth.

'Do you remember anything else?' she asked.

Savita shook her head, concern written all over her face. Realising that the atmosphere had changed, with mother and daughter wearing worried expressions, Anna smiled and attempted to lighten the mood.

To put them at ease, Anna decided to change the topic and started discussing various areas of London she was familiar with, including Harrow, where they were planning to visit the following day. She mentioned that she had spent her childhood in the borough of Harrow and her parents still lived in the same house they had purchased when they first arrived in London. Roshni joined in, pointing out a few landmarks in East London, saying she would be delighted to show Anna around whenever they both had a free weekend.

The late afternoon sun had dipped behind the buildings, casting the entire street into shadow. Anna glanced at the time. It was 7.30 p.m. Looking at her new friends, it felt as if she'd known them for years. They were good company, but it was time to take her leave. When she said goodbye, they both gave her a hug, as if they felt the same way. Assuring them that she would be in contact soon, Anna walked away, leaving them to enjoy the rest of their evening.

As Anna embarked on the long drive back to Finchley, her mind buzzed with the information she had gleaned from Savita. Foremost in her thoughts were the rumours. She realised that she needed to question other people like Savita. There might be someone out there who remembered something important. Was it possible that Mathew's birth parents were still in Zimbabwe? Or if his mother was from India, could she be alive and residing somewhere within that vast country? And who was Mathew's father? Overwhelmed by the multitude of questions swirling around in her head, Anna was determined to follow up on all that she'd heard when she went to Zimbabwe. It was going to be a busy trip.

# Chapter 7

As soon as she got home, Anna changed her clothes and settled down on the sofa to call her father. He answered on the second ring, so she knew he was sitting on his armchair with the phone at his elbow. The television was blaring in the room. She waited until he turned the sound down, then told him her incredible news. He remembered Savita right away.

'Savita? Yes, there was a Savita in my class.' He sounded calm, but Anna could tell that he was surprised and pleased. His response to everything was restrained, so it was normal for him not to show any excitement or obvious enthusiasm. But he did say he was amazed to learn about the way the two had met.

'You mean she just walked over to you because she heard your parents were from Zimbabwe?'

'Yes, she did. A real coincidence! She was so nice, Dad. I liked her. What do you remember about her?'

There was silence on the phone for a while. Anna pictured him scratching his head full of grey hair, thinking about this school friend after so many decades. Eventually, he said he remembered that she was friendly with everyone and always up for a laugh, making mischief of some kind.

'Do you remember any other girls?'

'Not really. This girl stood out because she was popular, especially with the boys.'

'Even with you?' Anna was teasing him.

'No. Not me.' She could tell he was smiling when he denied it.

'Was she pretty?'

'Yes, she was pretty.' Mathew paused. 'What's she like now?'

'She's a beautiful woman. Smartly dressed and stylish. She doesn't look sixty.'

'Over sixty. I'm surprised she remembers me because I didn't have much to do with her.'

'Well, she does. She remembers quite a lot about you, really.' Anna's mind flicked back to the things she'd heard about the rumours surrounding his real parents. Instinctively, she knew this was something she could not repeat to him. Skipping over that part, she continued.

'She recalls that you lived in Arcadia with your adoptive parents. She really wants to meet you. So here's the question. Would you like to meet her?'

'No.' His response was quick and emphatic. 'I wouldn't know what to say.'

'Oh Dad. Come on. You'll find lots to talk about. Honestly you will. And initially, I bet Savita will do all the talking. She's quite a talker.'

Anna tried hard to convince him that he would be fine. She promised to be with him all the time so that he wouldn't feel tongue-tied or awkward in any way. But he was adamant. It was only when she suggested that her mum could go with them that he paused to consider. He always felt more comfortable when Theresa was around. 'I'll talk to Mum and sort something out. Leave it to me,' Anna said.

She ended the call with Mathew still protesting. He hated having to make conversation. Meeting Savita after so many years would undoubtedly be difficult for him, but Anna believed it was important that he made an effort this time.

Leaving her phone in the lounge, she went to make herself a mug of tea. As the steam began to rise from the kettle, she suddenly heard the gentle chimes of her ringtone. Hurrying back, she answered the call. It was from Roshni.

'Sorry to bother you,' Roshni began. 'I hope it's not too late to call you?'

Anna was surprised to hear from her so soon. 'Not at all. How can I help?'

'It's my mum. She insists on speaking to you. I tried telling her she's being too pushy, but she's not having it. Will you speak to her?'

'I'm intrigued. Of course, I'll speak to her.'

In a nasal, sing-song voice, Savita greeted her as if they were old friends. First, she asked if Anna was okay, and apologised once again for bringing up Mathew's past. She said that after their meeting at the wine bar earlier, she'd had an idea. It had occurred to her that there was a golden opportunity for her and Mathew to meet up the very next day. Savita remembered Anna mentioning that her parents lived in Harrow, and since she and Roshni were already planning to visit from East London, she wondered if it would be possible to drop by and see them.

Dumbfounded, Anna found herself at a loss for words. She knew Mathew would be totally against the idea of Savita going to their house. And with so little notice, even her mother was likely to raise objections.

'Sorry to spring this on you, but I thought it would be foolish not to check if it's possible.' Savita was clearly someone who liked to get things done immediately. 'I'm not in London for long, and Roshni's house is miles away from Harrow. So, while we are there, it would be a shame not to pop in. Do you think we could?'

Anna knew this plan was not going to work. Not only would Mathew hate the idea, but she had already made arrangements to spend the weekend with Tom. Apologising, she explained that it would have to be another day. She promised to get back to her with a date.

Returning to the kitchen, Anna couldn't help but chuckle at Savita's eagerness to meet Mathew. She decided to call her mum the next morning to fix a date for all of them to get together. Knowing it would be easier for Mathew if they met outside their home, she thought of booking a table at one of the many coffee houses in the Harrow shopping centre. Perhaps she could arrange it for the following Saturday.

The weather forecast was predicting a warm and sunny weekend, perfect for the picnic Anna had planned. She and Tom were going to spend the next day at Hampstead Heath, relaxing by the lake near Kenwood House. In the evening, there was an open-air music concert at the quirky sham bridge. They had been to one the previous year and enjoyed the whole outdoor experience. Aware of how quickly summer events were booked up, Anna had purchased their tickets months in advance. She looked forward to the day ahead.

Before going to bed, Anna phoned Tom to confirm the time he would be picking her up. As soon as he said hello, she knew that something was amiss.

'What's wrong?' she asked.

'This bloody paperwork!' He sounded tired and frustrated. 'It's never-ending.'

As senior partner, Tom had more responsibilities than other GPs in the practice. He had numerous reports to write and submit to the NHS commissioners. While the admin team assisted with data collection and uploading, Tom had to ensure its accuracy and readiness for submission.

He let out a long sigh of exhaustion. 'These reports need to be submitted on Monday, and they are nowhere near complete. I'm sorry, but I won't be able to see you tomorrow.'

'You're joking! Tom, you promised me.'

'I didn't realise how much more work there is to do this year. I can't miss the deadline, Anna. This is going to take me all weekend.'

Anna wanted to scream. She was furious. He should have anticipated the time commitment needed. There always seemed to be other things more important for him to do than being with her. Whether it was his ex-wife, his children, work, or something else entirely, she was tired of keeping her days free for him, only to be let down and left with nothing to do. If she had any sense, she would end the relationship there and then. But when it came to Tom, Anna knew that sense never factored into the equation. She pressed her lips together, swallowing her scream.

'I'll make it up to you. I promise,' he said. That's what he always said. But it wasn't enough. Anna wanted more.

Later, as she lay back on her sofa, Anna made up her mind not to spend the entire weekend brooding over Tom in her flat. She thought she would call Fiona and join her at the swimming pool. Or if her parents were free, she would go to see them. Together, they could agree on a date and time to meet Savita.

Thinking of the meeting, a better idea flashed across Anna's mind. Reflecting over her conversation with Savita earlier, she thought it would be perfect if her parents could be persuaded to have the reunion in Harrow the next day. If they agreed, she would join them.

Glancing at her watch, Anna noted that it was already 11.30 p.m. Her mother would be asleep, and it was too late to call Roshni. However, she decided to send her a message on WhatsApp.

As she got into bed, Anna checked her mobile before putting it on silent mode. There was a text message from Tom. 'I'm sorry,' it said, followed by emojis of hearts and kisses. Still infuriated by the cancellation of their plans, Anna ignored the message. Reaching for her Kindle, she read a few more chapters of the novel she had started, before turning off the light and falling asleep.

~

Organising the get-together turned out to be surprisingly easy. Anna phoned her mother early in the morning and brought her into the picture. Mathew was still asleep and hadn't had a chance to tell Theresa anything about Savita.

As Anna had expected, Theresa readily agreed that Mathew should be encouraged to meet his old school friend. They both understood that his reluctance to do so was simply down to his reserved nature. Theresa was happy to go along with whatever arrangement Anna made. She was keen to meet Savita herself.

Roshni was also pleased when Anna phoned her. She confirmed that her mother was delighted with the plans and took note of the name and address of the meeting place – a coffee house in Harrow. She mentioned that her aunt and Savita would make their way there by 2.30 p.m., and since her own lunch date would be finished by then, she would also join them.

Feeling pleased with herself for not letting Tom's change of plan spoil her weekend, Anna looked forward to the gathering later that day.

# Chapter 8

The meeting at the coffee house was a huge success. As expected, Savita's bubbly and lively personality had everyone chatting like old friends. After a nervous start, Mathew also let go of his reservations and asked after several of their old school friends. Anna was pleasantly surprised when Theresa invited Savita to their home for a meal. When Theresa mentioned that they were going to Zimbabwe at the end of the year, Savita immediately insisted that they pay her a visit so she could introduce them to her family.

When Roshni's lunch date was over, she came to join the group too, accompanied by her potential suitor, Nikunj. She introduced him, then settled beside her mother and engaged in conversation with Mathew and Theresa. Poor old Nikunj was left to fend for himself.

This didn't appear to faze him at all. He took a seat next to Anna and began to talk to her in a relaxed and friendly manner. He had a deep, masculine voice and spoke with a cut-glass English accent. Dressed in jeans, tee shirt and summer jacket, he looked very smart. He had attractive features – brown eyes, a well-groomed beard, and neatly trimmed short black hair – and his smile revealed dimples on his cheeks. As he leaned towards her, Anna caught a hint of expensive aftershave. He had clearly made an effort for his introductory meeting with Roshni.

Aware that Roshni already had a boyfriend, Anna felt a little sorry for Nikunj. She decided to make an extra effort to be friendly towards him.

'So what do you do for work?' she asked.

'I'm in digital marketing. What about you?'

'I'm a GP.'

'Really? So's my sister.' Nikunj began to tell Anna where his sister worked, how many siblings he had and where they lived. He spoke about the places he liked in the city. Without prying, he asked Anna questions about her work, and her likes and dislikes about London.

While they chatted, Anna threw a quick glance over at Roshni. She was gazing at them with a cheerful smile. Anna wondered what Roshni was thinking.

She didn't have to wait long to find out. Roshni called her that evening to thank her for arranging the get-together. Her mother had been thrilled to see Mathew after so long and was looking forward to spending time with all of them in Zimbabwe.

'So, how was the intro meeting with your date?' Anna asked. 'What are his chances?'

Roshni laughed. 'None, I'm afraid. Much to my mum's disappointment. She really liked him.'

'Poor old Nikunj. How did you break it to him?'

'I didn't have to. He could tell there was no connection. To be fair, I don't believe he was keen on me either.'

'What makes you say that?'

'Because he made it crystal clear he found *you* more interesting than me.'

'What? Don't be daft!' Anna was incredulous.

'It's true.' Roshni chuckled. 'I can tell these things, you know. I bet he'll ask me for your number.'

'No, he won't! And if he does, please don't give it to him.'

Laughing heartily, Roshni promised she wouldn't. 'But don't be surprised if he finds your number some other way. I just have this feeling he's going to track you down.'

~

Weeks later, Roshni's prediction came true when Nikunj surprised Anna by showing up at her workplace without any warning.

It was the end of a busy day, and Anna was leaving the building with Tom. They were strolling towards their parked cars. The September weather was still glorious with blue skies and warm sunshine. They stood for a moment to feel the warmth of the sun on their faces.

Tom had been invited to a banquet that evening for NHS leaders. 'I hope the food's decent tonight. Sometimes these dinners can be pretty awful.'

'I'm sure you'll love it. You'd better get going or you'll be late.'

Tom was about to leave when suddenly, a voice called out: 'Hey! Anna.'

Hurrying towards them was a young man dressed casually in jeans, black tee shirt and white trainers. Anna squinted in the sun to get a better look at him. At first, she didn't recognise him, but as he approached, she realised it was Nikunj, Roshni's lunch date.

'It's you,' she said when he joined them. 'What are you doing here?'

'I'm glad I caught you,' he beamed with dimples in both cheeks. 'Were you just heading home?' Standing next to Tom in his formal suit and tie, Nikunj looked young, slim and handsome. Anna glanced at Tom and noticed a frown on his face, almost a scowl.

Nikunj held out his hand to him. 'Hi. I'm Nikunj.'

Still frowning, Tom took his hand. 'Tom Ingles,' he said in a gruff tone.

Nikunj turned to Anna and grinned. 'I was in the area, so I thought I'd drop by.'

Anna was momentarily lost for words. Why was he here? She hadn't told him where she worked.

'Is Roshni okay?' she asked, worried that he was here to give her some bad news.

'I wouldn't know. The last time I saw her was weeks ago in Harrow.'

'Oh! So, what brings you here?'

'Just thought you might like to go for a drink.' He glanced at Tom. 'If you're free, of course.'

Now it was Anna's turn to frown. 'Did Roshni tell you how to find me?'

Nikunj let out a short laugh. 'No. I looked you up on LinkedIn. I was with a friend who lives round the corner from here. Thought you might be finished for the day and thirsty for a drink.'

He had such a cheeky grin that Anna couldn't help but smile. She shook her head in disbelief. 'You just looked me up and walked over?'

'Yes. Is that bad?' His brown eyes sparkled mischievously.

Anna turned to Tom, and her smile faded. He did not look happy. For an awkward moment, no one said anything.

'No problem if you have other plans,' said Nikunj, looking from one to the other.

Tom made a grunt-like sound, then coughed. Shooting Nikunj an icy look, he said: 'I have to be somewhere else this evening, so I'm off.'

Using his key fob, he unlocked his car remotely and began to step away. 'Don't let me stop you, Anna,' he said over his shoulder. 'You go and have fun.'

There was a hint of sarcasm in his voice, and as she caught his eye over the car, she noticed disapproval and accusation on his face. Anna felt a surge of irritation rise within her. Tom had no cause to look at her that way. And he had been rude to Nikunj. She watched him drive away, annoyed and irritated by his abrupt exit.

Nikunj was watching her askance. 'Are you okay?'

Anna blinked, gathering her thoughts. 'I'm fine. Just embarrassed by my colleague's behaviour. I apologise on his behalf.'

Nikunj turned the corners of his mouth down, feigning sadness. 'He did rather hurt my feelings. But I'm sure I'll get over it if you come for a drink with me.'

He looked so silly that Anna had to laugh. His childish sense of humour amused her. He seemed unfazed by Tom's arrogance and completely unapologetic about turning up out of the blue. She really should send him packing. Instead, she found herself saying: 'Okay then. Where are you taking me?'

~

Sipping her glass of red wine, Anna sat at one of the bench tables set up in the sun at the back of a pub called The Wisteria. She admired the many potted flower plants around the small courtyard. Behind her, beautiful lilac wisteria vines draped along the back wall. Twisting her body to admire the blooms, she marvelled at the magnificent sight. The vines clothed the wall and the flowers cascaded down like a lush rainfall. Turning back, Anna smiled at Nikunj who was watching her with attentive eyes.

Sitting opposite her, he picked up his cold beer and glugged thirstily. Putting down his glass, he gave Anna another one of his dimpled smiles. 'I did ask Roshni for your phone number, but she wouldn't give it to me.'

'I told her not to,' Anna replied.

'Why not?'

'Because I'm seeing someone.'

'Oh.' He replaced his smile with a pretend pout, looking like a child denied an ice cream. 'That is a problem,' he said slowly. Pausing for a moment, he asked if it was Tom. When she nodded, he sighed in an exaggerated manner. 'Oh well. We'll just have to be friends then.'

Anna laughed. 'You really are presumptuous, aren't you? What makes you think I want to be friends with you?'

'Because you have no reason not to.' He looked at Anna with a playful look in his eyes. 'And also, you agreed to talk to me about your charity work.'

Anna puckered her brows. 'When did I do that?'

'When you asked your friend Fiona Christie to give me your email address.'

Anna gasped. 'I did no such thing! And how do you know Fiona?'

'We work for the same company. She told you about me. I'm the guy that runs fundraising events, Nick Gopal. You said you were happy to tell me about your medical advocacy role.'

'What? I thought you said your name is Nikunj!'

With a deep throaty laugh, he sat back and watched the confusion on her face. He took another glug of his beer, then smacked his lips together.

Anna shook her head. 'You're going to have to explain this to me. I'm completely confused. When we met with Roshni, everyone was calling you Nikunj.'

'Because that is my name. Actually, my full name is Nikunj Gajanand Gopal.' He grimaced. 'It's a real mouthful, so all my friends and colleagues call me Nick.'

Anna stared at him, not sure if she could believe him. 'So when we met in Harrow, why didn't you say you were Fiona's colleague?'

'Because on that day, I didn't know *you* were the friend she was talking about. Fiona only gave me your name and contact details after we met in Harrow. It took me a while to make the connection. When I did, I tracked you down to your surgery.'

Anna pursed her lips and shook her head. Still amazed that she was talking to Fiona's colleague, she sipped her wine slowly, making a mental note to call Fiona as soon as she got home.

'By the way,' continued Nikunj, 'I hope I didn't cause you any trouble with your . . . erm, friend.'

Anna shook her head but wondered again why Tom had been so ill-mannered. He couldn't possibly be jealous. If he was, she ought to be flattered. But all she felt was irritation. She resolved to give him a piece of her mind.

'So,' said Nick. 'How is Roshni?'

'She seemed fine when I last saw her.'

'Glad to hear it. I'd hate it if she was still pining over me,' Nick said with a smirk.

Anna laughed. 'I don't think she's pining. I'll be seeing her soon so I can give her a message if you like. Shall I tell her you've been thinking about her?'

'That won't be necessary,' he said with a grin. Changing the subject, he asked about her role as a medical advocate. 'I'm serious about finding out exactly what you do for your charity. Some of the charities I work with could do with a medical advisor. Fiona said you've been offering this service for quite a while.'

'About two years. What would you like to know?'

'Loads of things. We have a few projects linked to mental health care for vulnerable and disadvantaged people. We need specialists who can help people understand the clinical decisions made for them.'

Anna nodded. 'If it helps, I can send you my job description. It describes the role and responsibilities. There's a bit about the governance of the post as well.'

'That sounds great. Thanks.'

'What are you working on at the moment?'

He took a sip of his beer. 'Right now, I'm busy raising money for people in the developing world. We need funds for things like building schools and wells. We also do a lot for destitute women and orphaned children in Africa and India.'

Anna blinked. He seemed to be involved in things very close to her heart. 'What about women suffering domestic abuse?'

Nick considered for a moment. 'I think that would be included with the destitute women charities.'

Anna nodded. 'I always wish I could do more for them. It's heart-breaking to see their suffering.'

Nick looked at her with a sombre expression. 'I can let you know when we run another fundraising event for women and children, if you like.'

'I'd like that.'

He beamed a smile. 'In that case, shall we exchange phone numbers?' He pulled out his mobile, tapped on it, then offered it to her.

Without any hesitation, Anna punched in her number.

# Chapter 9

The first thing Anna did when she went into work the next day was confront Tom in his office. It was at the start of surgery, and he was preparing to see his first patient.

'What was all that about yesterday?' she asked him, her eyebrows knitted together. She had brooded overnight about his behaviour towards Nick, as well as all the different times he had cancelled on her. 'You can be so rude and arrogant sometimes.'

Tom narrowed his eyes. 'Rude and arrogant. Is that what you think of me?'

'Yes,' said Anna testily. 'I don't like it when you behave like that.'

Tom gave her a hard look. 'Seems to me there's a lot of things you don't like these days.'

'Well, I didn't like your treatment of Nick. You were very dismissive.'

'Dismissive?' Tom frowned. 'You don't think I had a right to be annoyed that you were going out with him?'

'I wasn't going out with him! It was just a friendly drink.' Anna was becoming increasingly irate.

Tom's expression hardened. 'You know, Anna. I sometimes wonder why you even stay with me. If you can't understand why I didn't want you to go with that guy, then you will never understand me.'

Anna was dumbfounded. She hadn't expected him to go down that route. He stared at her with his mouth twisted into a humourless smile. He was making it all about himself, not even trying to see it from her position. Her anger spiked. For a moment, she considered walking out on him in a huff. But his mocking tone infuriated her. She stood her ground. Giving him a cold stare, she opened her mouth to challenge him.

Suddenly, she found herself holding back her words. In a moment of clarity, for the first time, she saw him for what he was: a conceited, egocentric man. It was there, facing him in his office, that she finally understood how wrong they were for each other. Her anger drained away.

'You know what, Tom?' She held up both her hands. 'This is not working. It's about respect. I deserve more respect from you.' Turning on her heel, Anna held her head up and walked out, leaving Tom staring after her.

～

When Anna rang Fiona that evening, there were two important things she had to tell her. The first was related to her colleague Nick and the second was her argument with Tom.

Fiona was astonished to learn that Nick had been the Nikunj that Anna had met in Harrow. She laughed heartily at her confusion over his nickname. 'That's hilarious. And it's just like him to turn up at your workplace unannounced. He's a bit of a prankster, old Nick. But quite the charmer.'

'Well,' said Anna. 'I can tell you he didn't charm Tom.'

'What do you mean?'

'Nick persuaded me to go for a drink with him, and Tom became very possessive. It really pissed me off.'

'Tom pissed you off? I can't believe that. Don't tell me you've finally seen the light. Has he fallen off his pedestal?' Fiona teased.

Anna took a deep breath. 'He definitely has. We exchanged a few words about his behaviour this morning. You know what, Fiona? I'm done. I'm done with Tom.'

'What do you mean?' Fiona was astonished.

'I mean I'm going to break up with him,' Anna replied firmly.

There was silence on the line. Anna wondered if Fiona had heard. 'I know you've always wanted me to leave him. You never trusted him. You told me so. I think you were right.'

'Yes, I know, but Anna, this has to be your decision. Are you sure?'

'I am.' Anna paused, realising the gravity of what she had just said. 'We're not on the same wavelength. I've decided to tell him it's over and hand in my notice. That way, I'll be out of there by December and there won't be any danger of seeing him at work.'

'Wow. You really are serious.'

'Yep. I've thought it through. When I leave the practice, I'll locum for a bit then look for a position at another surgery.'

Saying those words out loud, she felt a weight being lifted from her shoulders. She realised that by holding on to Tom, she'd been placing an emotional burden on herself.

'It's strange, Fiona, but I feel relieved,' she said. 'I didn't expect that. It's as if I'm suddenly free to do whatever I want.'

'And what *do* you want to do?' asked Fiona.

'To go in search of my past,' Anna replied without hesitation. She paused for a moment to reflect on her conversations with Tom. 'You know, I tried hard to explain why that is so important to me. But Tom just couldn't see it. He didn't understand. Even my parents don't get it. I'm going to have to do this myself. I have to stop being indecisive and put all my energy into finding out what happened all those years ago. I don't know how successful I'll be, but I've got to try.'

She began contemplating her trip to Zimbabwe. Having given a lot of thought on how she would get started in Harare, she had prepared a plan of sorts. She knew what she had to do. With her mind made up to leave the practice, December couldn't come soon enough.

# PART 2

# Chapter 10

Anna looked out of the window as the plane touched down at Harare international airport. The tarmac was wet with puddles of rainwater and the sky was full of dark heavy clouds. This was the rainy season in Zimbabwe and Anna knew to expect scorching heat on some days and at times, thunderstorms and heavy rain. But most days would be sunny and warm with an average temperature of 25 degrees centigrade. Anna looked forward to soaking up the sun after the bitter cold of the British winter.

Waiting at the arrivals section was her Uncle Peter, her mother's younger brother. He beamed with pleasure when he spotted them coming through with their luggage trolleys. Tall and lean, he chuckled as he hugged the ladies and clapped Mathew on the shoulder. Grabbing one of the trollies, he led them to his Nissan saloon which Anna noticed had seen better days.

As soon as he'd parked the car on the gravel driveway of his home, Peter's wife Mary hurried out to welcome them.

'Hello my dears! You are here at last.' She enveloped Anna in a tight, warm hug, emanating a scent of lavender soap and sweet perfume. Auntie Mary was short and chubby with a cheerful personality. 'So nice to see you, baby! What took you so long to come see us?'

Without waiting for an answer, she linked arms with Theresa and led them into the house. As soon as they went through the front door, they were greeted with the inviting aromas of lunch.

'I hope you're hungry,' she said. 'Go freshen up, then we can eat right away.'

'Dominic is very excited to see you, Anna,' said Uncle Peter when they were all seated round the table. 'He'll be here straight after work.'

Anna was fond of her young cousin Dominic who always went out of his way to make her feel at home. She was counting on him to help her with her investigation.

'Where does he work now?' asked Theresa.

'He's got a good job at the *Zimbabwe Express*, one of the biggest national newspapers here. He's working his way up the ladder there. He just bought his first car last month and can't wait to show it off to all of you.'

Mathew looked pleased. Though he didn't say it, Anna could see that he was happy to be back in his hometown. Uncle Peter filled him in on the changes that had occurred in Harare since his last visit. They discussed President Mnangagwa, the man who had ousted Robert Mugabe in November of the previous year. After enduring Mugabe's destructive rule for four decades, Uncle Peter held hope for a better future under the new leadership.

After lunch, the men brought the luggage inside, placing Anna's case in the smallest of the three rooms. Like other houses on the street, this was a bungalow with a good-sized garden behind the kitchen. A covered veranda had been built at the back, complete with outdoor furniture for al fresco dining. They were in Marimba Park, a suburb conveniently located just ten minutes away from the shops. Anna knew her way around and was keen to take a walk by herself.

'Wear a hat if you're going out,' said Mary. 'The sun is very strong in the middle of the day.'

Anna changed into a sleeveless cotton dress and slipped on her sandals. She left the house with her floppy-brimmed hat, leaving the two couples to enjoy their reunion.

The street outside was a single-track tarmac road with verdant green grass on either side. Tall royal poinciana trees with flamboyant red blooms provided much needed shade every few metres. Anna marvelled at the vibrant red blossoms covering the beautiful green leaves of these magnificent trees. They were breathtakingly beautiful.

Also wonderful were the red and pink bougainvillea flowers growing wild on the boundary walls and hedges by the roadside. Harare city was famous for these amazing trees and flowering plants at this time of year.

The air was hot and humid, but after weeks of cold wind and grey skies in London, Anna was glad to feel the heat. She welcomed the sun on her bare arms and shoulders. The sound of Zimbabwean music floated over from one of the shops in the parade ahead. It got louder as she approached the row of grocery stores, food stalls and shops selling clothes, shoes, household goods and more. Due to the heat, only a few people were walking on the pavements outside the shops.

Anna stepped into one of the food stores which was more like a mini supermarket. The fresh scent of fruits filled the air, kept cool by strategically placed electric fans throughout the room. Anna's eyes were drawn to the mountains of big, round golden oranges. They were her favourite. Oranges from the Mazowe Valley just north of Harare were exceptionally juicy, unlike any she had tasted in the UK. She hoped her Auntie Mary had some Mazoe Orange Crush, the local fruit juice that she loved, in her fridge.

The shop owners and sellers went about their business looking relaxed and cheerful. They chatted and laughed a lot, and when she passed by, they gave her a friendly smile. It was good to be back in Zimbabwe. Anna felt a kinship with these people whose heritage she shared. Part of her belonged here and she readily returned the smiles. She understood some of what they were saying because her mother had sometimes spoken to her in Shona when she was little. However, lack of practice over the years meant that Anna was unable to carry out even a brief conversation in the local language.

Remembering there was an open-air market further on, Anna decided to make her way towards it. When she got there, she was disappointed to find it very rundown. Ten years after the economic crisis in Zimbabwe, she had expected it to be much improved. During that difficult period, the country went through an incredibly tough time with hyper-inflation resulting in extreme shortages of food and other essential goods. Despite that, the markets were still fairly lively. She remembered this market for its many traders selling all manner of goods for locals and tourists. Now there were only a few drab stalls selling second-hand items.

Anna found it distressing to see the weary and defeated faces of the people sitting around the stalls. These individuals were evidently the victims of the shattered economy resulting from years of government negligence. It saddened her to see the state of men, women and children sitting in rags, hoping to earn a few dollars by selling used goods.

Feeling disheartened, Anna turned around and slowly made her way back to her uncle's house. She was hot and thirsty, so she headed straight to the kitchen and helped herself to some water from the tap. As she downed the glass, she heard a familiar voice behind her.

'There's cold Mazoe Orange for you in the fridge.'

It was Dominic, standing with a broad smile across his face. Despite being twenty-five years old, he still had a youthful appearance, resembling a teenager. Anna smiled back at him and approached with open arms. Only a little taller than her, he was slim, with shiny dark skin and a head full of curly black hair. This was her happy-go-lucky, good-looking cousin.

'You're early,' she said as they hugged.

'Ach well, my boss told me I could scoot.'

'Good to see you.'

Dominic stepped back. 'Guess what? I've got my own car now. Did you see it parked outside?'

Anna shook her head. She'd been too hot to notice. He insisted on showing her, so she followed him out to the driveway, where his gleaming white pride and joy awaited under the late afternoon sun.

'It's a second-hand Subaru, but it looks brand new, doesn't it?' Anna nodded, smiling at his excitement. 'Let's go for a drive. You get in and I'll go tell the oldies.' He dashed inside and was out before Anna had even opened the passenger door. 'Come on, get in!' He waited until she was belted up, then reversed carefully and accelerated out on to the road.

They drove into the city, and Dominic served as her tour guide, showing her familiar sights and some new ones while providing information along the way. Anna sat back and enjoyed the drive. The seat was comfortable, and the air conditioning was a godsend. There were many potholes on the roads, but Dominic drove around them, taking care not to damage his tyres and suspension.

They arrived outside an ice-cream bar in a retail park opposite a large area of green fields. They settled at an outdoor table shaded by a massive umbrella. Anna ordered a Banana Split with scoops of different-flavoured ice creams and a drizzle of caramel sauce on top of the banana. Dominic had a Coke float – a scoop of vanilla ice cream in a tall glass of cola. The cream fizzed like a volcanic eruption inside the glass.

'I'd forgotten about your Coke float!'

'Best thing in the world,' said Dominic, drinking through his straw. 'It's nice to have you back here.'

'Thanks. This time, I'm going to need a lot of help from you. I've come with a purpose.'

Dominic raised his eyebrows. 'What kind of purpose?'

Anna explained her mission. Dominic was shocked to learn that his uncle had been a foundling, not an orphan. It seemed that only those closest to Mathew knew the truth. Anna told her cousin how much it meant to her to find out why her father had been abandoned. Dominic had grown up with a large extended family, knowing his grandparents and cousins from both sides of the family. He sympathised with Anna for being deprived of what he had enjoyed all his life.

'I can see where you're coming from. But where would we even start?'

Anna sighed. 'I've thought about this a lot. The first thing we need to do is find out where records of births and adoptions are kept. There may be some clues there.'

'Have you looked at your dad's adoption papers?'

'I have. There's nothing helpful in those. Only the name of the church and the names of Granny and Grandad Kotze who adopted him.'

Dominic pursed his lips in thought. 'How does Uncle Mathew feel about you doing all this digging? From what I remember, he was never keen to even talk about his past. I was told not to mention it in front of him.'

Anna nodded, looking regretful. 'He's not happy about it. He knows I want to find out what happened, but he doesn't know what I plan to do here.'

Dominic frowned. 'That's not good. If he's not happy about this, he won't like me helping you.'

'Don't worry about that. He'll be fine.'

Dominic still seemed sceptical. 'I don't know . . . Besides, it was a long time ago and I don't think records were kept from those times.'

'Why wouldn't they be? I'm sure they'll be archived somewhere. Dominic, you could easily find out for me.' He responded with a concerned shake of the head. 'Oh, come on, Dominic. You've got to help me. No one seems to understand how important this is for me. I was really hoping you would.'

Sipping his drink, Dominic remained silent.

'Look,' Anna continued, determined. 'I know the name of the church where my dad was found. It's somewhere near a town called Fort Victoria. I intend to find that place and go to see it. Will you tell me how to get there?'

'You can't go on your own.' Dominic's voice was firm.

'Then come with me. Come on, Dominic. Help me out.' Anna was not going to give up.

When he realised how determined she was, Dominic eventually relented. 'All right, all right, I'll take you. But if your dad gives me a hard time, you'd better speak up for me.' He paused. 'What if the church is no longer there?'

'It *is* still there,' said Anna with a grateful smile. 'I've searched online for it and there seems to be a school next to it called Rukuvoko Faith School.'

Dominic considered. 'Fort Victoria is now called Masvingo. It's about two hundred miles away, close to the Zimbabwe Ruins. If you insist on going, I can drive you there. I'm free from next week because my section at work closes early for Christmas. We can go sometime next week or the week after.'

'Thank you, Dominic. That's very kind of you. I want to go there because they must hold some record of my dad being found as a newborn.' Anna exhaled slowly. 'There's something else I want to do. In the UK, we often see news articles about abandoned babies being taken into care by the authorities. I'm sure that even here, there would have been something in the news if that happened. Where would I go to look through past newspapers? Do you know?'

'Yah. They'll be in the National Archives of Zimbabwe.' He paused and gazed at Anna with furrowed brow. 'I really feel sorry for your dad. It must be horrible to know you were rejected by your own parents. I can guess why he doesn't want to check out his past. He's afraid of the unknown and of being rejected again. He's scared you might uncover something horrible that will give him even more pain.'

Anna looked at her cousin in astonishment. 'When did you become so wise, Dominic?'

Grinning, he shrugged and slurped the last remnants of his Coke float. 'I'd better take you back. My folks will be worrying about you.'

'Won't they be worried about you?'

'Ach, no. I'm not a kid any more. By the way, I'll be staying with Uncle Simon. There's not enough room in the house.'

'I'm sorry. I know I've taken your bedroom. How's everyone at Uncle Simon's?' Anna knew that her mother's older brother lived only a few miles away.

'They're all fine. They want to come see you tomorrow.'

Once they were back in the car, Anna told Dominic that she had one other idea up her sleeve. 'I know this Indian lady called Savita Virani who lives in the suburb of Belvedere. I'm going to pay her a visit and ask her to help me talk to some Indian families. Somebody might remember something about an Indian baby abandoned in a church. It's a long shot, but worth a try. What do you think?'

Dominic made a short hooting noise. 'Good luck with that! You're clutching at straws. No one is going to remember something that happened so long ago. And even if they did, they are not going to talk.'

'Why do you say that?'

'Because I know Indian people. They are very tight-lipped. They show a united front and cover for one another. If they didn't say anything at the time that it happened, they will definitely not say anything now.'

Anna fell silent, contemplating this potential challenge. She thought of Savita and how open and talkative she was. There must be others like her who would be willing to help. Anna decided that she would call Savita that evening to let her know she had arrived. In London, she had not told her anything about her plans. But now, she was ready to explain the real purpose of her visit. She was counting on Savita to advise on how to ask people difficult questions about the past.

# Chapter 11

The following morning, Auntie Mary drove Anna and her parents to Savita's house. After announcing their presence on the intercom at the side of the electric gates, they proceeded down a paved driveway, passing a well-kept lawn and a charming flower garden on the left. Ahead, there stood a lovely bungalow where Savita awaited them outside the front door, sheltered by a covered portico.

'Welcome!' Savita said, smiling widely. She reached out for Anna and gave her a tight hug. 'It's so nice to see you again.'

A middle-aged man with greying hair came out to join them. Savita introduced him as her husband, Prakash. Of medium height, a paunch hanging over his belt, he wore casual trousers and a loose shirt. Shaking hands with everyone, he invited them all inside.

They gathered around a carved wooden coffee table, already set with glasses of water on a silver tray. Savita began talking about their time together in London, quickly putting everyone at ease. She mentioned that some of their old school friends had been enquiring about Mathew and asked if he would be interested in meeting them. Anna was surprised by how readily Mathew agreed, and Savita's delight was evident as she promised to start arranging a reunion for the following week.

Before long, Savita's maid served tea with snacks. A delicious aroma arose from the platters of samosas, bhajiyas, pooris and dhokras. An array of chutneys, arranged like a work of art on a tray, accompanied the dishes.

'You've gone to a lot of trouble, Savita,' said Theresa.

'Not at all. I'm hoping you will come back for dinner one evening. And Anna, you must meet my daughter Taruna, Roshni's twin.'

Anna smiled. 'Roshni told me about her. Does she live nearby?'

'Not too far. She and her husband live near the university where they both work. If you let me know when you're free, I can ask her to come meet you.'

Anna nodded. Thinking about the information she was after, she hoped to get a chance to talk to Savita privately. But it proved impossible with everyone around. When they were leaving, however, she managed to have a quiet word. She asked Savita if she could call her that evening to ask for her help with something important. Looking intrigued, Savita kissed her on the cheek and said she looked forward to her call.

∼

At Auntie Mary's house, a lively atmosphere awaited them as they arrived. The back garden was filled with guests, including Theresa's older brother Simon, his wife, and their three young grandchildren. Uncle Peter was preparing a barbeque lunch for everyone. He looked relieved when they walked in.

'Thank God you're back, Mary. While I do the *braai*, can you get the vegetables and salads going?'

After the happy greetings were exchanged, Uncle Simon poured Mathew a cold beer and drew him into a conversation about the good old days after independence before Mugabe ruined the country. Anna went to help Uncle Peter with the barbeque.

'Why do you call it a *braai*?' she asked.

'It's short for "*braaivleis*", meaning cooking on an open fire. It comes from Afrikaans, you know, from when the Dutch took over South Africa. Some words stick, don't they?'

Anna nodded. 'Sometimes my parents speak in Chilapalapa when they don't want me to know what they're saying. How come you don't speak that?'

'I don't like it. It's a racist language. The colonials used it to keep us black people subservient.'

Anna reflected on this while she watched the children playing on the lawn. Her Uncle Simon called out to say that they were all invited to spend Christmas Day with them at his home.

'It's usually a scorching hot day and we always have the whole extended family over for lunch by the pool. Everyone jumps in before we eat, adults and children, so I hope you've brought your swimming costume.'

Anna confirmed that she had and was pleased for her dad who loved being in the water. He had explained to Anna that Uncle Simon was a wealthy man. He had done well in the years after independence, building his small import-export business into a large successful company with many employees. Fortunately for him, he had decided to sell the company just before the economic downturn in 2008. Now enjoying his retirement, Anna looked forward to visiting his mansion in the more exclusive part of Marimba Park.

~

That evening, Anna waited until 8 p.m. before phoning Savita. She wanted to tell her the full story so that she would understand the importance of her mission.

'I've been waiting for your call,' said Savita. 'I can't imagine what help I can give you.'

Anna gave an audible sigh. 'It's a long story. I'm after some information and you're the only one I know who might be able to help.'

'Fire away.'

'Okay. When you were in London, you told me that you and your classmates knew that my father was a foundling. You were aware that he was left as a newborn at a church door.'

'Yes,' said Savita slowly.

'You also said there were rumours about him being abandoned because his mother was unmarried, and she came from one of the Indian families in Harare.'

'Well, yah. But it was all just gossip, you know. Nothing was for sure.'

'But you mentioned that those families are still around. What I would really like is to meet them to ask if they know what happened all those years ago.'

'Oh, my dear! That will be very difficult. If you ask questions like that, they might think you are accusing them of being involved in your father's abandonment.'

'I know. That's why I need you with me. I thought maybe you could help me find a way of asking for information without making anyone feel uncomfortable. I just want to know if they remember anything or have heard of anything about an Indian baby boy being left in a basket outside a church.'

Anna went on to explain why it was so important for her to learn the truth. She emphasised her need to know who Mathew's biological parents were, and why they had abandoned him.

Savita was clearly troubled. 'I'm not sure about this, Anna. Has Mathew asked you to do this?'

'No. He doesn't want to dig up the past. It's just me. I feel the need to do this for myself *and* for him. We have a whole chunk of history missing from our lives. For me personally, I'm searching for the missing part of my identity, the Indian part.'

Savita was quiet on the line for a long minute. 'I know it's a lot to ask,' said Anna. 'I just think someone in your community *must* know something. It would have been a huge decision for parents to give up their baby. There must have been extreme circumstances for them to do that. I'm sure of it. I *have* to find out what those circumstances were. And I *have* to know who left my father at that church.'

Savita sighed. 'You know Anna, we might be barking up the wrong tree. Mathew's mother might not be from here at all. Some people believed she came from India and went back after her baby was born.'

'Then she must have stayed with someone in the community. One of the families linked to the rumours perhaps. Even though it happened so long ago, that bit of information could have been handed down over the years and if we jog their memory, it might resurface and give us a lead to follow up. That's possible, isn't it?' Anna heard the catch in her own voice.

'Oh, Anna. I'm sorry this is causing you so much pain. Of course, I will help. But we must be realistic. After all these years, it's unlikely that people will remember.' She paused. 'Let me talk to my family. I'll call you tomorrow morning and maybe you can come to our house so we can discuss it together. My daughter is free on Saturdays so I will ask her to join us.'

Anna agreed to return at around 11 a.m. the following morning, with her plan to meet Dominic in the afternoon. They needed to find out where all birth and adoption records were held. She also wanted to firm up their trip to Rukuvoko Church where Mathew had been found. Time was of the essence. Before they knew it, it would be Christmas and it was important to do as much as possible before everything closed for the holidays.

~

Shortly after 11 a.m., Uncle Peter dropped Anna off outside Savita's house. She pressed the intercom button at the side of the gate and looked into the small camera. When the gate opened, Anna walked up to the front door. Savita opened it before she got there.

'Hello, my dear,' Savita said, enveloping Anna in one of her tight hugs. A young woman appeared behind her, looking similar but not identical to Roshni. She hung back until Savita drew her forward and introduced her as Taruna.

'Nice to meet you,' Taruna said, in a soft, shy voice. She led them through to the lounge where Prakash was already seated.

'So,' Prakash began, sounding grave. 'You wish to speak with some families from our community.'

Anna nodded. 'Just the ones that were linked to my father all those years ago. I know the links were just rumours, but they're all I've got.'

Prakash made a soft guttural sound and interlocked his fingers. 'It will be easy to take you to their homes, but I'm not sure asking questions about the past will go down well.'

'I know and I'm sorry to ask this of you.'

Prakash nodded. 'It will be tricky because I wouldn't want to offend anyone. But I can understand why you want to find out. We'll need to be careful how we do the questioning.'

Savita took Anna's hand and patted it. 'We've made a list. Prakash and I racked our brains to remember which families were likely to be around in 1954 and which ones are still here in Harare. Luckily, there aren't hundreds of homes in the Indian community. Many have left the country, of course, but there are some hardy old people still around. In some cases, the younger generations have left but their parents and grandparents are still here.'

Taruna had a notebook on her lap. She opened it and showed Anna a list of about twenty names. Savita pointed out five that were highlighted in yellow.

'These are the ones that we think were talked about in relation to your father. What we can do is phone them and say we have a visitor from the UK who would like to meet them.'

Anna puckered her brows. 'Won't they ask why I want to meet them?'

Savita shook her head. 'No. It would be impolite to ask, so they will always be welcoming. But once we're there, we will have to be ready with our reasons for the visit.'

'I've given this a lot of thought,' said Anna. 'What if we said I am doing some research on orphans and orphanages in Zimbabwe? Do you think people would be more likely to help?'

Taruna smiled. 'Funny you should say that because I was thinking along the same lines. Before you came this morning, I did a quick search on the internet to see if there was any information on orphanages here for Indian and mixed-race children in the 1950s. It seems there were separate children's homes for white and black orphans, but none for any other races. No one knows what happened to those children and you could say you are looking into that specific area.'

Anna nodded slowly, considering the idea. 'That's not only plausible but truthful as well. I *would* like to know what happened to those children. Where do you think they went?'

'I'm not sure,' Taruna replied.

'Are you carrying out this type of research at the university?' asked Anna.

'No,' she said with a soft laugh. 'I work in the science department.'

Savita reached out her arm and pulled her daughter close. 'My daughter is being modest. She is a senior lecturer in the science faculty. We are very proud of her.'

Taruna looked uncomfortable with the praise. She was clearly very different in nature from her twin sister in London. While

Roshni was lively and forthright, Taruna seemed more reserved. Looking bashful, she fiddled with the ring on her finger. Anna remembered Roshni saying her sister was in their parents' good books because she was married and already settled in life.

Anna brought the conversation back to visiting the families. She asked Savita when they could make a start on the visits.

'Tomorrow's a good day because on Sundays, people are likely to be home. I will make some calls today,' Savita replied.

Prakash pointed to the notebook and explained that only the five highlighted names were worth a visit. A telephone call to the others would be sufficient.

Taruna ran her finger down the page. 'I can make those phone calls. I will say I'm carrying out the research for you, which of course I am.' She turned the page and showed Anna a crib sheet she had produced. 'We should start by asking if anyone in their family was around in the fifties and sixties and explain the purpose of our research. Here's a draft of the questions we could ask.' She read out the list:

1.  'Was anyone in your family living in Southern Rhodesia in the 1950s and 1960s?
2.  Is it possible to speak to that person or those persons?
3.  Were you aware of any orphanages for Indians and mixed-race children at that time?
4.  Were you aware of any Indian or mixed-race orphans during that time?
5.  If so, do you know what happened to those orphans?
6.  Do you think they might have gone abroad?
7.  Do you know anyone who might have more information on this?'

'This is brilliant,' said Anna, in admiration. 'You've even mentioned the possibility of orphans going abroad. That might spark a memory of a woman going away after having a baby. Thank you so much.'

'No problem,' said Taruna.

Anna smiled gratefully at the kind and considerate nature of Roshni's family. They all knew it was a long shot, but they were willing to give it a try. Reflecting on it, Anna felt extremely fortunate to have met Roshni at the shelter for domestic abuse victims. That day had been incredibly lucky for her.

# Chapter 12

The minute Dominic parked his car, Anna was at the door to greet him. She led him through to the veranda at the back where her mother and Auntie Mary were sitting, having a chat. Anna began to tell them about her conversation that morning with Savita and her family. She updated them on all the details. Theresa listened with a scowl on her face.

'Your father will not be happy about this,' she said. 'He won't want you going around asking people questions about him.'

'I know, Mum, but I *have* to talk to these families. Someone might remember something.'

'Don't be ridiculous! No one's going to remember anything from so long ago.'

Auntie Mary put her hand on Theresa's arm. 'Let her do it, Theresa. The child needs to go back to London knowing she has tried everything.'

Theresa glared at Anna. 'As long as she knows that this could be painful for her father.'

'Best not to tell him, then,' said Auntie Mary. 'Only tell him if something good is discovered.'

'Thanks, Auntie Mary,' said Anna gratefully. 'That's what I'm planning to do.'

Theresa drew her lips into a thin line of displeasure, but she said nothing. Anna turned back to her aunt.

'I'm looking into every possible avenue. Dominic is going to take me to find past newspaper articles. A baby abandoned in a basket must have been featured in the papers, even in 1954.'

Mary was sitting with her eyebrows knitted together in thought. 'Someone was telling me about those DNA ancestor-finding websites. Have you tried anything like that?'

'I have.' Anna was surprised her aunt knew about DNA tests. 'I sent off my sample ages ago. I wanted Dad to do it too, but Mum wouldn't let me ask him.'

Theresa sniffed. 'As if he wasn't upset enough, you wanted to give him more stress! No thank you.'

Mary was curious. 'How does it work, this DNA stuff?'

'You buy a kit that contains a tube for your saliva sample, you post it off to the company and wait for their laboratory to do the analysis. Two months later you read the results online.'

Theresa tutted with impatience. 'It was a total waste of time.'

'No, Mum, it wasn't! I did learn something. The results mapped out my ethnicity going back several generations and worked out where my ancestors came from.'

'For heaven's sake!' Theresa glared at Anna. 'I could have told you that for nothing. Mathew's ancestors came from India and yours came from Africa and India.'

'Okay. Calm down, Theresa,' said Mary. Still curious, she queried Anna further. 'Doesn't the DNA match you up with living relatives? I thought that was the purpose.'

Anna sighed. 'Yes, it is. But it can only do that if your relatives have also sent in their DNA to the company. Unfortunately, there were no matches for me.'

Dominic joined the conversation. 'That doesn't mean there will *never* be matches. Someday, a distant cousin might send in a sample and who knows? It could lead you to Uncle Mathew's birth family.'

In silence, everyone pondered over this scenario. It did seem like a pipe dream. Anna had to admit that this would probably never happen. It was yet another line of action that fell into the *highly unlikely* bracket.

Dominic blew out his cheeks. 'Man, you guys need to lighten up. Why get so depressed? There are loads more things we can do, like checking out the birth and adoption records.'

With a grateful smile, Anna waited for Dominic to elaborate.

'All records of births, deaths and adoptions registered in this country are retained by the state. They are held at the Central Registry Office in the Registrar General's Department. We can go there sometime this week to find out what the process is for requesting access.'

'Why don't we just phone them?' asked Anna.

Dominic snorted. 'This is not the UK, Anna. Things don't happen here unless you physically go to these places. We might be told to go away and fill in some forms. I don't know. But it's best if we see someone face to face.'

Theresa still looked unsettled. 'What are you hoping to achieve, Anna? You have already seen your father's birth certificate, his adoption paper and his baptism certificate. What more will you find in the central records?'

'I don't know. I'm just hoping there will be a file on Dad. Maybe some notes or references that I can follow up on.'

Mary was curious about the legal papers they already had. Anna explained. 'Dad's birth certificate has the stamp and signature of the Fort Victoria District Registrar. It's dated twenty-fifth of March 1954. The date of birth stated is twenty-fifth of January 1954. Then in one line it says: Parents unknown. Baby found in basket at Rukuvoko Mission Church. That's it.'

Mary chewed her lip, reflecting on this piece of information. 'So that means Mathew was already two months old when he was registered. And I suppose the date of birth was a guess?'

Anna nodded. 'That's what we believe. That church is still standing, so I've persuaded Dominic to drive me to Fort Victoria to see if we can get more information.'

'Not Fort Victoria. Masvingo,' said Mary. 'What does the adoption paper say?'

'It bears the same stamp and signature of the District Registrar and the same date: twenty-fifth March 1954. It states that the baby boy of unknown parents is legally adopted by Mr and Mrs Kotze of a particular address in Fort Victoria. It mentions Dad's date of birth and the name and address of the church.'

'That means Mathew's birth was registered on the same day that he was officially adopted. Interesting,' Mary remarked, turning to Theresa. 'Mathew has never talked about this. He doesn't like to think back, does he?'

Theresa's face reflected the sadness that she felt. She pressed her lips together and slowly shook her head. 'For all these years, he has managed to bury this. Now it's come to the surface again and I am very worried about him. He's afraid of what might be discovered.'

Anna let out a sigh. 'I know. He thinks I might uncover something that will be too painful to bear. His fear is that if I find his family and they don't want to know anything about us, he will feel worse. Like being abandoned all over again.'

Theresa stared at Anna in surprise. 'Did he tell you that?'

'No, but I understand Dad better than you give me credit for.' Anna sighed. 'I hate to do this to him. But what choice do I have? You know how I usually doubt myself; how I'm never sure of things. Well, on this matter, I have no doubts whatsoever. I *have* to try and solve this mystery.'

Dominic was looking at her intently. 'Uncle Mathew might be worrying for nothing. If you get to the truth, and it's a big if, who's to say it will be bad news? It could be something nice that will make him really happy.'

'That's right,' said Mary. 'It could lead him to relatives who are lovely people, and they might be overjoyed to meet him. I wish you luck, Anna. I hope you find what you're looking for.'

At that moment, Matthew and Uncle Peter joined them, bringing the discussion to an abrupt end. 'Time for a sundowner,' said Peter. 'Who wants a cold beer?'

~

As promised, Savita called Anna in the evening to confirm their visit to two families the following day. Both visits were scheduled for the afternoon, between 2 and 4 p.m. Anna promised to be ready when they came to pick her up.

That night, Anna struggled to fall asleep until the early hours. Filled with a mixture of excitement and apprehension, she worried about upsetting or offending people when she asked questions about the past. She had no idea how she would be received. Remembering what Dominic had said about Indians being tight-lipped, Anna could only hope that the families they were about to visit would be as open and friendly as Savita and Prakash.

'No need to be nervous,' said Savita when Anna got into the car and confessed to being anxious. 'It'll be fine. Let me tell you about the first family we're going to see, the Patnis. There are three generations living together: grandfather Bhiku-*kaka*, Devika and Chandu who are my age, and their two grown-up sons. They should all be at home this afternoon.'

'So, I guess this is one of the families rumoured to have a connection with my father's birth?' Anna asked.

Savita nodded. 'Bhiku-*kaka* is in his eighties. He's quite a tough and demanding old man, but don't let him frighten you. His bark is worse than his bite. He was born and brought up in this country. In 1954, he would have been a young man in his twenties. I have a memory of people saying he was quite wild and rebellious, mixing with boys thought to be rough and tough. He didn't conform to the societal norms of traditional Gujarati families. The gossip about him being involved with Mathew's birth mother was based mostly on his reputation.'

'We must be careful not to jump to any conclusions,' warned Prakash. 'Lots of young men go through a rebellious phase. It doesn't mean the rumours are true.'

Anna agreed but decided to closely observe the old man's reactions when they discussed orphans and orphanages.

~

Mr and Mrs Patni gave them a warm welcome and offered them tea as soon as they went inside their beautiful home. The front room had double doors that opened to a patio overlooking a flower-filled garden. The back door must have been open too, as fresh air circulated, creating a cool and comfortable atmosphere inside.

Devika explained that her boys had decided to go out, but her father-in-law was currently having his afternoon nap. Anna's face fell but Savita was quick to speak up.

'Anna was hoping to gather some information about Southern Rhodesia in the 1950s. It's the older generation that would know more about that period. Is *Kaka* due to wake up anytime soon?'

'Yah. He's usually awake by this time,' said Chandu with a frown. 'I did tell him you were coming. Let me go and see.'

As Chandu left the room, Savita apologised for causing a disruption, but Devika assured her it was not a problem. However, when the old man entered the room, there was a noticeable change in the atmosphere. Anna sensed a tension in the air, and silence fell until he took his seat across from her.

Small and stooped, he had thin grey hair and horn-rimmed glasses on his nose. Dressed in an open-neck shirt, brown trousers, and slip-on mule sandals, he entered the room slowly, avoiding eye contact with anyone. Only after he took his seat did he raise his head and peer at Anna, his expression stern and forbidding.

Savita and Prakash greeted him respectfully with joined palms. '*Namaste, Kaka.* We've brought our friend Anna to meet you.' Their voices were hushed, as if they felt intimidated by this man who seemed to carry a lot of gravitas.

'*Namaste,*' he said. His voice was a little wheezy, but it sounded as stern as the look on his face. He addressed Anna. 'You are from London?'

'Yes,' said Anna, holding his gaze, keeping her voice strong. 'I'm doing some research on orphanages in 1950s Southern Rhodesia.'

He coughed and cleared his throat. 'And how can I help?'

'I'm trying to find out if there were any children's homes for Indian and mixed-race orphans. Would you happen to know if there were any at that time?' She watched his face carefully for his reaction. He screwed up his eyes and puckered his lips. He remained silent for so long that Anna wondered if she needed to repeat her question.

'You want me to tell you if there were any orphanages here in the fifties.' He spoke slowly, in a breathy voice. 'Orphanages for Indians and mixed-race children. Why?'

'Because . . . because I'm interested to know what happened to those orphans. It doesn't look like there were any safe places for them. There are records of separate children's homes for white and black children, but none for any other groups. I just wondered if anyone had personal knowledge of this.'

Bhiku-*kaka* responded with a sardonic smile. 'If there were any orphanages at that time, I would be the last person who would know about them. In the fifties, I was too busy doing other things to notice things like that.' Anna sensed a defiant glint in his eyes.

Prakash coughed and took a sip of his tea. 'I don't know about the mixed-race community, but if there were any Indian orphans, I'm sure we would have heard of them. Wouldn't you agree, *Kaka*?'

'Yah,' he replied, frowning at Prakash. 'I don't remember hearing about any orphans, Indian or mixed-race.'

Anna hesitated, then looked directly into his eyes. 'What about adopted children? Were you aware of any families with an adopted Indian child in their home?'

Giving her a humourless stare, he seemed to be considering her question seriously. The corners of his mouth came down and he shrugged his shoulders. 'I don't believe there were any.'

Anna pressed her lips together and nodded. Something in the way he pondered over the question while maintaining eye contact suggested to her that he was being truthful. He seemed genuinely not to know. She smiled. 'Thank you for your time.'

Screwing up his face again, he gave her the briefest of nods, then turned to Prakash. 'Why haven't I seen you at the *paana* club recently?' It was more an accusation than a question.

In a gentle and almost meek tone, Prakash apologised for not joining him and others at their club. It seemed they played cards together on a regular basis. There ensued a discussion about their games, and while they talked, the women chatted among themselves. When it felt acceptable to leave, they stood up and said their polite goodbyes.

It was clear to Anna that Bhiku-*kaka* commanded respect and fear in equal measure from people around him. But there was a directness about him that suggested he was not a dishonest person. Anna stepped away with the feeling that he and his family knew nothing about Mathew and any rumours linking them to him were probably untrue.

~

The next family they visited was a couple in their seventies. Sharda and Bipin Daruwala were both born and bred in Southern Rhodesia. They'd grown up as neighbours and been married for over fifty years. They would have been about nine years old in 1954. Savita explained to Anna that there had been talk about Sharda's late father being a womaniser. His name had often come up in connection with Mathew's birth parents.

Although Sharda had lost her father many years previously, her mother had only recently passed away. The hope was that Sharda's mother had said something to her about Mathew. Not necessarily about a possible link between her husband and Mathew, but perhaps an awareness of the rumours flying around.

Once again, they received a warm reception. The conversation flowed smoothly without any difficulties. Anna felt comfortable enough with them to ask her questions without concern about offending them. They responded openly and without hesitation, showing a willingness to be helpful. Unfortunately, neither of them knew anything of value to her.

'We were wondering about your mum,' said Savita. 'Did she ever mention any orphaned or adopted children to you? Especially Indian children without parents in the 1950s?'

Sharda knitted her eyebrows. 'No. I don't think so.' She paused to ponder a little more. 'I can't remember her saying anything like that to me.'

Disappointed, Anna pursed her lips and frowned. At that very moment, they heard the front door open and someone calling out.

'It's only me!'

Bipin smiled. 'That's our daughter Pratima. She pops in almost every day.'

Pratima entered the room carrying a large saucepan and took two steps forward before stopping. 'Oh, sorry. I didn't know you had visitors. I brought some biryani for you.'

'It's okay,' said Bipin, standing up. 'Let me take that to the kitchen.' She handed the pan over and came forward to greet everyone. In her forties, Pratima was a plump woman with a round face and wavy brown hair tied at the nape of her neck. She looked at Anna with curiosity and when she heard about the research project, she wanted to know more.

Anna was happy to go over the details again. She could tell Pratima was genuinely interested. 'Did you find the information you needed?' she asked.

Anna shook her head, looking regretful. Pratima sympathised. 'I suppose it is a long time ago. People won't remember that far back.'

Turning to her mother, she explained that she had to rush off but would be back the next day. Apologising to everyone, she got up to leave.

'It was nice to meet you, Anna. Best of luck with your research.'

Soon after she took her leave, Prakash thanked their hosts and led the way out. Sharda and Bipin stood at their door, smiling as they waved goodbye. Disappointed but grateful to them, Anna waved back, wondering if she would ever find the information that she was after. Finding people who could recall events from over six decades ago was proving to be as challenging as everyone had warned. Fingers of doubt began to close around her mind, but she pushed them away. She was determined not to give up.

# Chapter 13

On Wednesday morning, Anna was ready and waiting for Dominic to pick her up at 10 a.m. The day was bright and sunny, although the week had started with rain lashing down on and off for two days. Loud claps of thunder had made Anna jump and flashes of lightning cracked across the sky. As someone accustomed to the perpetual drizzle of London, she marvelled at the stormy weather in Zimbabwe.

Initially, Anna's Uncle Peter had planned to take them for a drive around town on Monday, followed by lunch at a riverside restaurant on the outskirts of the city. However, due to the rainy weather, they had stayed at home to enjoy some rest. Anna spent her time sitting in the veranda in between the downpours, reading from her Kindle or speaking to Fiona in London on her mobile. Fiona was keen to know how she was getting on with her detective work.

Allowing herself a little break from her investigations, Anna sat back and appreciated the honeyed scent of the Zimbabwean garden after the rain. It brought with it much needed cool air laden with a sweet earthy scent. It was so different from the post-rain smells back in London. The African sky remained overcast with clouds, and beneath this grey canopy, large raindrops cascaded from the damp branches of the towering msasa trees. Anna watched as they fell upon the lawn, transforming it into a brighter shade of green.

After each heavy downpour, Anna noticed a myriad of birds emerging from their shelters or flitting out from under bushes of refuge. They chirped and hooted in loud chirrups, making their presence known, as if calling one another to come out and play in the cooler, fresher air.

Anna enjoyed her two days of rest but was glad when the rain cleared. She was eager to continue with her enquiries. As Dominic drove her into the city, Anna looked with interest at the progress made since her last visit. New buildings had sprung up in many places and there seemed to be more greenery around. Compared to the suburbs where the roads were full of potholes, the city centre streets were smooth and even. Anna was surprised to see that the wide pavements were not filled with vendors. She asked Dominic where they had all gone.

'They're still around, just not in these parts. This is where the government buildings stand so no street vendors would be tolerated.'

Dominic steered his car past the main street and parked several blocks away from their destination. The area was bustling with office buildings, and well-dressed individuals walked purposefully, many clutching mobile phones or carrying files. Most of the parking spaces were taken with old and new cars parked nose to tail. Anna watched Dominic call out to a group of youths who seemed to be doing nothing more than chatting and watching people going about their business. He gave them some coins and pointed to his car.

'The parking meters don't work,' he explained. 'We pay these guys to keep an eye out for anyone trying to steal or tamper with our cars.'

They briskly walked to the State buildings and located the offices of the General Registrar as directed by the receptionist. Following the corridor, they entered a room with an open door, displaying the signage for 'Births and Deaths' above it. A man sat at the end of a long wooden counter, diligently typing on his desktop computer while surrounded by folders filled with documents. He seemed to be inputting data from paper to computer. Middle-aged with frizzy black hair, he had an officious-looking face with wire-rimmed glasses on his nose and an untidy stubble on his chin and cheeks. Anna and Dominic were the only two people on their side of the counter.

Behind the man, the room was filled with aisles of grey metal storage units arranged lengthwise, with letters of the alphabet stuck on at the front. Anna counted at least six aisles with shelves filled with cardboard boxes brimming with brown folders.

'Good morning,' said Dominic, forcing the man to look up. He grunted and frowned at them, peering over the top of his spectacles.

'Yes?' His voice was gruff and his mouth turned downwards at the corners.

Dominic gave Anna a nod, encouraging her to explain. For some reason, Anna felt her heart begin to race. She was nervous about asking for something that meant so much. Taking a deep breath to compose herself, she spoke with as much confidence as she could muster.

'I would like to view the birth and adoption records of my father, who was born in this country in 1954.'

The man blinked, his mouth contorting further. 'You have ID?' he asked with something akin to a sneer. From her handbag, Anna pulled out her passport and showed him the page with her photograph and details. He glanced at it and grunted again. 'Not *your* ID. Your father's,' he barked, his voice low, clearly displaying his irritation at being interrupted.

117

'Sorry.' Anna opened her handbag again and drew out Mathew's passport. The man inspected it, making grumbling noises as he flipped through the pages. Eventually, he handed the passport back and fixed his gaze on Anna, peering over his glasses.

'You need permission from the General Registrar.' He got off his stool and bent down to search for something from under the counter. When he surfaced, he pushed a grey A4 piece of paper over to Anna. 'Fill in that form and bring it back another day.'

Dominic moved closer to Anna and gave the man a broad smile. In a cheery voice, he said something in Shona. The man narrowed his eyes and barked out a reply. Dominic continued to talk to him in their local language. Anna could tell the man's grumpy mood was softening. She thought she heard Dominic say the word 'gift'. Eventually, the man glanced at Anna, then gestured to Dominic that he should move to the other end of the counter.

Picking up the form, Dominic led Anna away. He asked her for a pen. 'I persuaded him to let us fill in the form and hand it in today. He was saying you wouldn't hear back until after Christmas. I explained you don't have much time and got him to agree to speed up the process.'

'How did you manage that? Magic?'

Dominic gave her a grim smile. 'The magic of money. The promise of foreign cash is difficult to refuse.'

Anna's eyes widened in understanding before narrowing in concern. She was about to object when Dominic gave her a warning nudge to get on with completing the form. Realising that she was in no position to make a fuss, Anna filled in the information required. The form was straightforward, requesting basic details about her father, her own name and contact information, and the reasons for her request to access his records.

'If you have £20 sterling on you, just fold it into the sheet,' said Dominic, keeping his voice low, even though there were no other people around.

Anna did as she was told and went to hand over the folded form. Without looking at her, the man took a quick look inside, muttered something under his breath and placed it under the counter. Then, he ignored them. Anna wanted to ask when she could expect to hear back, but Dominic took her arm and led her out of the room.

'He said you'll get a letter very soon,' he said. 'Or an email. You'll be asked to come back at a specific time to view the records.'

Anna reflected on all the aisles behind the man filled with hard-copy reports. 'Is none of that information in digital format?'

Dominic shrugged. 'I think some of it might be. That man seemed to be transcribing from paper to computer. I guess eventually it will all be available electronically.'

Returning to Dominic's car, they drove towards the northern part of the city. The previous day, Anna had made a phone call to the National Archives of Zimbabwe to reserve a slot for browsing through their historical documents. She'd been told they had a repository of newspapers, catalogues and other print material available on microfiche dating from 1953 to 1963.

Walking through the doors into the spacious reception area, Anna was impressed with the quiet calm interior which exuded a sense of study and education. A smiling receptionist asked to see ID before directing them to the room that held the information she needed. They descended a flight of stairs to the basement level.

Looking around at the countless shelves and cabinets, Anna had no idea where to begin. It took a while to work out how to find the correct section for the archived newspapers. Eventually, they found them stored in a complicated arrangement in cabinets all around the enormous rectangular space. Three microfiche readers stood on one side of the room while long tables and chairs occupied the area on the other side. Anna counted eight other people working quietly in the room.

'The newspaper we should look for is the *Rhodesia Herald*,' whispered Dominic. 'That was the national paper at that time. It will include reports of anything interesting happening across the country.'

'Yes, but if what we're looking for is not in that paper, we will have to go through other newspapers too.'

Dominic made a face. 'Oh God! That will take us ages.'

'We'll have to do it,' said Anna with a shrug. 'Well. Let's see if the *Rhodesia Herald* was printed in 1954 and get started with our scanning.'

The microfiche slides were kept in individual envelopes arranged in chronological order. These were housed in narrow sliding drawers inside the cabinets. Fortunately, Anna was au fait with microfiche archives. Much of her medical research included trips to the university college libraries to trawl through papers on microfiche. While computer hard drives were more convenient for document storage, the old-fashioned microfiche and microfilm were still widely used in the UK.

Finding the relevant microfiche slides took Anna and Dominic an inordinate amount of time. No staff were around to help them, and Anna did not want to waste time traipsing up to the reception desk for assistance. With dogged determination, they eventually found what they were looking for.

'What month did you say Uncle Mathew was born?' asked Dominic.

'January. The birth certificate says twenty-fifth of January, but we should start from the first day of the year. We can't be sure of the exact date.'

Since no one else was using the microfiche readers, Anna and Dominic gathered all the envelopes labelled 'January 1954' and took a reader each to scan side by side. The *Rhodesia Herald* was a daily paper which meant there were a very large number of slides to get through. Anna instructed Dominic to look out for any reports of foundlings, churches, orphans, orphanages and adoptions.

As they checked the headlines and delved into the articles, Anna found herself engrossed in the content. She was fascinated by the things reported and printed in the middle of the twentieth century. Being a doctor, she couldn't help reading with interest about the details of the mass polio vaccination programmes for children, and the health of the nation at that time. The advertisements on medicines and home remedies were especially captivating. She realised Dominic was getting through the slides much faster than she was.

After an hour or so, Anna asked Dominic how he was getting on. 'There's nothing relevant here at all,' he replied, sounding frustrated.

'Same here.' Anna made a sad face. 'Do you want to stop for a while?'

'My stomach is growling,' Dominic said, making a playful expression.

Anna laughed softly. 'Okay. Let's go for some lunch and come back later to do the rest. I don't want you to faint on me!'

Lunch was a small burger for her and a large multi-layered one for Dominic with an enormous side of chunky chips. They sat in a restaurant at the end of a shopping and business complex not far from the National Archives. Anna noticed a detached building across the walkway that didn't look like a retail outlet. But people seemed to be going in and out without shopping bags.

'What is that place over there, Dominic?'

Noisily sipping his cola through a straw, Dominic glanced across. 'That's your kind of place: a doctor's surgery.'

Once he said that, Anna could see the signage at the side of the entrance stating that it was a medical centre. Her thoughts immediately went to the GP surgery she had left in London.

Her mind flashed back to the day she had handed in her notice and spoken to Tom about breaking up. He had been staggered by her decision. It had clearly never occurred to him that Anna would take that step. He'd tried hard to make her change her mind. His ego had been bruised and he'd reacted by being defensive about his behaviour. Thankfully, he did eventually come round, accepting that they needed to go their separate ways.

'Are you missing London?' asked Dominic, wiping his mouth with a paper napkin. 'Worrying about your patients?'

'I am thinking of London, but I'm not worried. It's all good.' She saw that his plate was wiped clean. 'Still hungry?'

Dominic laughed and said he was ready to return to work. They had until 5 p.m. before the Archives building closed. That gave them almost three hours to scan through the hundreds of slides from January 1954.

They worked steadily through the afternoon, stopping every so often to check with one another when they found something of interest. Anna was still slower than Dominic in getting through their envelopes and had to be reminded to stop reading irrelevant articles.

By 4 p.m. they were both flagging. Anna was losing hope of finding anything in the *Rhodesia Herald*. The thought of searching through other papers was too daunting to consider. But when she raised her concerns with Dominic, he made a helpful suggestion. While Anna continued with her set of slides, he proposed using the last hour to scan newspapers from locations near Rukuvoko Church.

He went off in search of newspapers printed in Fort Victoria in 1954. His enthusiasm made Anna feel a little less weary. She began to look through the slides with renewed vigour. So engrossed was she in her resolve to complete her objective that she jumped when she heard Dominic squeal with delight.

Sitting beside her, clutching a smaller pile of envelopes, he pointed to the microfiche under the glass, his eyes wide with excitement. Opening and closing his mouth, he finally whispered, 'I've found it!'

For a moment, Anna sat in stunned silence, staring at Dominic with a furrowed brow. Then her eyes shifted to the screen. Dominic got off his seat and gestured for her to take his place. After a moment's hesitation, she moved quickly to view his screen.

There it was, a photograph of a baby in the arms of a nun against the backdrop of a church spire. The headline screamed: BABY ABANDONED OUTSIDE CHURCH.

The picture was a 3 x 4-inch caption in black and white. The article, written by a James Rathbury, took up the space of one quarter of the front page. It was the *Fort Victoria Chronicle* dated 28 January 1954. Anna glanced at Dominic who was beaming with excitement. Giving him a dazed smile, she turned back to the screen.

Silently, with a racing heart, Anna read through the article twice – once quickly, then with more care and attention. Satisfied that all the facts correlated with what she knew about her father's circumstances, she leaned forward to inspect the photograph. The baby, her father, had a white blanket wrapped around his tiny body and over the back of his head. His dark-skinned face peeped out of the whiteness with tufts of straight black hair visible above his forehead. With a round face, plump lips, small chin and cute little nose, he resembled many other brown babies she had seen. His eyes were shut, but she could see tiny little eyelashes below the arched eyebrows.

The most significant aspect of the photograph was the pendant held up by the nun. She cradled the baby in the crook of her right arm and her left hand dangled a chain and pendant. In the black-and-white photo it was impossible to tell if it was gold and the inscription was not at all clear, but the size and shape of the pendant left Anna in no doubt that it was the same one she wore around her neck.

Dominic pointed to a button at the side of the reader. 'If you press that, we can get a printout of the report.'

In a daze, they obtained the printout, meticulously returning everything to its proper place before leaving. Clutching the report in her hand, Anna proceeded to the reception area to pay the required fee.

'Are you going to show that to Uncle Mathew?' asked Dominic as they headed home.

Anna considered for a moment. She had said she would not tell him anything that would cause him distress. But the newspaper article with his photograph was hardly negative news – it was simply confirmation of what he already knew. She decided that he should see it.

'He has a right to see this. He will be fine. I'm sure it won't freak him out.'

# Chapter 14

Anna waited until after dinner to tell her parents about the newspaper article. They were relaxing on the veranda with their hosts, enjoying a coffee liqueur. The night air was warm and the garden gave off a scent of earth, loam and fragrant flowers. Mathew gazed out at the illuminated lawn, bathed in soft amber light from a wall lamp behind them.

Anna drew his attention to the printout in her hand. 'I've got something to show you, Dad.' He turned to her with a questioning look, then glanced at the printout.

'Dominic and I went to the National Archives today to see if there were any newspaper reports about you. This is what we found.' Anna's tone was soft. She watched Mathew narrow his eyes, looking puzzled.

'I know you would rather I didn't go delving into your past, but while I'm here, I feel I have to do something.' Mathew drew his eyebrows together. Anna saw him inhale deeply then breathe out noisily. After a brief pause, she carried on. 'At the Archives, they keep all their old newspaper articles on microfiche. We searched for hours and just when we were about to give up, we were rewarded with this article.'

Anna placed the report on the table and pushed it gently towards him. He hesitated, then picked it up. It took him a moment to realise what he was looking at. When he did, he immediately jerked back in his seat. His eyes widened and he caught his breath in a loud gasp.

'Oh my God!' Mathew's voice was barely audible, almost a whisper. He dropped the report as if it were burning his fingers, and he looked at Anna in shock.

Theresa's hand shot out to lift the report from the table. She stared at the picture for a moment then turned to glare at Anna.

'Why have you brought this here?' Her voice seethed with anger.

Anna had expected surprise, curiosity and possibly a little hostility from her mother. But not from her father. Faced with the look on his face, she drew back. She didn't like to see him in distress.

'I just . . . I thought . . .' Anna trailed off, doubting the wisdom of her decision to share the news.

Theresa scowled. 'You thought what? You thought your father needed this reminder of what happened?' She raised her voice. 'What don't you understand about this? He doesn't want to know! I have told you time and time again not to bring this up. But what do you do? You fling it in his face. Can't you see the harm you are causing? Just leave it alone!' Theresa shouted at the top of her voice, waving the printout in the air.

Anna sat back from the table. When her mother was livid with fury, she knew it was best to remain silent. She shifted her gaze to her father. His face had been puckered up and his eyes screwed shut. But now, Anna noticed that he was looking fixedly at the report which was still in his wife's hands.

Theresa continued to rant, but Anna had ceased listening. She was watching her father. He seemed entranced by the article. Slowly, he reached out and took it from Theresa. With his other hand, he gripped her wrist, making her stop in mid-flow. Everyone round the table watched in astonishment. Mathew stared at the photo of himself as a baby with a peculiar expression on his face. He still looked shocked, but Anna sensed a nervous curiosity in the way he studied the picture. After a long silent minute, he turned to her and handed over the report.

His voice trembled with emotion as he gestured towards the article. 'Read it, Anna. I want to know what it says.'

Anna gaped at him, unsure if he was serious.

Theresa put a hand on his arm. 'Mathew, you don't have to do this,' she said gently.

'It's all right.' He sounded more composed. There was still apprehension in his demeanour, but he spoke with a bit more confidence.

Anna took a deep breath. 'You want me to read it aloud?'

He nodded, peering at her intently.

Anna took a sip of her drink, swallowed hard, then held up the picture to her dad.

'This is you as a newborn baby.' She kept her voice soft. 'You can see the chain and pendant I'm wearing and also the white blanket we've heard about. I've checked all the dates and facts. They confirm what we know. This article was posted in the local newspaper when you were only three days old.'

Anna glanced at her aunt and uncle who were sitting in silence. Tension had built up around them. Anna could feel it hanging in the air. She cleared her throat, then began to read.

> A baby boy has been found abandoned in a basket outside Rukuvoko Mission Church. The newborn was discovered sleeping peacefully in a basket placed outside the front door. An investigation is underway and the police are searching for his parents.

Sister Mary Angelou expressed her shock at finding the baby at 6.30 a.m. on 25th January. 'I couldn't believe my eyes,' she said. 'There was the little cherub warm and snug in a basket. I looked around but couldn't see anyone at all. I took the baby in and called Father Groober immediately.'

Wrapped tightly in a white sheet, red shawl with Indian motifs and a soft white blanket over it, the baby was sleeping in a sturdy brown wicker basket placed under the portico. With a white woolly hat on his head, the newborn was found on a velvet cushion keeping him warm and comfortable. Under the blanket, Sister Angelou found a gold necklace with a name inscribed on a round pendant: INDIRA. Based on the name and the facial features of the baby, the Fort Victoria Police believe he is of Indian heritage. They will be appealing to all Indian families in nearby towns and cities to come forward if they have any information on the identity of the baby's parents.

Rukuvoko Mission Church is located deep in the bushlands near Fort Victoria. With a small team of Catholic nuns, Father Groober, who founded the church, provides a valued service to local villagers. The newborn is doing well under the care of the nuns. He will remain there until either his parents are found, or he can be placed in a safe home.

Father Groober has expressed his own appeal. 'I would urge anyone who has information that could help us reunite this baby with his parents to come forward.'

Anna glanced around the table, observing Theresa's stern expression and Mathew's bewildered look. Her aunt and uncle stared at her with wide eyes. Only Dominic looked unmoved.

'I'm sorry I upset you, Dad, but I thought you should see it,' Anna said, offering a feeble smile. He didn't reciprocate.

Theresa scowled. 'This is all well and good, but how does this lead you to your father's birth parents?'

Anna shrugged her shoulders. 'It doesn't. But I'm going to keep searching. Dominic and I are going to return to the National Archives to see if there are any follow-up reports. I will also try to trace the journalist who wrote the report. He might still be around.'

Suddenly, Mathew leaned forward and slammed his hands on the table with a thump. 'No, Anna!' Eyes flashing, his voice was uncharacteristically loud. Startled, Anna moved back in her seat. 'You've done enough. You won't find anything more, so you must stop this now.'

'Exactly,' said Theresa. 'There's nothing new in this article. We told you all this. You are wasting your time and causing unnecessary agony for everyone.'

Anna let out a little cry of frustration. 'I wish I could stop, but I can't.' She looked her father in the eye, willing him to understand. 'I need to know where I come from. You do understand that Dad, don't you? Please say you do.'

It was a cry from the heart. But Mathew's face had turned to stone. He turned away to gaze into the gloom of the garden.

Anna felt an overwhelming sadness envelop her. Her father was determined to close his mind to his past. He didn't want to close the circle, to fill the gap in his history. She understood his reluctance to bring it all up, but she had already gone too far to turn back. She had to keep going. If there *was* any further information, she had to do all she could to find it.

~

The following morning, Savita telephoned to ask if she was free to visit two more families that afternoon. Both were rumoured to have some connection with Mathew's past. Although the older generation were no longer alive, Savita thought they might have passed on some useful information to their sons and daughters. Eager to jog people's memories, Anna said she would make her way to Savita's house after lunch.

'It's just you and me today,' explained Savita when Anna arrived. 'There are no men at these two houses so it's better if Prakash doesn't join us. Conversation will flow more freely, I think.'

Unfortunately, even with the free-flowing conversation, there was nothing to be gained that morning. The widow at the first house had no memory of any orphans or adopted boys. The woman at the second house did recall that there was one Indian boy adopted by a mixed-race family, but more than that she knew nothing.

Disappointed, Anna shook her head. 'It does look like we're wasting our time, doesn't it?' she asked Savita.

'It was always a long shot. But we mustn't give up. There's one more family to see, and who knows? That might be our lucky ticket.'

'I don't suppose Taruna's had any luck with her phone survey?'

'She hasn't finished yet, but so far, there's been nothing to report.'

On the way back to Marimba Park, Anna gave Savita an update on where she was with her other enquiries. 'Apart from the old newspaper report, I haven't really got very far. I'm beginning to think I won't find anything else.'

'Don't be so disheartened. Taruna thinks there are more things you can do. You could issue an appeal notice in the national newspaper without mentioning Mathew's name. Just something along the lines of *Please contact xxx if you have any information about an Indian newborn baby boy found in a basket outside a church in 1954.* You could do the same on social media.'

Anna shook her head, looking defeated. 'My dad would hate it if I did that. He's already fuming about my search activities.'

Savita looked thoughtful. 'What if someone else issued the notice?' Anna puckered her brows, puzzled by what she meant.

'I mean, what if I or Taruna placed the notice in the newspaper and posted the same on social media, giving our contact details? Do you think Mathew would mind?'

Anna chewed her lip, pondering over Savita's suggestion. Mathew would still be against that and so would her mother. Anna tussled with the idea for a while, weighing up what was more important: keeping her parents happy or grabbing the opportunity to jog someone's memory. Anna couldn't decide. Realising she was doubting herself again, she made an effort to do the right thing.

'Even if he minds, I think we should do it. We have to try everything.'

Savita nodded in agreement. 'Okay. I'll talk it over with Taruna and make it happen as soon as possible.'

'It really is very good of you to go to such lengths for me,' said Anna, her voice filled with gratitude.

'Think nothing of it. I'm also curious about what happened and would love to help you solve this mystery. Prakash said he was going to ask around at the temple and community centre where many of the elderly men get together. I might do the same at the women's gatherings. Let's stay positive. I know the odds are stacked against us, but miracles do happen.'

Biting her bottom lip, Anna nodded and hoped for better news soon.

# Chapter 15

That evening, Dominic came over to say that he was free at the weekend to drive Anna to Masvingo, the closest town to Rukuvoko Church. The famous Zimbabwe Ruins were also near the town. At her mother's insistence, Anna had not mentioned the trip to her father.

'You are not to upset him any more than you have already,' she'd said. 'Can you imagine how he would feel if he knew you were going to the very place where he was abandoned? It would traumatise him all over again.'

Auntie Mary sympathetically chimed in. 'I agree. So where will you say you are going?'

'To see the Zimbabwe Ruins,' said Anna. 'We will stop there, won't we, Dominic?'

'Only if we have time. Depends on how long we take at the church.'

~

Two days later, on Saturday morning, Anna and Dominic left Harare for the long drive to Masvingo. They had already booked hotel rooms and mapped out the church's location.

'This is the main road from the capital to South Africa,' explained Dominic. 'There is always heavy traffic on this highway. We have to be uber alert on these roads.'

'Are we going as far as the border?'

'No. We stop about 180 miles north of the Limpopo River. We should get to Masvingo before dark. Tomorrow, we'll need to drive into the bushlands to get to Rukuvoko. What time do we have to be at the church?'

'I spoke to someone called Marian Tembe who I think is an office worker at the school. She said that after their Sunday morning service, she'll take us to see one of the nuns at around ten a.m.'

'Did you explain what we're after?'

'Sort of. I didn't go into too much detail in case it puts her off. I mean, it might be *her* that ends up searching through old records. That could take a long time.'

Dominic fell silent as he concentrated on his driving. His little car wobbled a little every time they were overtaken by a large truck. Anna sat back and looked out of the window at the changing scenery. The forests, lush green fields and farms gradually gave way to a more arid landscape. They crossed several rivers, all with low water levels, exposing intriguing rocks and stone beds.

The further they travelled away from Harare, the drier the open space became. The land was less cultivated, but occasionally, when passing through small villages, Anna spotted small patches of vibrant green amidst the sea of brown and grey. Men and women, wearing old hats or scarves around their heads, tended to the land near their homes. Dotted around, looking picturesque, were the typical Zimbabwean round huts with mud walls and thatched roofs. Beside them were a few brick-built shacks looking less attractive.

'See over there.' Dominic was pointing to mountains in the far distance. Anna shielded her eyes from the bright mid-morning sun. 'Those are our Eastern Highlands. Beyond those mountains is Mozambique. Sometimes, we go for short holidays up to the peaks. It's really peaceful up there.'

'It must be cooler too.'

'Yah, sometimes it's freezing cold. We stay in cabins with real log fires to keep ourselves warm. But where we're heading, there's never any need for a fire. We're going to the lowveld where the climate is always hot.'

Anna noticed a sign indicating the way to a range of mountains called Chimanimani. Against the wide aquamarine sky, they appeared deep blue on the horizon. All around her she saw *kopjes*, grey and bald hills, and a scattering of sturdy mopane trees. The landscape was dry and dusty but still possessed a scenic quality.

Anna had been born and brought up in the UK, yet somehow she felt that she belonged here, in Zimbabwe. It was an ancient land, rich in history, legends and folklore from past African civilisations. She was proud of the fact that part of her heritage was rooted in this beautiful country.

Taking a deep breath, Anna pondered over her other heritage – the missing piece of her legacy. It pained her to know that she had no information about that side of her identity. Who were her biological grandparents? Who was Indira? She was desperate to find out. Until that happened, she would always remain in limbo.

By midday, Dominic grew too hungry to keep driving. He pulled over at a dusty lay-by with a wooden bench table. Anna realised this was the Zimbabwean version of the motorway services in the UK. It was a far cry from the super-busy, round-the-clock welcome breaks on the motorways offering food, rest, shopping, fuel and toilets. In many ways, Anna thought this quiet, scenic open space was perfect in its simplicity.

Mary had packed a sandwich lunch for them with water and juices in an insulated cooler bag. It was more than enough for the two travellers. Dominic pulled out a separate bag stuffed with sweet and savoury snacks. Among the many packets, Anna noticed the British sweets and chocolates Theresa had brought over from the UK. Every time she came to Zimbabwe, Theresa made sure her suitcases were filled with assorted items of confectionery to distribute among her relatives. They looked forward to such gifts.

Dominic ate with relish. He followed his doorstop chicken sandwich with crisps, biscuits and then chocolates. Anna shook her head in amusement, wondering where he put away all the food he ate because it didn't show on his thin frame at all.

Eventually, he licked his lips with satisfaction and asked: 'You've been to Masvingo before, haven't you?'

'Yes. We went there the last time we visited the Ruins.'

Dominic grinned. 'Believe or not, I have never seen the Zimbabwe Ruins.'

'What?' Anna was astonished. 'It's such a world-famous place. A UNESCO World Heritage site.'

Anna pictured the stone ruins of the ancient city from the Iron Age, where archaeologists had unearthed intriguing birdlike soapstone figures. They sat like proud eagles on solid stone seats. They were the national emblem of Zimbabwe, appearing everywhere on flags, banknotes, coins and stamps.

Dominic laughed as he drove on. 'I've never been there but I know all about it. One of my teachers had a brother working as a researcher at the local university here. There are archaeological digs nearby and the scientists are still trying to uncover the secrets of the ruins.'

Dominic slowed down before reaching the main street in Masvingo. Cars were parked on both sides of the road, bustling with Saturday shoppers. Attractive pine trees lined the pavements outside the retail outlets. They drove past an interesting bell tower and a few historic buildings.

'The early white settlers erected a fort here and called the town Fort Victoria,' said Dominic. 'They built it to stave off the local warriors who didn't want them on their land. We were taught at school that they came from South Africa at the end of the nineteenth century. Mostly they were Dutch people called Afrikaners, and their language was called Afrikaans.'

'It's a nice town,' said Anna, looking around. 'Are we staying here?'

'No. I've booked a hotel a few miles further out.'

Upon arrival, Anna was pleased to see that the hotel was modern and comfortable, with a bright reception area. After the heat of the drive, it was good to be in the cool interior. Anna was immediately drawn to the outdoor swimming pool beyond the wide windows at the back. As soon as they were given the keys to their rooms, she changed into her swimsuit and headed out for a swim. Dominic, exhausted from the long drive, decided to rest in his room.

The water from the pool was wonderfully refreshing. Anna swam several lengths before coming out to sunbathe on a deckchair. She had the whole place to herself. Closing her eyes, she breathed in deeply and relaxed.

Her thoughts turned to the reason for their visit. They were going to Rukuvoko Church the next day. Whether or not they found any new information when they reached there, Anna knew it would be an emotional day.

Opening her eyes, she stared at the cool water sparkling in the sun. The last time she'd gone swimming was with Fiona at the Finchley Lido. Acting on impulse, Anna reached over and pulled out her phone from the drawstring bag beside her deckchair. Keen to hear her voice again, she decided to call Fiona on WhatsApp. Clicking on the settings button, she connected with the hotel's Wi-Fi. London time was two hours behind Zimbabwe, so she calculated that at 4 p.m. Fiona was either at home with her son or still out doing her weekend shopping. Without sending a text message, Anna called. It rang for quite a long time before Fiona answered.

'Hello?'

'Hey, Fiona. It's me. Have I caught you at a bad time?'

'No. Hey Anna. How are you?' She sounded pleased and excited to hear from her.

'I'm fine. Just had a lovely dip in an open-air swimming pool and thought of you.'

Fiona was keen to know what progress Anna had made towards solving her family mystery. Giving her the latest update, Anna explained how nervous she was about seeing the place where her father had been found.

'You'll be fine. I know you'll handle it well, whatever you find.'

'I just hope there *is* something to find after all these years. I'll keep you informed.' Anna could hear Callum's voice in the background. 'How's your little swimming champion?'

'He's okay. But I can tell you who is *not* okay.'

'Who?'

'Our friend Nick. He keeps asking after you. I think he's missing you. Why don't you give him a ring?'

Anna smiled. Over the months since they first met at the surgery, she'd spent a fair amount of time with him to discuss their charity work, attend fundraising events or simply to have drinks at The Wisteria pub. They had become good friends.

'I might just do that. Tell him I'll call him when I get back to Harare. Right now, I need to prepare myself for what's to come. Wish me luck.'

# Chapter 16

Dominic turned off the highway and on to a dirt road with two narrow, parallel strips of asphalt. Keeping one set of wheels on each strip, he drove with confidence in the centre of the narrow route. Anna had never seen these strip roads anywhere else except in Zimbabwe. They made her nervous because if there was another car approaching from the opposite direction, they would need to make a quick move into the bushes.

'Can you take it easy round the bends?' she asked. 'You're driving too fast.'

'Relax! There won't be any cars coming at us. The locals will be walking or riding bicycles.'

Anna was not convinced, but she held her tongue and concentrated on the map Dominic had drawn by hand. She needed to make sure they didn't go astray. Rukuvoko Church was over twenty miles away, and she didn't relish the thought of being on these roads for all that distance.

They were going deeper and deeper into the lowveld or bushlands of Zimbabwe. The rural landscape was open, flat and dry with low scrub all around. There were some trees, but they weren't abundant, and those that Anna saw were sturdy mopanes or msasas. Here and there, she caught sight of a baobab tree with its massive trunk and compact crown. They reminded her of bottles with wide bases and narrow mouths at the top. She was fascinated by these ancient trees, which she knew could live for thousands of years. Looking around, she wondered if there were any wild animals in the vicinity.

'There might be some,' said Dominic, 'but usually you see them in national wildlife reserves. There's one not far away if you want to make a detour.'

'Maybe another time.' Anna was keen to reach their destination. Dominic maintained a steady speed, slowing down to a crawl every time they passed a village. Anna looked with interest at the people in and around the village areas. Dressed in clothes that seemed old and shabby, they stared at them in their passing car with idle curiosity. Anna noticed many barefoot children dressed in rags. The rural communities were clearly going through many hardships.

Most of the dwellings were the usual round huts with thatched roofs. But there were also some small brick houses with tin roofs. Anna noticed that some villagers had cattle grazing behind their homes.

'Where do they get their water from?' she asked.

'There are wells in some villages, and boreholes in others. I think outside organisations like UNICEF come to help them sometimes. Life is hard around here.'

'But I see they have electricity at least,' said Anna, looking up at the pylons with overhead power lines.

'I'm not sure about that. There used to be power in these parts, but with so many outages these days, I don't think these areas get a decent supply.'

Looking ahead, Anna saw that they were approaching a road sign. Dominic stopped the car at the wooden post to read the place names. The writing was faint and obscured by dirt and grime. 'I think it says Umzuma to the right.'

Anna checked the map. 'That's the one. We have to head that way.'

Dominic swung the car to the right and drove for fifteen further minutes before they reached another village. This one seemed more like a small town. Astonished, Anna peered out at the shops and people on either side of the road. She was not expecting this in the middle of the bushlands.

'This is quite a big place,' she remarked.

'It is. I'm just as surprised as you.' Dominic parked beside two other cars in front of a little store with Umzuma Shopa painted in white above the entrance. 'Let's get some cold drinks from here.'

There couldn't have been more than twenty people around, but they stared openly at Anna and Dominic, clearly not used to seeing visitors in their midst. Anna sensed no hostility from them. Just simple curiosity. Inside the shop, a young mother with her baby tied on her back in a large grey cloth, stood looking up at something on a top shelf. Dressed in an old skirt and tee shirt, she went on her toes to reach for a packet of mealie meal or maize flour.

Anna hurried over to help her. She pulled down a bag of the flour and handed it over to the mother with a smile. The woman placed the packet in the basket at her feet, and with a shy smile, she clapped three times with cupped hands. Anna was aware that this was the Zimbabwean gesture for thank you. It was such a sweet movement that Anna found herself doing the same. She wished her good morning in Shona: '*Mangwanani.*'

The woman was delighted and let off a long sentence in the local language that went right over Anna's head. The woman threw up her hands and laughed and her face crinkled into a grin. She picked up her basket and walked away amused. Smiling to herself, Anna joined Dominic who was at the till. She watched him pay for two cola drinks with a one US dollar note and move off to the car.

'The last time I came, you had to pay millions of Zimbabwean dollars for this,' said Anna.

'I know. That was when our economy crashed. Those million-trillion-dollar notes are worthless. You can have some as souvenirs, if you like.'

Anna pursed her lips. It was sad to see the economy of the country so damaged. The effect of that on people around her was plain to see. The poverty and struggle of the villagers were heart-breaking. Now that there was a new regime in Zimbabwe, she hoped things would soon start to improve.

Dominic steered the car away from Umzuma. As they drove out of the village, Anna was surprised to see a few brick-built dwellings that looked quite modern. They even had gates in front of their entrances. Dominic thought they were probably places that could be hired or rented by backpackers who wanted to have the real bushland experience.

When they finally reached Rukuvoko, Anna's pulse quickened. The name of the town was emblazoned on a side wall of the first shop they saw. Steadying her breathing, she looked around and saw that it was similar to Umzuma, except that there were more cars parked on the dusty main street. Anna directed Dominic to the end of the line of stores, then left on to a small dirt road.

The church building was recognisable straight away. There was no sign or steeple identifying it, but there was a large cross of Jesus carved into the front wall above the entrance. All white with a red high-pitched roof, there was no doubt that this was Rukuvoko Church. As they got closer, Anna found herself holding her breath. Dominic parked near the building and suggested they wait in the car as they were fifteen minutes early for their meeting.

Anna's heart was pounding in her chest. Thrilled to finally be here, she was also tense with nerves. This was not how she was expecting to feel. For some reason, she had imagined she would be calm and collected. But this was where her father had been abandoned and found as a newborn. Ever since her parents had told her the truth, thoughts and images of this location had whirled around in her head. To be here at last was momentous. Anna recognised that this was a significant moment. Taking a deep breath, she blew out slowly through her mouth.

'Are you okay?' asked Dominic.

'Not really.' Anna clasped her hands together on her lap.

Dominic pointed to the entrance at the front of the church. 'Look, there's the sheltered porch.'

It was a small, enclosed space with its own high-pitched roof made of red clay tiles. There was an open archway at the front and arched doors at the back leading to the interior. The main part of the church rose tall behind the porch with its matching red tiles. Anna thought the box-like sheltered space looked like it had been added on to the front of the church as an afterthought. Imagining a basket placed inside it, she could see how sheltered and protected it would be.

The church entrance could be reached from the street via a short stone slab pathway. There was no gate, and no trees or shrubs concealing the arched porch. Anna wondered how someone had managed to walk in with a baby in a basket and leave it there without being seen. But she thought that perhaps in the 1950s, there was more vegetation cover, and not many people around in the early morning.

From the car, Anna could see down the side of the building. There were three large arched windows, and beyond that, a low wooden gate. In the distance, she could see some low-lying premises with flat roofs. She imagined they were part of the school where the nuns taught the village children. Again, she pictured her father being cared for in that school during the first two months of his life. Anna said a silent thank you to the nuns.

Through her open car window, she could hear joyful music emanating from the church. The worshippers were singing at their Sunday service. Anna recognised the hymn, one of many that she had sung as a child with her mother. For a while, Anna let her mind focus on the devotional song. The soothing sounds had a calming effect on her. She felt more in control of her emotions.

Soon after the singing stopped, people began to emerge, chatting to one another, looking happy. They ambled away in different directions. There must have been about thirty people in total, adults and children, all dressed in their Sunday best. Although no one appeared to be barefoot, Anna noticed that most of the clothes were well-worn.

'We should go in now,' said Dominic when everyone had dispersed.

Together, they walked up the path to the front porch. Stepping away from the brightness of the sun, the space under the roof was shady and cool. There was just enough room for about four people. Anna looked at the concrete floor and pictured a wicker basket with a handle set to one side. The nun who opened the door must have seen it immediately. Anna imagined her shock when she realised there was a tiny baby inside.

Dominic had gone through the open door into the church. Anna followed, and a young woman came forward to greet them.

'Welcome,' she smiled. 'I'm Mariam Tembe. Pastor Joseph will see you straight away.'

Anna was surprised. 'I thought we were meeting one of the nuns.'

'Sister Mary Consilio was going to speak to you, but she has been called away. Pastor Joseph is also needed elsewhere but he has agreed to see you for half an hour.'

Anna was disappointed. She didn't think half an hour was going to be sufficient time to ask all the questions she had. 'I was hoping someone would check through past records for us.'

'I'm sorry, but that won't be possible today.' Anna's face fell. She had come with high hopes. 'But don't worry,' continued Mariam. 'Pastor Joseph Kabandure is the best person to help you. He has been here a very long time.'

'How long?'

'More than forty years. He is the full-time teaching elder and pastor of this church.'

They followed her through a passageway that led them to a large office. Sitting at a desk was a grey-haired man with a clerical collar and black jacket over a white shirt. Behind him, on a wire hanger, was a long robe that he must have worn for the sermon. It was a splendid purple velvet robe with gold crosses at both shoulders and sleeves. Looking down at some papers with spectacles on his nose, he was reading something with concentration.

Mariam cleared her throat, and immediately he looked up. When she introduced them, he stood up and gave them a broad toothy smile.

'Please sit down.' His voice was warm and friendly. 'What can I do for you?'

Anna gave him a brief explanation of her quest. She told him how much it meant to her to find out as much as she could about the day that her father had been found. From her handbag, she produced the printout of the newspaper article describing what had happened.

Pastor Joseph listened with attention, his face puckered into a frown. He heard her out without saying a word. Picking up the report, he read through it in silence. Then, over the top of his glasses, he fixed his eyes on Anna. Thinking he was waiting for her to speak, Anna continued.

'I know you were not here in 1954, but I wondered if you'd heard anything about what happened the day he was found. Anything at all.' Anna heard the pleading in her voice.

The pastor gave a slow nod. 'I don't know too many details, but I heard about the shock it caused at the time.'

Anna and Dominic both sat up straighter. The pastor leaned back in his chair and turned to look out of the window. With a faraway expression, he spoke as if he were in another place.

'Father Groober founded this Mission in 1948. He was a remarkable man. It was a privilege to know him. When I joined in 1976, he told me a little about the Indian baby in the basket. It was an unusual case, so I remember it.' He swivelled his chair to face Anna again. 'But it was a long time ago. What is it you hope to find?'

Anna shrugged in despair. 'Maybe some clues that were missed at the time. Did anyone have any idea who left the baby? Were any records made? What happened to the cushion, woolly hat, shawl and blanket that came with the baby? There seems to be no trace of them. I thought perhaps there would be something about that and other things in your church records.'

The pastor tapped his fingers together and gave her an intense stare. He seemed to be thinking hard about something. Eventually, he looked at his watch and tutted.

'I'm sorry but I don't have much time today. If you want to search through our registers, you will have to come back another day. But I don't think you will find the answers to your questions there. Our records are always very brief, just one or two lines recorded for events like births, deaths, baptisms, marriages and so on.' He paused and stared at Anna again.

She puckered her brows and stared back at him, looking wretched. He pursed his lips and gave her a sympathetic smile.

'I don't want to raise your hopes, but there is something I can tell you that will not be recorded anywhere.'

Anna leaned forward, sensing he was about to say something important.

'There was gossip in the village after the baby was abandoned. Father Groober told me that there was talk of an Indian baby being delivered by a local midwife in Umzuma. He tried to find out if there was any truth in that. He even went to Umzuma to search for this midwife, but no one could tell him anything.'

Anna was not sure if she'd heard him correctly. 'Sorry. Did you say the baby was born in Umzuma? The village nearby?'

'In Umzuma, yes. But there was no proof.'

'Did Father Groober report it to the authorities?' Anna realised she had raised her voice.

The pastor shook his head, looking sad. 'It was just gossip. Father Groober would not want the church to be spreading stories without any evidence.' He paused for a moment before continuing. 'I'm sorry but that is all I know about it.' He looked at his watch. 'You must excuse me now. I must prepare for my appointments.'

'Please,' said Anna with urgency. 'This is really important. Do you have any idea who was involved? Maybe the name of someone who could lead us to this midwife?'

'No. I'm very sorry.' He turned to Mariam who was still in the room, standing by the door. She hurried forward. Anna could not move from her seat. Dominic stood up and took her by the wrist.

'Anna, we must go.' Turning to the pastor, Dominic thanked him for his time. Anna threw him a pleading look, but Pastor Joseph had returned to his folder. Dazed and distressed, she followed Dominic out of the office, her mind in a whirl. She couldn't process what she had just heard. Her questions had not been answered and now she had even more questions to add to her list.

# Chapter 17

'What do we do now?' asked Dominic before starting the car engine.

Anna was staring out of the window, her mind focused on what they'd just been told. She visualised the scene of a baby being delivered by a midwife in the nearby village, in a house with brick walls, a tin roof, and a gate, similar to the one they had seen earlier in Umzuma.

'We have to go there,' she murmured. 'To Umzuma.'

'You think the rumour about the midwife is true?'

'It makes sense, Dominic. The baby was left at this church early in the morning, so the birthplace was probably close by. A midwife from the next village could have delivered the baby then brought him here to the church.'

Dominic pondered for a moment. 'But Umzuma is at least half an hour away by car. How would a local midwife transport a newborn baby such a long distance? It's unlikely she would have a car.'

'Maybe it wasn't the midwife. Maybe it was the father.'

They both fell silent, imagining the fateful event. Anna pictured a pregnant woman coming to Umzuma just for the delivery of the baby. This area in the bushlands was ideal for an Indian couple to hide from everyone they knew. A local midwife, sworn to secrecy, could have been found beforehand. Everything would have been planned and preparations made before they came.

Anna allowed the scenario to play out in her medical head: the midwife encouraging the mother through labour, delivering the baby, cutting the cord, checking that mother and baby were healthy, then wrapping the newborn first in a clean sheet, then a red shawl and a soft white blanket.

Anna's heart began to race as she considered what might have happened next. Someone, maybe the midwife, placed the baby on the soft cushion inside the basket, then covered him with the blanket. Perhaps at that point, the mother removed the gold necklace from her neck and gave it to the midwife to place under the blanket. After that, someone, possibly the father, took the basket and drove to Rukuvoko Church.

If that was what happened, it must have been heart-breaking for him to leave the baby and drive away. Did he wait until the nun opened the door in the early morning? And what about the mother? How did she feel? Anna refused to believe that it was the parents' decision to give up their baby. Someone must have forced them to do it or their circumstances had made it impossible for them to keep him.

Anna played with the chain and pendant around her neck. It *must* have belonged to Mathew's birth mother. But what were the circumstances? One thing she was certain of was the parents' intention for the baby to survive. He had been left in a safe place where he was bound to be found and taken care of.

Dominic's voice shook her out of her reverie. 'We're nearly there.' She'd been so wrapped up in her thoughts that she hadn't even realised he'd started driving. He was soon parked outside Umzuma Shopa.

'Now what do we do?' he asked. Anna took a long breath. She didn't have a clue. Casting her eye over the stores in front of them,

151

she watched the few people walking in and out. It was difficult to know where to even begin.

'Give me a minute,' she said as she racked her brain for ideas. She couldn't think straight and felt drained of all energy. How was she ever going to find out what had happened here over six decades previously? No one living here now was going to know anything about it. She pondered over it for a long time while Dominic waited patiently.

'Okay,' she said eventually. 'Let's go into this shop and tell the owner that we are trying to trace someone from a very long time ago. We can ask him if he's ever heard anyone mention an Indian woman staying in this town in the past. And if there was any gossip about an Indian baby being born here and abandoned in Rukuvoko. It would be such an unusual occurrence that it's possible it would stick in someone's mind. What do you think?'

Dominic lifted his shoulders and dropped them with a sigh.

'Look,' continued Anna. 'There aren't that many shops. Let's go into each one and ask if they know anything about it, or if they know anyone old enough who might remember. We can give them your phone number so if they hear something relevant later, they can call you. Would that be okay?'

Dominic shrugged again. 'It's crazy, but at least it's a plan. Let's do it.'

For the next half hour, they both got busy talking to whoever would stop to listen. Everyone they spoke to looked too young to have any helpful information. All Anna could hope for was that they would spread the word and someone in their community might remember something useful.

Back in the car, Dominic offered Anna a chocolate bar and unwrapped one for himself. 'I don't know about you, but all that talking has made me very hungry. Let's go straight to Masvingo now and find somewhere nice to eat. It will take us around forty-five minutes.'

As they drove along, she made a mental list of all her lines of enquiry. It was depressing to note that apart from unearthing the newspaper article from the National Archives, she had not made any concrete headway into her search.

'I've been here over a week and haven't really made any progress,' she lamented. 'I've heard nothing back from the Central Registry Office.'

Dominic clicked his tongue in annoyance. 'They should have contacted you by now. I'll chase them up tomorrow.'

'We also need to follow up on that journalist who wrote the article. I wonder if he's still around.'

'He's probably long gone by now. Most white people left the country in 1980 after independence. But I'll help you search for him. How are you getting on with the Indian families?'

'Not very well. I have one more to visit, but the other families knew nothing. The telephone survey Taruna carried out has also been disappointing. No one remembers anything.'

'And what about the plan to advertise in the local paper?' asked Dominic. 'When will that happen?'

'I'm not sure. I'll ask Savita tomorrow. There's also going to be a message on social media. I know it's usually young people who use those platforms, but Savita thinks someone may ask their parents or grandparents and maybe, just maybe, we will get lucky. It's worth a try, I suppose.'

~

By the time they got back to Harare, it was well past 10 p.m. Both sets of parents were relieved to see them home. They had been worried. Uncle Peter explained that the highways were not safe to drive on, especially after dark. The truck drivers were not known for their careful driving, and there were frequent reports of car accidents.

'You must be hungry,' said Aunt Mary. 'Come and have some shepherd's pie. Dominic's favourite.'

Anna was tired but not hungry. Dominic was always hungry and ready to tuck into his mother's cooking. Anna played with the food on her plate. She wanted to tell her aunt and uncle what they had seen and found in Rukuvoko, but with her father present, she was unable to discuss it.

It was not until the next morning that Anna had a chance to talk to her aunt. They happened to be alone in the garden before breakfast. As quickly as she could, Anna updated her.

Mary was astounded to hear about the pastor's surprising disclosure. She was angry that the authorities had not been told about the midwife from Umzuma. 'Even if it was a rumour, that Father Groober should have mentioned it. A thorough search at that time could have led them to the midwife and the birth family.'

Anna agreed. 'Dominic and I have made enquiries in Umzuma, but I think it's unlikely it will get us anywhere.'

'Yah. It all happened too long ago.' She pondered for a moment. 'But it does make sense to me. If a couple needed to have a baby in secret, no one would know about it if they went deep into the bushlands and found a local midwife to help with the delivery.'

Anna nodded. 'I am certain they didn't want to give their baby up. They made sure he was safe and sound when they left him. Someone or something forced them to give him away.'

Mary pressed her lips together. 'Maybe.'

Anna pulled out her necklace and held up the pendant.

'I *am* right. This is the proof. It's a message from Dad's birth mother saying she loves him and hopes he will find her one day.'

Mary gave Anna a hug, tutting in sympathy. 'I'm sure you are right, child.' Anna buried her face in Mary's ample bosom, wondering if she was ever going to discover what happened all those years ago.

~

The news from Savita was not encouraging. She phoned the next morning to say that she and her husband had not had any joy at their community centres. No one had heard of an abandoned baby or an orphaned boy from the 1950s. Taruna had drawn a blank with her telephone survey. She was planning to post a message on social media that morning. And Savita was ready to place an advertisement in Zimbabwe's largest daily newspaper, the *Herald*.

'We'll have the ad in the paper every day this week,' said Savita. 'I've included my contact details, so fingers crossed I get a response. And before I forget, are you free any evening this week? The last family on our list, the Mehtas, are happy for us to pop in around six p.m. Bharat Mehta's ninety-year-old mother lives with them. She suffers from dementia, apparently, and harks back to her childhood all the time. She might say something helpful.'

Hoping they would be in luck, Anna readily agreed to call on the Mehta family the next evening.

In the meantime, she borrowed her uncle's laptop and started searching for James Rathbury, the journalist who had written the article about the baby found at the church.

A quick Google search on James Rathbury provided several results, but Anna realised she needed to narrow down the search. She added 'Zimbabwe journalist' to his name and found some unrelated reports. When she replaced 'Zimbabwe' with 'Rhodesia', she finally found what she was looking for. However, it wasn't good news. James Rathbury had died in 1978 at the age of forty-six.

Disappointed, Anna read that he had become a prominent journalist who was killed while covering Rhodesia's Bush War. He had died during the height of the war between the white-minority government and the black nationalist fighters. Anna's hopes of learning first-hand from someone who'd seen Mathew in 1954 were completely shattered.

Later that morning, Dominic called to inform Anna that he had visited the Central Registry Office and spoken to the man they had seen before. Dominic had urged him to chase it up because time was running out for Anna. The man made a phone call to someone in the office that handled the request forms and promised that Anna would soon be granted access to Mathew's records.

Anna immediately checked her emails but found none from the Registry Office. Disappointed once again, she went through her other emails and was pleasantly surprised to find one from Gita Thakur, now at her brother's house in Mumbai where she sounded quite settled. Anna calculated that she'd been there just over two months. Gita described her happiness at being back in India and finally feeling safe from harm. She ended by once again inviting Anna to visit her if or when she made a trip to Mumbai.

That night, as Anna lay in bed, she drifted off to sleep, thinking about a woman giving birth in Umzuma and her baby being taken away. She had a clear picture in her mind of the very church where the baby was abandoned. The image of her father's sad face flashed through her mind. For his sake and hers, she hoped her search for the truth would be successful.

# Chapter 18

Anna and Dominic were granted permission to access Mathew's records at the Central Registry Office the next day through an email. They were given a time slot between 10 and 11 a.m. to view the file. With Christmas approaching and the office set to close on Christmas Eve, time was of the essence.

When Anna and Dominic arrived at the office, there were two staff members at the counter and three groups of people scattered throughout the room, looking through files on tables. A low murmur floated over to Anna and Dominic as they walked up to the man they'd seen before. They greeted him and without a word, he handed over a thin brown folder and gestured towards a table at the far end of the room.

Eager to see the documents, Anna opened the folder and pulled out two certificates and one A4 sheet of paper. Frowning with disappointment, she stared at Dominic.

'Is this it? Just three pieces of paper?'

'Shh,' he said, looking around the room.

Anna lowered her voice. 'There must be more than this, surely.' Dominic looked pointedly at the sheets. She spread them out and examined them one by one. The first was a copy of the birth certificate that Mathew already had in his possession. It had the stamp and signature of the Fort Victoria District Registrar. The date of registration was 25 March 1954, and Mathew's date of birth was stated as 25 January 1954. A single line at the bottom read:

> Parents Unknown. Baby found in basket at Rukuvoko Mission Church.

The second sheet was the adoption certificate, which was identical to the one Mathew already had. Below the stamp and signature of the District Registrar was Mathew's date of birth and the name and address of Rukuvoko Church. Beneath that was a statement about the baby boy of unknown parentage being legally adopted by Mr and Mrs Kotze of a specified address in Fort Victoria.

The final sheet of paper was a report from the Department of Social Welfare, Southern Rhodesia, dated 15 March 1956. Signed by a Mrs Jennifer Williams, it stated that she had visited the home of Mr and Mrs Kotze at their address in Arcadia, Salisbury. As part of the Children's Protection and Adoption Act, she was carrying out a routine inspection of an adopted child at the home of his adoptive parents. In quotation marks, she stated:

> 'The health and development of this 2-year-old boy appears to be good and the family environment suggests that there is nothing to prevent him from enjoying a successful adult life.'

This was something new. Mathew had never mentioned this inspection. Anna guessed that the Kotzes had never told him about it. While the report confirmed that Mathew had been well cared for by his adoptive parents, it didn't provide any new information about his birth parents. Anna felt disappointed and set the report aside.

'I can't believe there is so little information.' She shook her head in frustration. 'I thought there'd be lots more, like police reports and investigation records. There's no mention of the cushion, the hat, the red shawl or the white blanket found in the basket, so we still don't know what happened to those.'

Dominic made a tsk sound. 'You were expecting way too much, Anna. You're forgetting we're talking about an event from sixty-four years ago.'

'Even so! Let's go and ask the man.'

As Dominic expected, there was no further information. In an irritated tone, the man at the counter informed them that they were lucky to have even those three documents. Most records that went that far back were only one or two lines scribbled in a register. He added that in the future, when all data were transcribed on to electronic records, there would be even less to see.

Disappointed, Anna followed Dominic out of the office. Nothing seemed to be going her way and she was fast losing hope of finding anything useful. All her enquiries had yielded no fruitful results. With only three more avenues to explore – the last family visit, the newspaper advertisement, and the social media posts – Anna started to doubt herself once again. She questioned whether she was doing the right thing and whether she was causing unnecessary anguish for her father. Perhaps she should stop chasing after information and simply enjoy the rest of her stay in Zimbabwe.

~

That evening, when she went with Savita and Prakash to visit the Mehta family, Anna was not feeling at all optimistic. Mr Mehta's ninety-year-old mother suffered from dementia, and although she was very talkative, Anna doubted she would learn anything from her. As soon as she saw Savita, the old woman began to chatter like an excited little bird.

Calling her Manju-*masi*, Savita tried to get a word in edgewise. She asked a few questions and old Mrs Mehta twittered her answers with a wide smile on her face. The conversation was all in Gujarati, so Anna sat watching their body language, trying to work out what was being said.

At one point, Savita put her hand on Manju-*masi*'s arm and said something in a grave voice. The old woman stopped talking and fell into a reflective mood. Her eyes glazed over, and she seemed to be thinking hard. Eventually she locked eyes with Anna and said a few words that sounded important. Anna held her breath, hoping someone would translate. But before anyone could say a word, the old woman reverted back to the joyful, chattering bird that she was before. It was as if someone had flipped a switch.

Soon after that, Prakash indicated that they should leave. Back in the car, Anna couldn't wait to hear the translation. 'What did she say? Did she remember something?'

Savita gave her an apologetic shake of the head. 'Nothing useful, I'm afraid. For a moment, I really thought she was going to say something important. I asked her if she knew anyone in the community who'd fallen pregnant, gone away somewhere, then returned without a baby. When she fell silent and stared at you, I felt certain she was connecting you with a distant memory. But all she said was: *she disappeared!* Then she blinked and snapped back to the present. I couldn't get her to go back. Over and over again I asked her to tell us *who* disappeared, but she had no answer for that.'

Anna breathed in slowly and chewed her lower lip. 'That is so disappointing.'

'You know,' said Prakash. 'Maybe she *was* remembering a woman who disappeared. In 1954, Manju-*masi* must have been in her mid-twenties. She might well have known someone in her circle who was pregnant. Maybe they were friends. If that person went away somewhere, she would wonder what happened to her. Let's imagine that *was* your grandmother. If so, she could have had her baby in Rukuvoko, then gone away somewhere for good, and Mrs Mehta would have noticed her absence.'

Savita nodded slowly. 'That would mean Mathew's mother was a local woman who had her baby, then disappeared to another country, perhaps.'

'It's still possible that she was from outside the country but friends with Mrs Mehta,' said Prakash. 'She could have had her baby here, then gone back to where she came from.'

Anna put her head in her hands and groaned. 'Arrgh, this is too much! It's hurting my brain.'

Savita clucked in sympathy. 'Don't upset yourself, Anna. This was always going to be a difficult mystery to solve. But I'm not giving up yet. Someone might see the advert or the social media posts and get in touch. Let's stay positive, and I'll call you tomorrow.'

~

But it wasn't the next day that Savita called. That very evening, just as Anna sat down for dinner with the family, her mobile phone rang.

'Don't answer it!' commanded Theresa who was fervently against interruptions at mealtimes. 'Eat first.'

Anna looked at her plate filled with lamb stew, rice, green beans and salad. It would take her a long time to finish it all. She looked back at her mobile on the sideboard behind her and saw that the call was from Savita. She was itching to pick it up. But seeing her mother's severe expression, she refrained. The call went to voicemail. But within seconds, it started to ring again.

'Sorry, Mum. This might be urgent.' She grabbed her phone and hastened away to the front room. 'Hello?'

'Anna! I have news.' Savita sounded breathless.

'What is it?'

'Pratima Daruwala came to see us. She just left.'

'Who's Pratima Daruwala?'

'Don't you remember? You met her last Sunday at the second house we went to. She was the woman who came in with food for her elderly parents.'

Anna remembered. Pratima had only popped in for a bit, but she'd been very interested in their research. She had asked a lot of questions and wished them luck.

'She knows someone who can help us,' continued Savita. 'Her friend, Seema Rajah, has information about a child in her husband's family who was given up for adoption.'

'Her husband's family?'

'Yes! It seems there is a skeleton in their cupboard. Seema knows about it because when her husband's grandfather was alive, he spoke about having a sister whose son was adopted. That would have been in the 1950s.'

Anna gasped. 'Oh my God! His grandfather's sister? Is she still around?'

'We don't know. Nobody was aware he even *had* a sister. Laxman Rajah, the old man, passed away about five years ago and there was no mention of any siblings.'

'Amazing,' breathed Anna.

'We can meet this Seema Rajah tomorrow, if you're free. She'll be at Pratima's house around six p.m.'

'Of course, I'm free. This sounds like a breakthrough.'

'It does. But we mustn't get too excited. You never know. It could turn out to be a damp squib.'

If recent experience was anything to go by, Anna knew Savita was right. But she couldn't help feeling that this time, her luck might be in. Before returning to the table, Anna took deep breaths to compose herself. When she joined the others, she said as calmly as she could that the call was from Savita inviting her out the next day. Thankfully, no one asked for details. They continued with their conversation and dinner.

~

Just after six in the evening, Savita steered her car into Pratima's driveway. It was a modest bungalow not dissimilar to Peter and Mary's. She parked behind a shiny white Mercedes-Benz.

'That must be Seema's car. The Rajahs are wealthy people.'

Pratima welcomed them at the front door and walked them past the lounge where Anna had a fleeting glimpse of a man with two small children watching television. They entered the kitchen where a young woman stood leaning against a worktop with a drink in her hand. Dressed in stylish clothes, she was attractive with big brown eyes, thick black lashes and dark hair falling in a bob round her shoulders. She greeted them with a friendly smile.

'Nice to meet you,' she said to Anna. 'And good to see you, Savita-*masi*. How are you?'

'I'm fine, thanks. Long time no see.'

Pratima, whose house they were in, asked them all to sit down and offered everyone a drink. There was an assortment of dry snacks like chevdo, sev-mamra and ganthia on the table, along with fruit juices and colas. After a few pleasantries, Savita thanked Seema for coming forward with information.

'We were surprised to hear that Laxman-*kaka* had a sister,' she said.

'So were we. We had no idea Chetan's grandfather had a sister,' said Seema. Turning to Anna, she explained that Chetan was her husband. 'It was only a few years before he died that his grandfather started speaking about her. He'd never mentioned her before. He kept saying his sister had a baby who was adopted.'

Savita puckered her brow. 'But what about Chetan's father? Didn't he know he had an aunt? She would have been *his* father's sister, his *foi*.'

'My father-in-law insists there was no *foi*. Both he and my mother-in-law have told us not to believe Laxman-*dada*'s story. They think he made it up. A figment of his imagination. But I believe it's true and they are in denial.'

Anna leaned forward. Her stomach had started to do somersaults. 'What makes you say that?'

Seema sniffed, expressing her disdain. 'My father-in-law doesn't want a scandal in the family. If word got out that his father had a mystery sister, people would start to wonder why no one spoke about her. And if they heard she'd had a baby, there would be tongues wagging about her married or unmarried status. Chetan's parents told us not to mention this to anyone because Laxman-*dada*'s stories were just the ramblings of an old man.'

'But you believe the stories. Why is that?' asked Anna.

'Because there is so much detail in them.' Seema looked at Savita with a knitted brow. 'I don't know how well you knew Laxman-*dada*, but I can tell you, he was no rambler. Right to the end, his mind was as sharp as a knife. He was a good man. Unlike my father-in-law who is a real bully. I feel no allegiance to him. That's why I'm telling you all this. A little boy in the Rajah family was definitely given up for adoption in the 1950s.'

Anna took a breath. 'What were the details?' She tried to tone down her mounting excitement.

'What Laxman-*dada* said is that when he was about nine or ten years of age, his older unmarried sister had a baby boy. His father was an angry man, shouting at everyone constantly. His sister was taken away somewhere to have the baby delivered. When she returned home, there was no baby with her. Laxman-*dada* was told that his father had given the newborn up for adoption. His sister and mother were crying all the time. One day, not long after she'd had the baby, his sister packed a suitcase and went away somewhere with their father. His father returned, but his sister never came back home. Laxman-*dada* kept asking for her, but his father told him to forget her. He made him promise on his mother's life that he should never mention his sister's name again!'

Anna felt her heart pounding in her ears. She closed her eyes and tried to breathe normally. For a moment, she thought she was going to pass out. Savita put a hand on her arm and asked Seema the questions burning in Anna's heart.

'Tell me, Seema. Why do you think Laxman-*kaka* decided to speak about his sister so late in his life?'

Seema blew out a breath. 'He was diagnosed with liver cancer. He knew he didn't have long to live. When he started to tell us about her, it was as if he wanted to unburden himself. He said she was like a captured butterfly hiding in his heart, and he wanted to release her before he died. I remember those words clearly because it sounded like poetry to me.'

Anna was trying hard to calm her racing heart. When Seema turned to her, Anna gave her a weak smile. In a hushed tone, she asked: 'Did your husband's grandfather ever go looking for her? For his sister?'

Seema shook her head. 'No. He'd sworn on his mother's life. He was the sort of man who kept his promises. But I believe he regretted never going in search of her.'

With her brow furrowed in concentration, Pratima said: 'Sounds like he wanted someone else to go looking for her.'

Seema gave her a rueful smile. 'That's exactly what I thought. I said to Chetan that we should try. But he disagreed. He thought we should leave well alone.'

Pratima shrugged. 'It would have been impossible to find her anyway. Where would you even start?'

'Well,' said Seema. 'Laxman-*dada* did give us a clue. He said he'd found out where his sister had been taken.'

There was deathly silence in the room. Anna could feel the tension as they all waited for Seema to continue.

'India,' she said. 'He took her to India.'

Anna let out a long breath. She could hardly believe what she was hearing. Everything seemed to point to the fact that this sister was Mathew's biological mother. She *had* to be. And she was taken to India!

Seema was still speaking. Looking directly at Anna she asked in a kind voice: 'I can't help thinking this information means more to you than just data for research. You need this for personal reasons. Am I right?'

Anna blinked. She realised that they were all waiting for her to speak. With a slow nod of her head, she explained.

'You are right. I'm searching for my father's birth parents. He was born in this country in 1954 and left as a newborn in a basket outside a mission church.'

Pratima let out a loud gasp and gaped at Anna with wide eyes. Seema's expression softened to something sweet and sad.

Savita continued the story. 'Anna's father was adopted by a mixed-race couple. He has no idea who left him in the basket, and why. He grew up in Arcadia and went to Mountford High School. He and I were in the same class. I lost touch with him for years but by a happy coincidence, I met him again in London a few months ago. His name is Mathew Kotze. I don't suppose Laxman-*kaka* mentioned that name, Mathew?'

'No. Not *that* name. But he did give us another name.' She paused for effect. 'His sister's.'

Anna had stopped breathing.

'Her name was Indira.'

As soon as Seema uttered the name, a low choking moan escaped Anna's lips. She realised she had finally discovered who Indira was. In truth, she had always imagined that Indira was the name of Mathew's mother, and that she had left her chain and pendant with her baby. But now she had confirmation. Seema's account of Laxman Rajah's story *was* the truth. She felt it in her bones. Indira was Indira Rajah, blood sister of Laxman – Seema's husband's grandfather.

'Finally!' she whispered, her eyes filling with tears.

Savita put her arm around Anna's shoulders. Pointing to the chain round her neck, she asked her to show it to Seema and Pratima. They were staggered to see the name engraved on the pendant and fascinated to hear all about the search so far. Blinking away her tears, Anna gave them a brief account of her investigations.

'She's your real grandmother,' said Seema, her voice filled with awe. 'And you are named after her – Indira. Will you go to India to look for her?'

Filled with emotion, Anna couldn't speak for a moment. Eventually she said: 'Yes. Without a doubt. I'll go as soon as possible.' She paused for thought. 'I have to accept that she may not be alive any more. But even if she's not, I'm going to try to find people who knew her, to find out what happened the day my father was born.'

Seema gave her a sombre look. 'India is a vast country. You'll need to know *where* in India she was taken.' She puckered her eyebrows in thought. 'I'm not a hundred per cent certain, but I do have a theory about that.'

All eyes were on Seema.

'Whenever my in-laws go to India, they always visit some relatives living in Mumbai. They are a part of the extended Rajah family. If Laxman-*dada*'s sister was taken to India, I think she would probably have gone to visit that family. If I was looking for her, that would be my starting point.'

Anna's eyes widened. 'Do you have their address?'

'I do,' smiled Seema. 'You can have it with pleasure. If you find your grandmother, you will be finding Laxman-*dada*'s sister. For sure that would make him very happy. I wish you all the luck in the world.'

Anna and Savita exchanged a look of disbelief. They had finally discovered who Indira was. Overwhelmed by what she had just learnt, Anna tried to calm her breathing. It was a very significant milestone in her search for Mathew's biological parents. Now she had to concentrate her efforts on finding her, wherever she was in India, and discovering why she had given her son away.

# PART 3

# Chapter 19

## INDIRA

### Sonwadi, Gujarat, India, 1954

7 May 1954

Dear Diary

This is the first day of my life.

It is my seventeenth birthday today, but I am declaring my life before this moment null and void. I want to cancel everything that has happened to me thus far. My past is gone, wiped out, written off. I have no choice but to bury it deep inside my soul, in a place where it can't easily be reached.

I'm not allowed to talk about it. *Bapuji* has made me swear on my mother's life that I will tell no one what has happened to me. He said that if I do, I will suffer more. Nobody will understand my problem, and nobody will believe I am innocent. But dear Diary, I *have* to speak to someone! If I keep things locked up inside me all the time, I will explode. There has to be some release for my feelings – my feelings of grief, anger and pain.

I have decided that *you* will be my confidante, my one and only friend who will help me get through this. From time to time, whenever the pressure builds up inside and I feel the urge to release the tension, I will speak to you by writing on these pages. I'll keep you hidden, so no one will see you except me. The good thing is that people around here don't read or write English; they are all Gujarati. If they see me with you, I'll say I am writing English poetry. My teacher always said I was good at English. She also said I had a flair for writing. I don't know about that, but I do know that putting my thoughts on paper has always made me feel better.

*Bapuji* has banished me here, in this village, and gone for good. Out of my life. I have been discarded, like a piece of potato peel, into the rubbish bin. My mum, my brother Laxman, my cousins, uncles, aunties and all my friends are gone from my life forever. I will never see them again.

My whole family is lost to me and my grief is indescribable. There are moments when I can hardly breathe because my chest feels tight, as if a snake has coiled itself around me and is squeezing with all its might. It's a strange thing but until I came to this village, I didn't feel anything at all. Nothing seemed real. My grief must have been suspended up in the clouds. But when I arrived here, it came crashing down on me, hitting me so hard that I was struck dumb.

For almost a month, I did not utter a word. It didn't seem possible to open my mouth and form any words. When anyone asked me a question, I nodded or shook my head in response. When asked to comment, I simply turned away. All I wanted to do was curl up and die. I didn't want to be in this world.

But gradually, over the last few weeks, I have started to feel a little stronger. The shock and horror of what my body and mind have suffered is slowly beginning to recede. I am able to talk to people now, though I say as little as possible. But there is so much going on in my head. I desperately need someone to share my thoughts with. Dear Diary, you will have to bear with me and give me the strength I need to go on with my life. I will be pouring my heart out to you.

The reason I'm starting life anew is because my old life is too painful. The last twelve months have been unbearable. I have suffered so much trauma. *Bapuji* has arranged this different life for me where no one knows anything about me. I have to start again.

My *bapuji* is a hard man. I always knew that. But now I know his heart is made of stone. I cried, screamed and begged to be allowed to stay home. But he just closed his ears and his heart. He ignored *Ba* too. She implored him not to send me, their eldest child, so far away. But he would rather cut me off than have the family name ruined by scandal.

I'm here now, and it's no good feeling sorry for myself. *Ba* told me that I should be brave. Her face was twisted in anguish as she hugged me for the last time. She said I was the strongest person she knew, and she made me promise that I would be good and build a happy life for myself. I'm going to try to do that, accept my fate and get on with whatever lies ahead.

It's been three and a half months since I had my baby. My body seems to have recovered. But my mind is another matter. Every time I think about that awful day, when they didn't even let me hold my baby, I am in bits. I can't go on like that. So I'm going to try really hard NOT to think back.

But it's inevitable that at times, I will fail. Maybe as time goes by, it will get easier to forget. But for now, when my thoughts turn to the past and my loss and grief become too much to bear, I will offload on to you. Bit by bit, I will tell you what happened to me. But only you will know.

I also want to talk to you about my new life. There are good and bad things about this place, and maybe if I describe it all, it will help me settle in. Right now, I am sitting under a shady tree at the back of the house where I live with my husband and his mother. Yes. I have a husband now, and he has brought me here to live with him in his village on the outskirts of the small town of Sonwadi.

With my back resting against the tree trunk, I can see the back of our house, and I can hear the sound of the river flowing behind me. It's a good spot to sit and share my thoughts with you. This is my go-to place for a bit of peace and solitude.

The house is an end-of-terrace made of timber, mud, cow dung, straw, and rice husk. The roof has clay tiles and straw, similar to thatched roofs in Africa. But it's not a hut. It's long and narrow with windows along one side, one wooden door at the front entrance, and one at the back. It's got a front room, leading into a back room, then the kitchen which opens out to this yard. The rooms are quite big, and there is a curtained-off section in the kitchen that is used as a shower. We use a bucket of water and pour it over ourselves with a pitcher. The toilet, one of those with a bucket that needs cleaning out every day, is out here in one corner of the yard.

When I first came here a month ago, it was a shock to my system. Everything seemed so backward. It is so different from what I've been used to in Southern Rhodesia. Our house there is beautiful with a front and back garden, a wide gate and a veranda with steps on which I loved to sit and read. Our bathroom has both hot and cold water on tap, and my mother's stove is electric.

At first, I couldn't believe that I would have to live with no electricity in the house and no running water. How was I ever going to manage? But surprisingly, as the days have passed, I've grown used to it. We use oil lamps at night to see what we're doing, and we fill up water in large pots from a communal water tank near the house. Clothes are washed at the riverbank behind me, and cooking is done on a Primus stove. It all sounds like hard work but to be honest, it's not that bad. The house is actually very clean and airy.

It's quite tranquil on this side. There is a lot of activity and noise in the front, with children playing, scooters and bicycles hooting and cows ambling by. There are also a lot of stray dogs. But they're usually sleeping during the day. It's at night they seem to come alive with their incessant barking.

The land is dry at the moment. But I'm told the monsoon rains will start soon. Then everything will turn green. People seem excited when they mention the monsoon. They are looking forward to the rains. Behind me, the land slopes downwards to a river called Ambica. At the moment, it's more like a stream, but my husband says that when the river is swollen, it will be full of fish. He is a fisherman who cycles twelve miles every day to the nearest seaport. He goes first thing in the morning then takes his catch to sell at the Sonwadi fish market. He comes home for a quick shower and lunch, then goes to town for his second job as a salesman in a shoe shop.

His name is Manoj Jhinwar, so I am now Indira Jhinwar. He is devoted to his mother, who is a widow, in her mid-fifties and blind. I'm told there are many blind people in rural India, caused by vitamin A deficiency in childhood.

My impression of Manoj is that he is a hardworking, decent man. I don't see much of him, and when I do, he treats me like a house guest. Most of the day he is out, and at night, he has asked me to sleep in the back room with his mother who needs help with going outside at night. Needless to say, I am extremely satisfied with this arrangement, and relieved that he does not expect more from me.

The reason why Manoj chose to marry me is no secret. He needed someone to look after his mother. Not many girls were willing to do that. Despite his mother's attempts to find a wife for him, no family was willing to give their daughter's hand in marriage to a poor fisherman living with his blind mother. Then six weeks ago, Manoj's mum heard from her sister Mohini who is married to my uncle Narayan-*kaka* in Bombay. She told my mother-in-law that she'd found someone who might be just right for Manoj. That someone was me.

As soon as we arrived from Southern Rhodesia on March 25th, we went to stay with *Bapuji's* cousin Narayan Rajah. *Bapuji* asked if they knew of any suitable boys for me to marry. Mohini-*kaki* mentioned her nephew Manoj and promptly asked him to travel up from Sonwadi. He came, he saw me, and within a week we were married by a Hindu priest in a small temple nearby. I had no say in the matter. Narayan-*kaka* said he would file the papers for the court marriage to take place at a later date.

Did my father ask me if I wanted to marry Manoj? Of course not. Did he ask if Manoj had the means to take care of me? I don't think so. He wanted me off his hands so he could return to Africa as soon as he could. When he said goodbye to me, the day Manoj and I left for Sonwadi, I saw only relief in his whole demeanour. He was glad to see the back of me. I was lost in a haze and can't remember feeling anything. But I did notice a tear in Narayan-*kaka*'s eyes. He patted my back and said I should contact him if I ever needed any help. Mohini-*kaki* had made herself scarce when we left their house. I got the feeling she was not interested in me or Manoj. It left me wondering why she'd taken the trouble to be a matchmaker. Maybe she just wanted to make sure I didn't end up as her responsibility.

At the time, my mind was in a fog. I was made to feel like a burden, someone dirty and unwanted. I did what I was told to do in a robotic fashion. When Manoj came to see me, I sat in silence with my head lowered and my hands folded on my knees. Dressed in one of Mohini-*kaki*'s saris, she made me cover my head with the *chedo*, the end of the fabric, like an old married woman. I didn't look up even once. And the wedding was a brief affair, over in what seemed like a flash. It was only when we were on the train heading for Manoj's home that I registered his appearance in some detail.

I was sitting beside him, looking out of the window, noticing nothing beyond the fact that we were no longer in the city. He spoke to me in a surprisingly gentle tone of voice.

'Are you thirsty?' He held out a silver-coloured thermos flask.

I looked up. My first thought was that he appeared old. He had a bony face with a large forehead, high cheekbones and long nose. With his thin black moustache, closely cropped hair and dark skin, he wasn't my idea of handsome. But there was something in his eyes that captured my attention. They were sympathetic eyes. Without words, he seemed to be saying I should not worry. But he was a stranger to me. How could I not worry? If there was one thing I have learned from my unspeakable experience is that I should never trust a man.

It occurred to me that he might also have found *me* unattractive. I know I'm short and a little plump, and my face is round with big cheeks. Unlike my beautiful *Ba*, my eyes and mouth are on the small side and my nose is a bit flat. But *Ba* told me that my beauty is within, and it shines brighter than anyone else's. My crowning glory is my thick dark-brown hair which usually tumbles over my shoulders and back. People always comment on it. But since my problems began, I have not bothered to take care of it. Brushed away from my face, I now tie it back with a clip at the back of my neck.

If that's how my husband finds me, then he has kept it to himself. Like me, he says very little. We've been married for over a month now, and

179

these days, I feel a little more comfortable with him. I've learnt that he is almost double my age. Hard physical work has made him look older than his thirty-two years. He lost his father when he was eight years old and had to stop attending school. Taking any jobs that were available, he toiled long hours so that he and his mother would not go hungry.

His mother's name is Kastur. Being blind, or mostly blind, she can't do very much. She's able to move around the house without too much trouble, and thankfully, she can manage her own personal hygiene. But all the household chores are done by me. My job is to cook and clean for the three of us and always be at Kastur-*ba*'s beck and call. When she shouts my name, I have to stop what I'm doing and rush to her at once. If not, I get a telling-off. She can be very impatient. I do try to follow her instructions, but when something goes wrong, she doesn't hold back. She's quite scary and I must admit, I find her very intimidating. She's small and thin with shoulders that are perpetually stooped. But there is nothing wrong with her tongue.

I have never been a noisy, chatty person. My friends described me as reticent and reserved, a bit of an introvert. Being in this new environment has made me withdraw into my shell even more. Kastur-*ba* is the complete opposite. She says whatever comes to her mind without stopping to think. Having a companion like me who speaks only when spoken to must be frustrating for her.

I can see that. All day long she wants to chat. She told me all about the neighbours, the village, how she became progressively blind and how she managed before I came to live with them.

She also told me what she'd heard about me before Manoj came to see me in Bombay. Her sister Mohini had described me as 'not all there'. Apparently, I am physically strong but mentally slow. *Bapuji* made up this cruel story about me to explain why he was arranging my marriage to someone impoverished like Manoj. He said he would never find a boy from his wealthy connections who would be willing to marry me with my mental disability.

*Bapuji* lied and said that I am mentally impaired. Not crazy or unstable, exactly, but not very clever. How hurtful is that? But he has caused me so much pain that this new gut-wrenching untruth is just another example of how shockingly uncaring he is of his own daughter.

There is no point in denying anything. I am damaged and broken. But I have to make sure Manoj and his mother never find out what happened to me. *Bapuji* said that if they did find out, they would throw me out of their house.

Dear Diary, the thought of having nowhere to live terrifies me! I hope that in time, my husband and his mother will see that I have no mental impairment. I do think it's strange, however, that neither of them considered this supposed mental condition a problem. It didn't stop them from accepting me into their family.

I can only assume that they were desperate to find a wife-cum-carer, and anyone who agreed to marry Manoj would do.

Dear Diary, I think I will stop for today. It's nearly time for Kastur-*ba*'s afternoon chai. I also need to start preparing the evening meal. Every morning, I wake up with a heavy heart. Now that I've shared my feelings with you, it does feel a little lighter. So I'll write again in a few days' time. For now, I'll say goodbye.

# Chapter 20

12 July 1954

Dear Diary

It's been a horrible day today. For some reason, Kastur-*ba* is in a foul mood and nothing I do seems to please her. We've been stuck indoors for three days because the monsoon rains have arrived, and they haven't let up for a moment. It's coming down in torrents. Sheets of water are lashing down, flooding the roads and sending everyone scurrying for shelter.

It *is* a wondrous sight, though, especially after the heat and dust of the Indian summer. I can see why everyone looks forward to the monsoon season. The air feels fresh and there's a pleasant earthy smell that reminds me of home after our Southern African downpours. But now, there is a pause in the deluge, so I have come outside to write in the open air. I was tired of being at home with Kastur-*ba* night and day without a break. The non-stop torrential rain adds to her frustrations, and she takes it out on me.

'You are a stupid girl!' she screamed when I gave her lunch earlier. I cooked spicy slices of aubergines for her with hot rotlis. I even made kichdi – rice with lentils, and kadhi – the yogurt that goes with it. It took me hours to cook. 'Did your mother teach you nothing?' she barked. 'This food is tasteless.'

I wish Manoj was here. She doesn't berate me like this when he is around. He seems to have a calming effect on her. I know I'm not a good cook, but that's only because I haven't had much experience. I'm still learning. If only Kastur-*ba* would show me how she likes her food. I'm frightened to ask her to teach me because she might fly into another rage.

She's not at all like my own *Ba* who is kind and gentle. With the utmost patience, *Ba* taught me how to cook the basic daal, bhaat, shaak, rotli – lentils, rice, vegetable curry and chapattis. But I was still at school so I couldn't spend too much time in the kitchen. Dear Diary, I miss my *Ba* so much. My heart aches for her today.

I wish I had appreciated her more. She was such a loving mother. But if I could change one thing about her it would be that she had more courage. I wish that she was able to stand up to *Bapuji* when he was cruel. I think she was scared of him, and she was conditioned to be subservient. Waiting on him hand and foot, she allowed him to control her. Unilaterally, he made every family decision.

That's what he did when he found out I was pregnant. I will never forget the fire of fury in his eyes when he stormed into my room and pulled me out of my bed. He shook me by the shoulders and shouted foul words into my face. He slapped me so hard that my nose began to bleed. *Ba* was crying and begging him to stop. She tried to pull him away, but he yelled at her and continued to rant and rave at me.

I was whimpering and trying to move away. But he had a firm hold of me.

'I am going to kill you! Do you hear me, you dirty filthy whore. How could you prostitute yourself like this?'

*Ba* was on her knees. 'It's not her fault! She didn't know what was happening.'

Pushing me backwards on to my bed, he turned on her. 'What do you mean, she didn't know what was happening? She's not stupid. Didn't you teach her anything? And why did you wait to tell me when it's too late to do anything about it?'

I didn't know what he meant. There was so much I didn't know because they had given me such a strict and protected upbringing. Whatever I did and wherever I went, I had to ask for their permission. After school, I was required to come straight back home. No staying late to be with friends. My social life revolved around family and community activities. And conversations never involved the cold hard facts about relationships between men and women.

*Ba* could not have told *Bapuji* that I was pregnant any earlier because neither she nor I had any idea ourselves. We both realised the awful truth at the same time only the week before he was told. It was when *Ba* was helping me wear a sari for the wedding of a family friend. As I stood there with my blouse and petticoat, she asked me to make a slow turn so she could tuck the upper end of the sari into the petticoat at my waist.

All of a sudden, she stopped. Standing back, she stared at my tummy. I thought she was going to say what she often said: that I should go on a diet. I'd been battling to lose my girlish chubbiness for quite some time. Aware that my waistline had been expanding, I'd resolved to eat less so that I could slim down a little. But *Ba* was looking at me with an expression of horror. In a voice full of urgency, she began to ask me questions. All kinds of questions about my menstrual cycle, about new friends, specifically boys I might have met. I was bewildered.

After counting on her fingers, she pinpointed a time five months in the past and asked me if I had been alone with any boy around that time. When I said no, she thought for a moment then gasped and took a step back. She asked if anyone had come into my room, apart from our family members. That's when I realised what she was getting at. Someone *had* come into my room but there was no way I could admit that. If I did, I would have to tell her about the terrible thing that I had done, and that would get me into very deep trouble.

*Ba* began to look frightened. With wild eyes, she asked me a direct question, staring into my face with such intensity that my heart began to pound, and I had to steady myself by holding on to the bedstead. I couldn't answer her. I couldn't even look at her. But she shook it out of me.

She made me tell her everything. How someone who had come to visit us entered my room when I was alone one day. It was a visitor from India staying with us for four weeks in April. Handsome, funny and good company, he charmed all of us, even my usually dour *Bapuji*.

One day, in the last week that he was with us, I came home from school to find him on his own, reading the newspaper in our sitting room. After greeting him, I went upstairs to make a start on my homework. I was hard at it when he knocked on my open door and invited himself in. He sat on my bed and began to talk to me about his life in India. Living with his parents and other siblings, he was single and worked in their family store.

He made me laugh with some of the stories he told. I felt at ease with him and happy to know that he liked my company. My hair was tied back with ribbons in two plaits. He asked me to remove the ribbons and let it loose. When I did, he said he'd never seen such beautiful hair and began to play with it. At the same time, he paid me lots of other compliments. No one had ever done that before and I was flattered.

He was my elder, someone from my parents' generation. So I didn't mind when he hugged me and kissed me on my forehead. I trusted him. But then he kissed me on my lips. That made me uncomfortable. When I moved back, he smiled and told me that I shouldn't worry. He convinced me that because we liked each other, it was perfectly normal for us to be close. To my shame, I allowed him to get too close. It was too late before I realised that it was all wrong. He shouldn't have done what he did, but then, I should have run away. It was my fault and I blame myself for what happened.

A few days after that shameful afternoon, the visitor left our home and returned to India. He told me not to tell anyone about what we had done because they would never understand how much we cared for each other. He needn't have worried because I had no intention of doing that. I don't think he realised how ashamed I felt.

But now, *Ba* had guessed what had happened. I could see from the shocked expression on her face that she knew exactly what had occurred. With my heart hammering in my chest, I told her everything and watched her expression change from shock, horror, anger and fear. At that moment, I was sure she was going to scream at me and tell me how disgusted she was with me. She would hate me forever.

Instead, her body started to shake and with a strangled sob, she pulled me to her and crushed me in a hug so tight that I couldn't breathe. We both cried as we held one another for a long time. Then she sat me down and explained that I was not to blame for what had happened. The visitor had taken advantage of me, and she would make sure he paid for it. But that one act had resulted in something terrifying. I was carrying his baby and at five months, my pregnancy was beginning to show.

It might sound strange, but I honestly did not know I was pregnant until *Ba* told me. Apart from gaining a little weight, I had no symptoms at all. My monthly periods had stopped, but I didn't know the significance of that. And it was not something we ever spoke about openly. It was one of those things you kept private.

Dear Diary, can you imagine how scared I was to hear that I was going to have a baby? And *Ba* seemed even more frightened than me. She was afraid for me, but she was even more afraid of how my *Bapuji* would react when he was told. In my naivety, I asked if we could hide it all from him. Shaking her head sadly, she said she would handle it. But she warned me to be prepared for a very difficult time ahead.

It took her a whole week to tell *Bapuji*. I can only imagine how much she must have suffered in that week, agonising about how she was going to explain it all to him. Every day during that week, she spoke to me about how much she hated that man from India, and how she was going to see to it that he was punished. Over and over, she assured me that I should not blame myself.

You see, dear Diary, how lovely my *Ba* is. How many other mothers would have understood straight away what was going on inside my head? I love her more than I can say. She tried to make things work for me. But it was not enough to stop the chain of events that followed.

Kastur-*ba* is calling for me again. I had better go. I'll write again soon.

# Chapter 21

20 August 1954

Dear Diary

Manoj was right about the river swelling up with the monsoon rains. I can see it flowing swiftly as I sit on its bank at the back of our house. Someone has placed a few boulders around the trunk of a mango tree, and I've covered one with an old sack of rice before perching on it. There is a lull before the next rainstorm, so I'm making the most of being outside.

Up on the branches, there are birds tweeting their melodies and the sound of the river flowing is pleasant and relaxing. The sweet scent of mud rising from the wet land is all around me. I've left Kastur-*ba* having her afternoon nap, but any moment now, she could call me to do some more housework.

Last Sunday, Manoj asked me if I wanted to go into a larger town called Gandevi, which is about five miles away from our village. Needing a change of scenery, I agreed without hesitation, and for the first time, I sat at the back of his bicycle and went on an outing with my husband. His manner towards me is still polite and respectful, so I have no fear or concern about being alone with him. We left Kastur-*ba* chatting to Jamila-*masi*, her friend and next-door neighbour.

I have been into Gandevi before, but never with Manoj. He does all the food shopping, so there is no need for me to go. But a few times, I have accompanied Jamila-*masi* when she wanted to buy something for her own house. The only reason she asks me to join her is because she needs my help to carry things back. I try to stay out of her way, generally, because she asks too many questions. Being Kastur-*ba*'s friend, I am wary of saying anything to her in case it gets me into more trouble than I usually am with my *sasu*.

I must confess I enjoyed going into town with Manoj. We didn't say much to each other, but there was a feeling between us that I can only describe as relaxed. The bicycle ride was bumpy, but it was also fun, weaving in and out of the traffic and avoiding the puddles on the roads. Carrying our umbrellas, in case it rained again, we walked around the busy shops and stalls. There was a festive carnival-like atmosphere around us.

The sights and smells of Indian streets are not new to me. When I was eleven years old, just before I started high school, *Bapuji* brought us to India for a four-week holiday. We came on a huge steamship across the Indian Ocean. My brother Laxman was only four years old. We arrived in

Bombay and stayed with Narayan-*kaka* for a few days before going by train to see my *Ba*'s parents and siblings in Ahmedabad, Gujarat.

Lately, I have been thinking a lot about that man from India. That's what I'm going to call him: That Man. The entire course of my life was changed because of what That Man did on that fateful afternoon. I know I am also to blame, and I doubt this feeling of guilt will ever leave me. But more and more I am thinking that if he had not come into my room, none of this would have happened. Here I am, far away from everyone that I love, and he is still enjoying life surrounded by his family.

The thought of him makes me sick to my stomach. I hate him. I couldn't sleep last night wondering if he was ever punished for what he did. *Ba* said she would see to it, but I have no idea if she did. It makes me so angry to think of That Man. Does he even know that I am now living in India? Did anyone tell him he has a child? A child that I gave birth to but lost straight away. I want him to know because he needs to realise how much damage he has caused.

My heart breaks when I think about my baby. *Ba* was with me at the birth, but she wouldn't let me hold him. I know it's a boy because that is all she would say. Stroking my hair and kissing my forehead, she wept as she told the woman who delivered my baby to take him away.

'It's for your own good, Indira,' she cried, holding me down when I tried to get up.

I loved that baby. How could I not? After carrying him inside me for so many months, it's only natural that I would want to see him, hold him, feed him. But I was not allowed. All I saw was a little bundle in white being whisked away, out of the room. We were staying in a small house hundreds of miles away from home. Just me, *Ba* and our maid, whom we called Nanny. She had been with us as a house servant for years, from a time even before I was born.

*Bapuji* had taken me and our maid to a rented house deep in the bushlands where no one would find us. He'd made enquiries and found this place from one of his customers. Trusting no one, he had driven us there himself and arranged for a local woman to deliver my baby. How he was able to find such a woman who knew how to deliver babies is anyone's guess.

The night he tore into me accusing me of being a 'dirty filthy whore', he ordered me to stay at home. He warned me, *Ba* and Laxman not to speak to anyone outside our family of four. We were all too scared of him to disobey. A few weeks later, he told us of his plan to drive me and Nanny to the rented house. We were supposed to leave the very next day. *Ba* was needed at home to look after Laxman, so she would only be allowed to join us in January, when the baby was due. Poor Laxman. He looked so sad and confused. I hope he is okay.

*Bapuji* made it clear that my baby would not be coming back home with me. At the time, my mind was in a whirl. I couldn't take anything in. *Ba* had to explain that after the birth, my baby would be given to a good family. I was distraught. It was my baby and I wanted him to be with me! I cried and cried, but there was little I could do. *Bapuji* refused to even talk about it. He had made up his mind. And his heart of stone was already making further plans to remove me from the shame that I had caused him. He was preparing to banish me to India.

But that is another story, dear Diary. I cannot bear to tell you that today. It fills me with pain and sadness because I was forced to leave behind my baby and everyone that I loved, especially my *Ba*. I can see her face now, filled with despair, holding back her cries of anguish. But I am going to wipe that picture away and replace it with one where she is smiling, showing me how much she loves me.

I think I'll stay here for a while, rest my eyes on the calming flowing waters of Ambica River, and think positive thoughts. I will write again another time.

# Chapter 22

14 December 1954

Dear Diary

It's been almost four months since my last communication. I have been busy. Manoj and I have had a meeting of minds. We got married in April, but it took us seven months to feel we were ready for a proper marital relationship. He truly is a thoughtful and considerate man. In all the months that I've known him, he has shown me nothing but kindness. He seems to sense my sadness and pain. Being so much older than me, I think he can see how vulnerable I am. Allowing me these months to get to know him and feel comfortable with him, shows me how mature and understanding he is.

Four weeks ago, he came home early from work and found me sitting in my favourite spot by the river under the mango tree. The rainy season is over, but there is still a lot of water flowing by on its way to the sea. As I said before, the sights, sounds and smells of nature here are very relaxing. They give me a sense of peace.

Hearing a twig snap, I looked over my shoulder and saw him coming down the slope. He was about to sit on a boulder a little distance away from me, but I smiled and moved over so he could join me on mine. We sat in silence for a while, looking out at the flowing river. Then, in a voice filled with nostalgia, he began to tell me about how he used to love going fishing on a small boat with his father. Though still a child, he helped throw the fishing net into the river and gather it in at the right moment.

A smile played on his lips as he gazed at the river, recollecting a happy time in his past. Then a shadow passed over his face and he became silent once again. He looked sad and I knew he was missing his father. It was a sadness I was all too familiar with. In my case, it was my mother I missed. Instinctively, I reached for his hand and took it in mine. We looked at each other and I felt a connection that was good and strong and real.

Speaking in a low voice, he leaned towards me. 'Do you think you will be happy here with me?'

His quiet gentleness made my breath catch in my chest. I wanted to say yes but the word would not come out. I couldn't answer because I didn't know if I could ever be happy with any man. He searched my face and seemed to understand. Pursing his lips, he nodded.

'You can trust me, you know. I will never hurt you.'

The tenderness in his voice made my throat constrict and tears stung my eyes. I released his hand and looked away. I could feel him watching me.

'I know you have been hurt,' he continued in the same gentle voice. 'Maybe it was your father. Or maybe someone else. Whoever it was, you don't have to tell me. But you must know that you are safe with me. I will look after you.'

His kindness and compassion unlocked something deep inside me. A strangled sound escaped my lips, and tears began to spill down my cheeks. I began to sob, my face in my hands, my chest heaving and my shoulders shaking. For a moment, Manoj sat beside me, just watching, doing nothing. Then he tutted and pulled me towards him. With both his arms around my shoulders, he locked me against his chest, holding me tightly, as if he was worried that I might pull away.

I cried like a baby, sobbing and howling, salty tears and snot dripping on to his shirt. Deep emotions of grief, sorrow and pain came gushing out of me. Staying silent, he made no attempt to stop me. He just held me in his arms, rocking gently, until I had tired myself out. Exhausted, I finally stopped crying. It was comforting to be inside the circle of his arms, my face pressed against his heart. I felt sheltered and protected. We stayed like that for a long, long time.

That night, when it was time to go to sleep, I saw that my roll-up bedding had been laid out on the floor in the room where Manoj slept. Kastur-*ba* was lying awake in her usual place. When I knelt down to ask if she needed anything, she shook her head, gesturing with her hand that I should go to the front room. I don't know what Manoj had said to her, but she seemed unfazed by the altered arrangements. Lying down next to Manoj, I asked him how Kastur-*ba* would manage without me in the dark.

'She will manage,' he said with certainty. It made me realise that the only reason Manoj had asked me to sleep in his mother's room was to give me the time and space I needed to gain his trust.

Dear Diary, now that Manoj and I are living as husband and wife, I do feel a little more at home. But it is still not *my* home. It is very much my *sasu's* home. She is the queen bee, and she never lets me forget that. It really isn't a problem because I have no desire to take her place. Manoj is her son, and the special bond which they share is absolutely fine with me.

What is not fine is having to accept her constant rebukes and admonishments. I am certain she doesn't like me very much. We have little in common because we come from different worlds. She probably would have preferred a daughter-in-law whom she could understand more and whom she could chat to all day long.

Sometimes when my chores are finished, I find that I have nothing to do. That's when I start to feel gloomy and depressed. It would be nice to have another activity which would keep my

mind occupied and take me away from Kastur-*ba*.
I wonder if Manoj would consider allowing me to
take on some kind of job in town. One of these
days, I will pluck up the courage to ask him.

16 February 1955

Dear Diary

I am pleased to say that Manoj did agree that I
should find an activity away from home. It wasn't
an immediate agreement because he had to
consult with his mother. She was not at all happy
that her *vahu* would be out and about on her own.
In her eyes, a woman's place was in the home, tied
to the kitchen. I could hear Manoj talking to her
in his usual calm and patient way, explaining why
it was important for me to keep busy.

In the end, they reached a compromise:
I would go out only after I had finished the
cooking and cleaning for the day. Manoj spoke
to some elders in the village and came back with
a very good suggestion. He asked me if I would
be happy giving English lessons to the pre-school
children in and around our area. It would only be
for two hours every afternoon. The local temple
had a side room which could be made available.
There would be no payment for my time, but it
would get me out of the house.

Without hesitation, I agreed. The classes
started four weeks ago with only five children on
the first day. News of the free lessons given by

an English-speaking resident of the village spread fast, and the number of pupils has been increasing steadily.

Dear Diary, I can't tell you how much this has lifted my spirits. It's like a nice little hobby for me. I have been speaking English from a very young age and going to English school since kindergarten. You could say it's in my blood. I also attended Gujarati school, so I am fluent in both languages. No preparation on my part is needed to teach the little ones who are such a joy to be with. They are quiet and shy at first, but soon become cheerful and chatty.

When the mothers or grandmothers bring the children in, they do seem a little guarded initially. Some are openly suspicious. I suppose they see me as an outsider because unlike them, I am not Indian born and bred. To make them feel at ease, I always invite them to stay in the class either to observe or to help with tasks such as setting up activities or helping children with their drawings. Slowly but surely, I think I am winning their trust.

These classes are very much in the domain of women. I am glad I don't have to speak to any fathers or grandfathers. They are usually at work, so I feel safe and comfortable at the temple. I also feel more secure walking the half mile there and back in the daylight. More often than not, there are other people coming in to pray or to carry out certain Hindu rituals. While I am busy with the children in the side room, it's good to hear the buzz of activity in the main temple area.

So, dear Diary, I am in better spirits these days. Kastur-*ba* is as difficult as ever, but at least I can escape from her for a few hours every day. And knowing Manoj is supportive of my teaching venture, I can just about cope with what life has thrown at me. When I start to think about what could have been, I try to turn my mind to the children in my class. Their happy faces and inquisitive minds do somehow lighten my burden of grief.

# Chapter 23

12 June 1955

Dear Diary

Last month, on the seventh of May, I turned eighteen. Manoj walked into the house carrying a paper bag full of multi-coloured sweetmeats. He laid out the pendas, barfis and halwa on a *thali* and offered them to me with a smile.

'Happy birthday,' he said in English with his clipped Indian accent. Over the months, he had learnt to say a lot of things in English. He wanted to learn, and I was happy to teach him.

Manoj had checked the date in my passport which had been handed over to him by *Bapuji* on the day we left Narayan-*kaka*'s house in Bombay. Unbeknown to me, Manoj had been given a parcel containing my passport, birth certificate and a 22-carat gold necklace and bangle set before we left for Sonwadi.

My state of mind at that time was such that I'd paid no attention to anything. When we arrived here, Manoj opened the parcel in front of me and described it all to his mother. She told me to wear the bangles and the necklace every day, and she gave me her own pair of gold earrings to put on.

Every morning when I get dressed in one of the many saris I seem to have acquired, I wear the jewellery, make a big round *chandlo* on my forehead with red vermillion powder and apply kohl under my eyes. Without being told, I knew that these were the essential trappings for all Hindu women who were married.

Dear Diary, turning eighteen is quite significant here because that is the minimum age for girls to be lawfully married. Manoj explained to me that although we have had a Hindu wedding, we need to go through the legal channels to obtain a registered certificate of marriage.

This is where he gave me a shock. He told me that Narayan-*kaka* was coming down from Bombay in two weeks' time to take us through the process at the nearest marriage registry office. It was nine miles away in a town called Bilimora. Mohini-*kaki*, my *sasu*'s sister, was also coming. They would arrive in the morning by train and return on the same day. While we went to see the marriage officer, Mohini-*kaki* would be spending time at home with Kastur-*ba*.

As soon as I heard this, my heart began to race, and my stomach clenched with fear. I didn't want to see them because they represented *Bapuji* who had disowned me and cast me out from the family. I felt hot all over, and my palms began to sweat. Thoughts that I had succeeded in putting aside suddenly came crashing into my mind.

Manoj could not understand why I was so fearful. 'There's nothing to worry about. It will be over very quickly. Narayan-*masaji* has prepared all the paperwork and I have all the necessary documents.'

But he had no idea what I'd had to go through. All I could think of was the look on *Bapuji's* face when he told me I was to go away for good. His cold, brutal words had cut me to the bone.

'*You have brought shame into this family and don't deserve to be a part of it. If anyone finds out what you've done, the family reputation will be in ruins. I have to think of your brother. Your deeds must not tarnish his honour. I've made my decision. You have got to go.*'

Dear Diary, I have already told you how much I suffered. *Bapuji's* cold heart would not budge no matter how much my *Ba* and I cried and begged for mercy. In his mind, the blame was all mine. Not once did he mention that That Man might be at fault. How I hate and despise That Man. He ruined my life. I want him to suffer too.

Until Manoj's aunt and uncle arrive and the court marriage process is completed, I will be a bag of nerves. I long for it all to be over so I can go back to my usual routine.

29 June 1955

Dear Diary

It's over. Manoj was right about the procedure being quick. Because all the documents were in order and the booked appointment was not delayed, the marriage officer was able to complete the task quickly. He checked the details, got all the required signatures and provided the stamped certificate within the space of an hour.

The difficult bit was hosting our guests in our home. Narayan-*kaka* was fine but Mohini-*kaki* gave me such a look of disdain when she walked in that I wanted to shrink and disappear. Any confidence I might have built up over the past months simply evaporated into the air. It was clear for all to see that she didn't think I was worthy of even a civil greeting from her.

I offered them water in two of our best stainless-steel tumblers. She ignored me and left me standing there, holding out the glass to her, unsure of what to do. Manoj took pity on me and accepted the drink for himself. Narayan-*kaka* drank thirstily then said we should leave for the registry office straight away. The plan was for us to leave the sisters to chat and take a bus to Bilimora.

I had already prepared lunch so that when we completed the process and received our marriage certificate, we could return home and have a meal without delay. Dear Diary, you can imagine how nervous I was when I prepared the dishes that day. I woke up early in the morning to start the cooking which took me three hours to complete.

We have only one Primus stove, so all the dishes had to be cooked one at a time. When I first started using the Primus, I was terrified, convinced that I would burn myself, or set the house on fire. It was Jamila-*masi* from next door who showed me how to sit on a low stool, light the kerosene burner and handle the cooking pots on the steel ring at the top. After a week or so, I did get used to it. I'm not afraid of it any more, though it is very different from the electric stove in my mother's kitchen back home.

With all the practice that I've had, I think my cooking has improved because Kastur-*ba* doesn't complain about my food as much as she used to. I hoped that Mohini-*kaki* would find it to her liking. And if she didn't, I prayed that she would see how much effort I'd put into it, and not be too critical.

I prayed in vain because as soon as she took a mouthful of my green bean curry, she gasped and asked for water, saying that her mouth was on fire. Kastur-*ba* immediately started complaining that I always put too much red chilli into all my dishes. There ensued a barrage of complaints about how slow and stupid I was. Sitting right in front of them, I had to endure their criticisms and verbal abuse without saying a word.

Manoj and Narayan-*kaka* had already had their meal and were out in the backyard. I was glad they weren't present to witness my humiliation. It was embarrassing to be told off in front of guests and I could feel hot tears threatening to spill over. Sitting silently with the women staring at my own *thali* in front of me, I was too choked up to eat. But somehow, I managed to stay focused until the meal was over.

Dear Diary, I need to tell you something very important. Narayan-*kaka* gave me some news that made me stop in my tracks. He spoke to me when we had a moment alone in the backyard. Mohini-*kaki* sent me outside to tell her husband that it was time they made a move for the station. He was chatting to Manoj. I called to him respectfully from the back door. Manoj immediately started walking towards me, but Narayan-*kaka* stayed where he was. He was giving me a strange look. I could tell he had something on his mind. It made me remain standing by the door, even after Manoj went past me into the house.

Narayan-*kaka* gestured with his hand that I should join him. Surprised and curious, I walked towards him. As soon as I reached him, he spoke in a low, secretive voice.

'There is something I want to tell you. It's important you should know. It's about the man who came to visit you in your home in Africa, the man who hurt you. He was involved in a car crash two months ago. He died in that accident. You understand? He is dead.'

I was speechless. This was the last thing I expected him to say. Not knowing what to make of it, I just stared open-mouthed at him.

'Your father told me what he did to you, but don't worry. I'm the only person that knows. He has no idea that I'm giving you this news about the man who has died. I'm telling you this so you can put him out of your mind. Forever. You understand? You must do that, Indira. Put him out of your mind.' His voice was gruff, and his face was screwed up in a frown. But underneath that, I sensed that he wished me well.

With quick steps, he walked away into the house, leaving me standing where I was, unsure of what to do next. Dear Diary, what am I meant to think? Is That Man really dead? Can it be true? It must be. Why would Narayan-*kaka* lie? He didn't need to say anything to me. I feel that he has given me this information so that I can get on with my life. That Man is no longer in this world.

Did he suffer at the end? I hope so. He deserved to feel pain. I can picture him bleeding to death somewhere. Maybe in his car crushed underneath another car, or truck or whatever. I will never know how it happened. But that doesn't matter. What matters is that he is dead. My emotions are all over the place. There is relief but also anxiety. Everything he did to me has come bubbling to the surface.

Last night, I didn't sleep a wink. Thoughts of That Man tortured me throughout the night. Dear Diary, how do I get rid of these images and memories? They are dragging me down and making me feel ill.

When I got up this morning, I felt nauseous. My stomach hurt and I felt unsteady on my feet. Taking my time, I had a bucket shower and got dressed. My first task of the day is always to tidy the shrine with pictures of Lord Vishnu and his consort Laxmi. I said a little prayer as I picked up the brass diva lamp to clean. Picking out the cotton wool and wick, I got a whiff of the stale solidified ghee at the bottom. It smelt sour and rancid. My stomach turned. I had to dash out to the yard and be sick into the bushes.

I didn't feel well at all. Manoj was at work already, and Kastur-*ba* was still sleeping. I made myself a hot drink with turmeric and *ajwan* seeds and took it outside. Sitting in the fresh air under the shady tree, I sipped the bitter drink. I'm sure my body is reacting this way because I am reliving the nightmare of what That Man did to me. He was a monster and I'm glad that he's dead. But how do I stop thinking about him? It's easy for Narayan-*kaka* to say I must put him out of my mind. I just can't seem to do it.

As the home remedy began to take effect, my stomach settled a bit, and I went back to my chores. I even managed to enjoy the afternoon class with the nursery children. I'm teaching them all the English nursery rhymes that I learnt as a child in Southern Rhodesia. It amazes me how quickly they learn and how much they love singing the songs. As always, they put me in a good mood, and I am determined to try harder at forgetting the ghosts of my past.

21 July 1955

Dear Diary

I'm still feeling ill, and I've been vomiting on and off every day for the last three weeks. There is a constant metallic taste in my mouth and the nausea is getting me down. I'm just so tired all the time. I'm trying hard to forget what That Man did to me and most of the time, I am able to push him out of my mind. But my body is saying something different.

Last week, Manoj noticed that something was not right, and he asked if I wanted to see a doctor. When I said that wasn't necessary, he suggested I talk to our neighbour, Jamila-*masi*, who is something of a natural healer. He gave me some rupees to pay her for her time.

Her front door was open when I went to her house. I called out her name and she came out after a few moments. We sat down together on the charpoy outside. She questioned me about my symptoms, and immediately looked as if she knew what was wrong. She wanted to know how long it had been since my last menstrual flow. I had to think because I couldn't remember. When I did remember, I knew exactly what she was getting at.

Dear Diary, you will be very surprised to hear this. It is big news. I am pregnant. There is no doubt about it because the dates tie in with the start of my bouts of sickness. Jamila-*masi* was giving me a triumphant smile, watchfully waiting for my reaction. I was stunned into silence. I shouldn't have been surprised, but I was. With so much on my mind, I hadn't given much thought to having children. I honestly believed I was ill because of my tormented memories. Jamila-*masi* was beginning to wonder at my silence. I fixed a smile on my face and breathed out slowly. I thanked her and handed over the cash Manoj had given me.

'I can give you something to stop you feeling sick.' She went indoors and returned with some seeds wrapped in paper. They had an aromatic smell of earth and mint. She told me they were a mixture of crushed cardamoms, cloves and an assortment of natural herbs, and instructed me to chew a handful whenever I felt the nausea coming on.

Back at the house, I found Kastur-*ba* sitting up from her nap, using a wet cloth to wipe her face and neck. It was a hot afternoon with very little breeze. I offered her cold water to drink, then made tea for her, boiling the milk and water together, carefully adding the tea leaves, sugar and chai masala just the way she liked it.

'What did Jamila say is wrong with you?' she asked, scowling, as if it was my fault that I was unwell.

I couldn't tell her. It was too soon to share my news. At that moment, I needed to go outside and think things through.

'She's given me some seeds to make me feel better,' I said, hastening away through the back door. I heard her mutter something under her breath, but I was gone before she could ask any further questions.

It was cooler by the river where I sat under the mango tree, mulling over what I'd just found out. I was going to have another baby. A tremor of excitement ran through me. Only a year ago, I gave birth to a baby boy. I don't know who he's with or even what his name is. I saw him only for a few seconds before he was whisked away. He will be eighteen months old now, walking, smiling, crying, laughing. It hurts to know that someone else is seeing him grow up. It should be me taking care of him, giving him all my love.

But now, I have a chance to love and cherish another baby. A brother or sister for the son I had to leave behind. The thought of this fills me with joy. My firstborn child will never know me. But by keeping the new baby close to my heart, I pray that he will always feel the mother's love that he deserves.

I'm going to cancel That Man out of my life. When I hold this new baby in my arms, I will think of my son so far away and I will remember that he belongs to me. Just me.

# PART 4

# Chapter 24

## Mumbai, India, January 2019

Anna stepped on to the balcony of her hotel room and looked down at the sprawling metropolis of Mumbai. She was on the sixteenth floor of a towering modern building with a view of the city on one side and the sea on the other. She gazed in wonder at the busy, noisy, crowded streets teeming with people and traffic below. On the opposite side, the Arabian Sea offered a stark contrast, its waters calm like a lake. The sun glinted off the wide expanse of blue and a slight breeze floated over to the balcony.

It was six o'clock in the evening and the golden light of the setting sun spread over the horizon, painting the western sky in red and orange. Anna marvelled at the sight as she dabbed the beads of perspiration on her face with an already damp tissue. The heat and humidity of Mumbai had hit her as soon as she'd stepped off the plane. Her flight had arrived on time, but it had taken three hours to get through passport control, collect her luggage, and make her way to the hotel by taxi. She was glad to have finally arrived.

Anna surveyed her luxurious room in the 5-star hotel recommended by the travel agent in Harare. She had taken his advice because of the favourable exchange rate, and because it was her first visit to India. She wanted to have the best experience possible.

Her body ached with physical and emotional exhaustion. The past few days in Harare had been extremely stressful. Deciding to leave her unpacking for later, Anna stretched out on the large deluxe bed and closed her eyes. She tried not to think about the arguments she'd had with her parents, but it was impossible to avoid. They had been furious with her when she announced her impromptu journey to Mumbai in search of Indira. She'd pleaded with her father to join her, but he would not even consider it.

He refused to believe that Indira Rajah could be his biological mother. Both he and her mother were in complete denial. No matter how hard Anna tried to convince them, they remained sceptical. With great care and sensitivity, Anna had sat her parents down and shared the information she had learned from Seema Rajah, whose husband's grandfather was Laxman Rajah. But they were not prepared to accept the word of an old man who was dying. And they were completely against her decision to fly out to India on her own.

Anna was aware that it would be difficult and possibly dangerous to travel around alone in a big city like Mumbai. She knew only one person who lived there, Gita Thakur. Anna had reached out to Gita and made plans to meet up, and Gita was thrilled to hear from her, offering to be her companion for as long as necessary. But her parents were still not satisfied. Her mother had raged at her, and her father had shaken his head, disappointed and aggrieved.

Anna didn't like to leave without their blessing. But she knew, without any doubt in her mind, that she could not give up with her search. She had to continue.

At some point, Anna must have dozed off, for when she woke up, it was already 7.15 p.m. Her stomach was rumbling, so after a quick shower and change of clothes, she decided to see what dining options were available at the hotel. She'd noticed an advertisement in the lift for an in-house restaurant offering traditional Indian cuisine from the various states. Eager to try authentic Indian dishes while in the country, Anna headed out to find this promised dining experience.

All the restaurants were situated on the second floor, each with its own unique decor and alluring aromas. Anna gravitated to the aptly named Spirit of India. As she stepped through the entrance, she found herself enveloped in a cosy and welcoming atmosphere. The tantalising scent of spicy food filled the air, and soft melodic music in the background created a calming mood. The dining area was spacious, modern and stylish. The ceiling was high and the lighting was soft. Wide windows overlooked the sea, and in the darkness, lights twinkled from ships moving across the water.

The maître d' led Anna to a table near the entrance. Looking around, she admired the contemporary design and lay-out of the room. The furniture was all grey marble-effect with matching velvet seats. Small Indian-design vases filled with colourful scented flowers adorned all the tabletops. Silver cutlery lay on black napkins folded neatly at each place setting. A low hum of conversation and the tinkling of cutlery filled the room.

Anna picked up the menu and selected the dishes she was most familiar with, those she usually enjoyed when eating out in London's many Indian restaurants. She chose items from the state of Punjab: lamb biryani, cucumber raita and mixed kachumber. Anna thought the food was outstanding; possibly the best Indian meal she'd ever had.

After dinner, she decided to take a stroll along the seafront outside the hotel. From her balcony, she had seen a wide walkway below with a low concrete wall separating it from the rocky beach. It was a lovely walk without the sun and many other people were out enjoying the cool evening breeze, just like her. Anna knew there was safety in numbers and thought it best not to stray too far from her hotel.

After a while, she took a seat on a bench facing the sea and watched the people walk by in front of her. Breathing in the cool night air, she contemplated her plans for the next few days. She was going to be in Mumbai for two weeks, after which her flight was booked for her return to London. She had thought long and hard about her length of stay and decided that two weeks were probably sufficient for what she hoped to do.

The first thing was to let Gita know that she had arrived in Mumbai. She intended to tell her all about her search for Indira and ask for her help and advice. Before leaving Harare, Anna had looked up Borivali East on Google, the area in Mumbai where the Rajah family lived. The map indicated that it was quite a distance away from her hotel. She hoped Gita would be able to advise her on how best to get there.

While in India, Anna wanted to take the opportunity to find out about local charitable organisations and aid agencies. She hoped to connect with those that helped victims of domestic violence. Before flying to Mumbai, Anna had contacted Nick in London to ask if he could pass on any relevant links. He had been delighted to hear from her and had promised to make enquiries and get back to her. As soon as she could, Anna planned to visit the charities and see if she could offer some support.

Sitting back, Anna continued to watch the people walking by, alone, in pairs or in groups. From the way they dressed and spoke, Anna could tell that there were both locals and others from around the world strolling along. Most of them looked a bit like her with her South Asian appearance. They were people with the same heritage as her father. She was also part of that heritage, and yet she felt no affinity with them at all. In Zimbabwe, she always had a sense of belonging. She felt a kinship with the local black Zimbabweans. But here, she felt like a foreigner. She was saddened by this feeling and hoped that while she was in India, she would find a way to relate to the people around her.

Before she retired for the night, Anna rang Gita's brother. A man answered, and when she gave him her name, he immediately called Gita.

'Dr Kotze! Hello.' Gita's voice was happy and bouncy, different from the subdued person she had become in London.

'Yes, it's me. I've arrived in Mumbai.'

'That's wonderful! You are here at last.' Gita sounded delighted and wanted to meet her the very next day. When she heard which hotel Anna was staying in, she was even more delighted because it was only a twenty-minute walk from her brother's house.

'Is it easy for you to get here?' asked Anna. Gita assured her that it was. 'Okay, great. Let's meet at the hotel reception at ten in the morning. And Gita? Do you know how far we are from Borivali East?'

'Borivali? I'll just ask my brother.' Within seconds, she was back with the answer. 'It's about an hour away by train. Do you want to go there tomorrow?'

'I do. Will you come with me? I'll explain everything.'

'Sure, I will take you there. We can talk on the train. There is so much I want to tell you.'

'All good, I hope?'

'Yes. All good. See you tomorrow.'

# Chapter 25

When Anna came down from her room at 9.50 a.m., she found Gita already waiting in the reception area. She was sitting in an armchair, looking excited and happy. Anna was surprised to see her in jeans and Western top. Her head was uncovered, and she'd tied her long dark hair back from her face. She looked like a modern Mumbai city woman unburdened by problems, a stark contrast to before.

As soon as she saw Anna, Gita stood up and came forward. With an affectionate smile, Anna gave her a hug, then took her hands and stepped back to admire her.

'Is this the same Gita from London? I don't think so!'

Crinkling up her eyes, Gita laughed. 'It's still me. But much happier. How are you, Dr Kotze?'

'You must call me Anna now. We are friends.'

Looking pleased, Gita gazed at Anna with shining eyes. 'I'm so glad you came.'

'I was always going to come, but I didn't think it would be this soon. How long have you been here now?'

'Two months.'

'Well, I'm glad you're here because I really need your help.'

Gita nodded. 'You want to go to Borivali East. My brother says we should go by train. It will take us about an hour.'

Anna shook her head. She had spoken to the receptionist and discovered that there was a faster and more comfortable way to get there. A taxi could get them to Borivali in twenty-five minutes at a cost that seemed very reasonable to Anna. The British pound against the Indian rupee was strong, giving Anna a healthy exchange rate.

'Let's take a taxi,' she said. 'We can talk on the way. There is so much I have to tell you.'

Together, they walked out of the hotel entrance to the long line of black and yellow cabs waiting patiently for customers. Gita spoke to the driver of the first cab in Hindi, and they were soon on their way.

The traffic was heavy, with vehicles of all kinds manoeuvring past: buses, cars, auto rickshaws, and people in what seemed like a chaotic frenzy. Anna had heard about the notorious driving in India, so she closed her mind to the sights and sounds outside and focused on her conversation with Gita.

Pleased to hear that she was keeping well, Anna asked Gita how things were working out at her brother's house. Smiling broadly, Gita said she was enjoying her life with the family, contributing to the household income by sewing and altering clothes for customers. She explained that her concerns about her sister-in-law begrudging money spent on her had proved to be completely groundless. She had given Gita a warm welcome into her home. When Anna asked if she'd heard from her husband and family in London, her face clouded over. She hadn't heard, and didn't like to even think about them. But she was certain of one thing: at some point in the near future, she was going to take the first steps in the divorce process.

Changing the subject, Anna gave Gita an abridged account of her father's history and her recent discoveries in Zimbabwe. Gita looked shocked and captivated at the same time. She seemed touched by the fact that Anna had been given the middle name Indira because of the engraving on the pendant left in the basket.

When Gita learned that Indira was confirmed as Mathew's mother's name, she gasped and tightly held Anna's hand. By the time they reached Borivali, Gita was just as invested in the search for Indira as Anna was.

'This is the address, madam,' announced the driver as he stopped outside a block of apartments in a built-up residential area. The taxi had veered off from a busy main street on to a narrow, uneven road that led to four identical six-storey apartment buildings. Each appeared worn-down and covered in years of dust and dirt, their once white walls now faded.

Anna looked up and unexpectedly, her heart began to race. The thought that Indira might have been brought to this place all those years ago filled her with awe. She could imagine the fear and anxiety that the young Indira must have felt. At only sixteen years old at the time, this place must have been a real culture shock for her. As Anna alighted from the taxi, she felt a strange nervousness about what she might learn from the Rajah family who lived here.

She paid the driver and followed Gita to the entrance of the building in front of them. The apartment they were looking for was on the fourth floor, so they decided to take the lift. It was one of those old-fashioned lifts with a collapsible gate. Gita pulled it to one side then slid it back again once they were inside. She pressed the button for the fourth floor, and a loud whirring sound reverberated around them as the lift chugged slowly up the shaft. There was space for only four people, and an unpleasant smell of urine and stale curry surrounded them. Anna held her breath for as long as she could.

Upon reaching the fourth floor, they found themselves facing four doors branching off from a small square landing.

'Number 401,' Gita said, pointing to the left as she started moving towards it.

'Wait!' Anna's voice came out as an urgent whisper. 'I'm not ready.'

Gita turned around, surprise written all over her face. She stared for a moment, then came to stand beside Anna, looking sombre. 'This is an important moment, isn't it?' she asked.

Anna exhaled heavily. 'I've been searching for a long time and finally, I might be standing in the same place that my grandmother did over sixty years ago.' She gazed at the door with trepidation.

'I understand,' said Gita, her voice filled with empathy. After a brief pause, she gently took Anna's arm. 'Shall we see if anyone is in?'

'Okay.' Taking a breath, Anna lifted her chin and stepped forward as Gita knocked four times. The sound rang out loud and strong. They heard a woman's voice from inside the apartment, followed by a man's response. Anna's heart was pounding. Who would answer the door? Would they believe her story? What if they didn't like what they heard?

With all these questions racing through her mind, Anna felt lightheaded when the door opened and a middle-aged woman peered at them questioningly. She was wearing a white cotton *salwar kameez* and was using her long *odhani* to wipe her hands. She said something in Hindi to Anna. Gita stepped forward and answered in a respectful tone. They had a little discussion that involved the woman giving Anna curious looks.

Eventually, she smiled and spoke in English. 'Please come in.'

They stepped straight into what looked like a sitting room. Indicating that they should sit on a sofa bed near the window, she walked away through an open door on their left.

'That's Mr Rajah's wife,' Gita explained in a hushed voice. 'She doesn't know anyone in his family called Indira. I told her we are looking for a relative of his who is also related to you.'

Before long, a man entered the room, smiling politely. '*Namaste*,' he said as he sat down on a chair across a small coffee table in the middle of the room. His wife followed with two glasses of water on a tray, placing them on the table before sitting down next to her husband.

'You do not speak Hindi or Gujarati?' the man asked Anna.

'I'm afraid not.'

The man wobbled his head. 'No matter. We can speak English.'

Anna gave him a grateful smile, feeling relieved by their welcoming demeanour. She began to relax and introduced herself. 'My name is Anna Kotze and I'm from London. This is my friend Gita Thakur.'

'Welcome to India. I am Hemant Rajah, and my wife is Surekha. You have come to find family members?'

'Yes. I found out recently that I'm related to someone from the Rajah family. Your address was given to me by your cousin in Zimbabwe.'

'I see.' Hemant nodded, pausing for a moment. 'If you are related to the Rajahs, then we must also be cousins, no?'

Anna smiled. 'I think we must be. But very distant.'

He looked at her with curious intent.

After a brief silence, Anna grew serious. 'I'm looking for someone by the name of Indira.' She watched his face closely for any signs of recognition. His expression did not change. 'I think she might have come to this house with her father in 1954.'

'1954? That's a long time ago.' Hemant pondered. 'Indira. I don't know anyone in my family by that name.'

'She would be quite old now,' said Anna. 'Probably over eighty years of age.'

'Achha. It's a pity my parents have passed away. They would probably know this lady. How is she related to you?'

'She is my grandmother, my father's mother. She was brought here from Zimbabwe after my father was born. He grew up without ever knowing her because she came to India and never returned home.'

Exchanging a look with his wife, he asked: 'Who looked after your father?'

'He was adopted.'

Hemant frowned. 'What about his father?'

'Nobody knows anything about him. Nothing at all. And I've only recently found out that Indira Rajah is my father's biological mother. It's a long and sad story that has affected us all our lives. Indira was unmarried when she gave birth, and her baby was taken away from her. He was left as a newborn in a basket outside a church. That was my father. He was a foundling.'

There was stunned silence in the room. Hemant was still frowning, and his wife had a shocked expression on her face. After a while, Hemant puffed his cheeks and blew out. 'I'm sorry to hear that. I can see why you want to find her. I wish I could help you, but I don't see how I can.'

Surekha tugged at his arm and asked him a question in Gujarati. He responded, then went into a lengthy discussion with her. Eventually, Surekha spoke to Anna in English: 'If your grandmother came to this house, maybe my father-in-law met her. He lived here all his life. Did you say she came in 1954?'

'Yes,' Anna replied, her anticipation growing.

'Well, my father-in-law was born in 1943. So in 1954, he was eleven years old. It's a shame he's not with us any more. He might have remembered her.'

For a moment, Anna was speechless. She gaped at Surekha, her face a picture of disappointment. Gita sat forward and asked Hemant: 'Did your father ever mention the name Indira?'

Hemant pondered over the question for a long minute before answering. 'I'm sorry. I don't remember.'

Gita gave him a rueful smile. 'It's okay. But do you have any elderly relatives we could ask? They might remember Indira or know something about her. Maybe she went to another town.'

Hemant shook his head. 'The old people are all gone. We're the elders in the family now.'

Gita grimaced. Bitterly disappointed, Anna sighed and looked at her hands.

'*Ek minute*,' said Surekha. Anna looked up in surprise. 'What about your relatives in Gujarat?' she asked her husband.

Hemant looked quizzical. 'What relatives?'

'Your mother told me that your grandmother, Mohini-*ba*, came from a village near Navsari. They were fishing people.'

'I don't know anything about them,' said Hemant, looking puzzled.

Surekha tutted. 'You don't remember anything! I know for sure that your grandmother came from a fishing family. There might be some relatives of hers still living there. And maybe someone will remember a girl called Indira.'

Both Anna and Gita were leaning forward. Anna's eyes shone with hope. 'Can you remember the name of the village?' she asked.

Surekha puckered her lips, her eyebrows pulled together in concentration. The silence was deafening. Eventually, she gave a triumphant smile.

'I remember now. Sonwadi. That's the name of the village.'

Anna turned to Gita, her eyes shining with excitement. 'Do you think we could go there?'

Gita blinked. 'I . . . I suppose so. We can find out where that is. But we'll need to know who to ask for.'

Surekha looked regretful. 'I don't know any names in that family. I just know that Mohini-*ba* came from a fishing family. In a small village, people know one another so I don't think it would be too difficult to track them down. If your grandmother went to Sonwadi, even as far back as 1954, someone might remember her, especially if she arrived from a foreign country. I think it would definitely be worth it to go there and ask around.'

Anna took a deep breath, her determination solidifying. 'I think you're right. You've been very helpful. I may be clutching at straws, but my next stop will have to be this village.' Turning to Gita, she added, 'I need to go there tomorrow.'

Gita nodded. 'We'll go together.' After expressing their gratitude to Hemant and Surekha, Anna followed Gita out of the room, her heart brimming with hope and her spirits lifted by the possibility of finding answers in Sonwadi.

# Chapter 26

Anna lay on her hotel bed and waited to hear from Gita. She had promised to find out about the easiest way to travel to Sonwadi. It wasn't long before she sent a text message saying their best option was to first take a train, then a bus or taxi. She thought they could take the train leaving Mumbai Central station at 8.30 a.m. the next day. Anna agreed and suggested they meet at the hotel reception an hour before.

As Anna considered the information they had gathered from Hemant and Surekha Rajah, her thoughts centred on Sonwadi. It was a village in the neighbouring state of Gujarat, a significant distance from Mumbai. Anna wondered how long the journey would take, but having Gita by her side made it bearable.

Anna realised she was probably expecting too much. Indira may never have gone there. Or if she did, in the years since 1954, she might have moved to another place. There was also the sobering possibility that she might have passed away. But if there was any chance of the puzzle being unravelled, Anna knew that she *had* to visit the village.

She tried and failed to curb her growing excitement and expectation of a positive outcome. Imagining the rural setting of Sonwadi, Anna envisioned the slow-paced activities of an Indian village. The mere thought that someone there might know Indira or have heard of her filled her with wonder. The icing on the cake would be if one of them was Indira herself. Anna closed her eyes and tried to calm the butterflies fluttering in her stomach.

~

The next morning, Gita was waiting at reception, looking bright and cheerful. Her eyes were fixed on the lift doors, and a childlike smile graced her lips. As Anna approached, they embraced warmly. This time, Gita was wearing a floral cotton *salwar kameez* with full sleeves. Her hair was uncovered again and the *odhani* was draped beautifully over one shoulder. Bending down, Gita pulled out a white, lightweight shawl from a backpack at her feet.

'This is to cover your bare arms,' she said. 'We're going to the countryside where people are very conservative. They will stare and make you feel uncomfortable.'

Grateful for her thoughtfulness, Anna accepted the shawl and draped it over her shoulders. She herself was dressed in a white linen top paired with coffee-coloured wide-leg trousers, designed to keep her cool in the hot and humid weather. In her large shoulder bag, she had stuffed a soft silk jacket that she thought she might need later in the day. For now, Gita's shawl was ideal.

The taxi ride to Mumbai Central Station took around twenty minutes, navigating through the crowded and bustling traffic. Anna was acutely aware that she was in one of the most populous cities in the world. Over twenty million people lived in Mumbai. It was a city experiencing rapid economic growth. But it was also a place where dire poverty was visible at every turn. One minute she was looking up at luxury tower buildings and the next she was facing shanty huts by the side of the road with people dressed in rags.

When their taxi was stuck in a traffic jam, little children stepped up to their windows begging for a few rupees. Anna resisted the urge to wind down the window and tell them to get back to the safety of the pavements. She wished she could offer them some money, but she'd been advised not to do that because it would result in an immediate crowd surrounding the taxi, causing further danger and disappointment all round.

Mumbai Central Station was a hive of activity. People were rushing about on the many platforms. Fortunately, Gita knew exactly where to find their train. She manoeuvred her way through the crowds and led Anna to their carriage. Without the burden of heavy luggage, they swiftly boarded and found their seats.

Anna blew out her cheeks. 'Phew! I'm glad I've got you with me.'

Gita laughed. 'It's chaotic but quite organised really. A bit like London.'

'I suppose it is. You must have found it difficult when you first arrived in London.'

Gita's expression turned serious. 'I did. It would have been a different experience if my in-laws had supported me.'

'What you went through was terrible. Instead of support, you endured physical abuse, repeatedly. It makes me furious just thinking about it.' Anna reached for Gita's hand. 'I'm glad it's over now. You're safe and free. It's incredible to see you thriving.'

The heat in the carriage was stifling. Removing the scarf from her shoulders, Anna bunched up at the end and fanned herself with the fabric. The windows were all closed.

'This is a first-class carriage so there will be air conditioning,' said Gita. 'But it will only come on when the train starts to move.'

Relieved to hear that, Anna looked around. The long seats were in rows all facing forward, arranged with the aisle running through the middle. The carriage was only half full. Several well-dressed businessmen and women were engrossed in their smartphones, a couple of families with children were chatting among themselves, and a few individuals sat alone, reading or gazing out of the window.

Outside on the platform, people hurriedly moved about. Passengers searched for their assigned carriages, porters pulled luggage on trolleys, and vendors sold food and drinks. Anna felt sorry for those heading for carriages with no air conditioning. She heard the hue and cry of the people outside and the pungent scent of curry flowed in from the open doorway, making Anna nauseous.

Gita offered her water in a stainless-steel bottle. 'That's for you. I've got my own.' She pulled out another bottle from her backpack.

'What else have you got in there,' asked Anna, taking a gulp. 'It looks pretty full.'

'Just a few home-made snacky foods. It's a three-and-a-half-hour journey so we will need something to keep us going.'

The train departed promptly as scheduled, and once the air conditioning kicked in, Anna started to feel more comfortable. It took some time, but the queasiness gradually subsided.

The nearest city to Sonwadi village was Navsari. She calculated that they would reach there at midday. From Navsari, it would be a half-hour bus ride or a quicker taxi ride to the village. She estimated that they would reach their destination around 1 p.m. Gita had not bought their return tickets. Depending on how long they stayed in the village, they hoped there would be seats available on the train back to Mumbai.

'I spoke to my brother last night about our search for this family,' said Gita. 'He thinks we should ask where the fishing families live and make our way to that area straight away.'

'Is that how it works? Different areas for different occupations?'

'Not always, but it's usually like that. When people have something in common, they tend to live near one another, don't they? I found that in London too.'

Anna agreed. She looked out of the window and began to imagine her grandmother travelling in the same direction over six decades previously. She must have been extremely anxious, wondering what lay in store for her. Anna was anxious herself, thinking about what she might discover. Sitting back, she tried to relax by enjoying the passing scenery.

When they arrived at Navsari Station, Anna was pleased to see it was nothing like Mumbai Central. There were fewer people on the platform and things seemed much calmer. They disembarked and made their way to the road beyond the station concourse, where rows of taxis and auto rickshaws awaited. Not spotting any buses in the vicinity, Anna decided to opt for a taxi ride.

Sonwadi was only fifteen kilometres away and the drive was short and uneventful. As they left the bustling streets of Navsari behind, the landscape became increasingly lush with farmland stretching on either side of the road. For the first time since she'd arrived in India, Anna breathed in air that seemed fresh and clean. She wondered what the village would be like.

'I did a Google search for Sonwadi last night,' said Gita.

'What did you find out?'

'There are around nine hundred households there. And the population is something like three thousand.'

'Is that all?'

'Yes. It's a small village. That's good because it will make our search easier.'

It wasn't long before they spotted a road sign for Sonwadi written in both Gujarati and English. The driver slowed down when the road suddenly widened. Two-storey terraced houses lined up on both sides, elevated about a foot above the ground on a long stone platform. The narrow homes, made of brick and timber, featured small balconies and tiled roofs. Some looked old and a little rundown, while others were well maintained. A few with blue or green painted walls stood out. There were shops on the ground floor and homes above them. The stores had open shutters made of wood or metal. Anna imagined these were closed at night for security.

The scene on the tarred street was surprisingly calm. Only a few people went in and out of the stores while cows and dogs ambled along, and scooters stood stationary outside some stores. Further along, smaller roads crossed the main street, leading to what looked like more houses. They rounded a sharp bend and a bus appeared, going in the opposite direction. There seemed to be a lot of people on it. Anna thought it probably went from village to village and ended up in Navsari.

Up ahead, Anna read a sign for the bus terminus. A few people sat in the shade of a covered area with small cloth bags on their laps. The driver stopped and parked a short distance away from them. When they got out of the taxi, Anna was conscious of the fact that every one of the seated travellers was staring at them in open curiosity. She pulled Gita's *odhani* tighter around her shoulders. They asked the driver for directions. He wiggled his head and said a few words before turning his taxi round to drive back the way they'd come.

'He doesn't know this village,' Gita explained. 'But he did say there's a river somewhere nearby. We should find out where that is.' She looked up and down the road, shaking her head. 'I don't know which way to go. Let's walk to the shops and ask someone there.'

As they headed towards the bend in the road, Anna's thoughts turned to Indira again and wondered if she was walking in her footsteps. She imagined a young girl living nearby, going to the shops, buying groceries and taking them back to whoever she lived with. She must have been very unhappy, living in a place so different from her home city. Anna hoped that as time went by, she'd have become more settled. If she was still alive, perhaps she now had a family of her own who looked after her.

On the other hand, this could just be a wild goose chase, with Indira living somewhere else completely. What had happened to her? Where was she? And how was she?

'Anna, be careful!' Her reverie ended abruptly as she stopped in her tracks to see what Gita was pointing to. It was a lump of wet cow dung directly in front of her feet. One step forward and her sandal would have been covered in it.

'Ugh! Disgusting.' Moving back quickly, she wrinkled up her nose. A peal of laughter rang out and Anna saw that Gita was finding the near accident hilarious. Anna rolled her eyes. 'It's not funny.' But seeing Gita chortling in hysterics, Anna had to join in.

'You have to watch where you're going in India,' said Gita when she was eventually able to speak. 'And here in the countryside, we'll be seeing a lot more of this stuff.'

'Isn't cow dung supposed to be collected up and used for fuel or plastering walls or something?'

'It is. But this dung has just been deposited.' Gita grinned and pointed to a cow sitting at the side of the road a few metres in front of them.

Anna took hold of Gita's arm and walked round the offensive dung. 'Come on. Let's get on with our mission.'

It didn't take long to confirm that fishermen *did* live in houses near the river which was only a short walk away. Gita spoke to several shopkeepers, asking if they knew a woman called Indira who had arrived in the village from Africa in the 1950s. It was a long shot, but the question had to be asked. Unsurprisingly, no one had heard of her.

They began to walk down one of the side roads that they were told led to the riverside. The time was 12.45 p.m. and Anna was beginning to feel peckish.

'Shall we have something to eat?' she asked.

'Yes. The man said there was a nice seating area by the river. Let's find that and have a picnic. There's plenty to eat in my bag.'

The side road was wide and tarred but full of dust and dirt. More cows and dogs lazed under the shade of trees. Anna noticed that the houses were different from those on the main street. These were single-storey detached homesteads. Some were small with tin or thatched roofs, while others were larger brick houses painted in white or bright colours. A few looked quite palatial. As they walked along, Anna could smell the spicy aroma of curry in the air.

'It's lunchtime,' Gita reminded her. 'Most people go home to eat and have a short rest.'

'Oh. That's why no one's around. We shouldn't be out at this time of day either. It's too hot.' Anna quickened her steps to stand under a tree. She felt as if she were melting. Thankfully, there was more tree cover as they walked further towards the river. They seemed to be going down a gradual slope. Close to the end of the road, a slight breeze touched Anna's cheeks.

'I can smell the river,' said Gita. 'It can't be far now.'

Anna sniffed the air. Sure enough, there was a faint musty scent of water and riverside vegetation. There was also the distinct smell of fried fish emanating from some of the houses they passed. Anna could feel her stomach rumble with hunger.

Straight ahead was a row of individual houses separated by leafy trees and narrow footpaths. Through the gaps, they could see the unmistakable sparkle of water. Some of the homes were shabby little shacks while others were fairly large and sturdy. They all backed on to the riverside.

Gita looked on both sides of the dirt road in front of them. She pointed to the left. 'Let's go this way. It seems to be heading downwards.'

She was right. Within two minutes, they were at a square concreted area right beside the river. Shaded by tall trees with thin trunks, the square had metal benches along two sides. The riverbank was a mixture of dry mud and grass. It dropped steeply to the riverbed. On one side of the square, wide steps led down to the water in a gentler slope.

They walked up to the edge and looked down from a height of about a metre. Anna was disappointed. The water level was very low. The valley was wide, but only the middle section had any water. Exposed below both banks were rocks, stones and pebbles.

'January is the dry season,' said Gita. 'Everything will change when the rains come. This will be a wide flowing river at monsoon-time.'

In the distance, down by the waterline, Anna could see a small group of women in brightly coloured saris squatting beside what looked like rattan baskets. 'What are they doing?'

'Those are the *dhobi*-women. They earn their living by washing people's clothes.'

'They have to go in a long way.'

'I'm sure they are used to it.' Gita looked around. 'It's not a bad life out in the open like this.' Her expression became wistful. 'I grew up in a small village and sometimes, I do miss this slow way of living.'

'Do you think you might leave Mumbai one day?'

Gita shrugged. 'Who knows what lies in the future? Right now, I think we should eat. Come.'

There was no one else around, so they selected a bench and sat down with Gita's backpack between them. She pulled out a tiffin carrier and separated the different compartments. 'I've got tikhi puri, batetanu shaak, thepla, dhebra and patudi, all homemade. There's also dhana chutney at the bottom.'

'Wow! What a feast.' Anna took a swig of water before diving in, making appreciative sounds as she tasted each item. Licking her fingers, she relished the traditional Gujarati food, something she had not eaten in any Indian restaurants in London. She made a mental note to root out these hidden gems when she returned home.

They were almost finished with their meal when the *dhobi*-women climbed up the steps and walked across the square with their baskets of washed clothes. There were four women in their twenties or thirties. As they walked by, they stared at Anna and Gita with intense curiosity. Seeing two strangers having lunch at the riverside was clearly not a common occurrence. Anna gave them a friendly smile.

'Do you think we could ask them if they've heard about Indira?' asked Anna.

Gita shook her head. She didn't think there was any point because they looked very young.

Anna persisted. 'It's worth a try, don't you think? They seem very friendly, and they might know something.'

Gita shrugged her shoulders and pressed her lips together as if to say she didn't agree, but she would have a go. She stood up and walked over to them. They stopped to hear what she had to say. Putting down their baskets, they peered at Gita looking quizzical. They didn't seem to mind answering her questions. There was a lot of shaking and wobbling of heads and excited chatter. They seemed eager to engage and talked over one another. Eventually one of them let out a little cry and they all turned to Anna and wiggled their heads with huge smiles on their faces.

Picking up their baskets, they waved at Anna, said a cheery goodbye to Gita, and went on their way, smiling and talking in loud excited voices. Gita stood where she was for a moment, watching them. Then she walked back to the bench.

Anna looked at her face and knew straight away that she had something important to say. 'What is it?' she asked, her heart skipping a beat.

Gita's eyes were sparkling. 'One of those women said something really interesting. It seems there is a family here that might know something about Indira. She said there's an old woman living nearby who we should go to. She used to be an English teacher.'

Anna was on her feet. 'Did she say where we can find her?'

Gita grinned. 'She did. Come on. Let's go.'

# Chapter 27

Two little boys were running around a patch of lawn in front of a gated house. It was situated on a road parallel to the one Anna and Gita had strolled down earlier. This was by far the nicest residence they had seen in Sonwadi. Painted in white, it was a house full of balconies. Three storeys high, it looked modern and well maintained. Each floor had a balcony with sleek railings. The stainless-steel tubular bars glinted in the hot sun. Concrete steps on one side led up to the wide tiled porch on the ground floor. Two windows and an open front door were visible from the road.

A short path from the gate reached up to the steps. It separated the lawn from a driveway on their left. Two scooters were parked in front of what looked like a garage with closed shutter doors. Shading her eyes with her hand, Anna gazed up and saw two sun loungers through the railings on the top floor. She realised it was a terrace open to the sky.

'Wow!' she breathed. 'I wasn't expecting anything like this in an Indian village. It looks like a villa on the Mediterranean coast.'

'It's not as unusual as you think,' said Gita. 'Sometimes people go abroad, make some money, then come back to build this kind of home for themselves or for their relatives.'

The boys had noticed them standing by the gate and ran up the steps calling for their mother. A young woman appeared from inside and peered out at them. Gita held up her hand and shouted a greeting.

Looking slim and pretty, the woman walked over with a questioning look on her face. She was clearly trying to work out whether or not she knew them. Wearing a casual blue *salwar kameez* and chappals on her feet, she came down to the gate and greeted them in Gujarati.

Gita began to explain who they were, gesturing towards the riverside and then to Anna. The woman gave Anna a polite smile.

'You are searching for someone?' she asked in perfect English.

'Yes. We were told you might be able to help.'

The woman nodded and opened the gate to let them in. 'Please come in. My name is Aditi.'

Anna and Gita introduced themselves and followed her up the path. The boys were back on the lawn. They looked identical in their shorts, tee shirts and open-toed sandals. Anna guessed they were twins aged around four years old.

Aditi led them into the house. They went through a wide hallway leading straight into a large kitchen. It was contemporary and Western-style, complete with all mod cons. The pleasant smell of fresh coffee followed them out to the back on to a covered veranda.

An elaborate garden swing, an outdoor table and several cushioned chairs were arranged around the stone tiled space. Anna and Gita took the swing and looked out at a flower garden with trees, shrubs and colourful flowerpots. It reminded Anna of her Uncle Peter's house in Harare. The set-up was very similar.

Aditi excused herself, then returned with ice-cold drinks on a tray. 'I hope you like limbu-pani? It's lemon-flavoured water.'

Anna took a sip. 'It's delicious. It's kind of you to welcome us like this.'

'It's the Indian way,' she replied with a smile.

'You have a nice house,' said Gita. 'Have you been here a long time?'

'I came four years ago when I got married.' Taking a seat at the table, she turned to Anna. 'You are looking for information about someone?'

'Yes. I've come to India in search of my roots. I've asked a lot of people and looked in many different places. Everything I've learnt so far has led me to this village. Some women at the riverside directed us to your house. They said there was an English teacher living here.' Anna paused for confirmation. Aditi nodded her head.

'I'm looking for a family with the surname Rajah.' Anna held her breath.

Aditi puckered her brows. 'Rajah? I'm sorry I don't know anyone with that name.'

'Oh.' Anna fell silent. She cursed herself for being foolish enough to think she had found the Rajahs so easily.

'May I ask what your surname is?' asked Gita with the utmost respect.

'It's Jhinwar.' Aditi was still thinking. 'I'm not from this village, but my husband is. He might know the name Rajah.'

Anna looked up. 'Do you think we could speak to him?'

'He's not here at the moment. He works in Navsari with my father-in-law in the family business.' She pursed her lips. 'I think you should talk to his grandmother. I can go and call her.'

'Oh.' Anna's pulse quickened. 'Your husband's grandmother?'

'Yes. She's been here a long time and might know someone with the Rajah surname.'

'We would love to meet her,' said Anna, breathing fast. He heart had begun to race.

As soon as Aditi left the room, Anna turned to Gita, her eyes glowing with hope. 'Do you think the grandmother could be her? Indira?'

Gita spread her hands in a gesture of helplessness. Anna waited with butterflies in her stomach. It wasn't long before Aditi returned.

'She's just coming,' she smiled.

Sitting forward, Anna asked in a hushed voice: 'What is the name of your grandmother?'

'Sharda-*ben*,' came the prompt reply.

Anna was crushed. Swallowing her disappointment, she gave Gita a tight-lipped smile.

A woman in a blue cotton sari stepped on to the veranda. Anna and Gita both stood up. '*Namaste*,' said Gita, palms joined together in respect. Anna did the same.

The woman was short and plump, wearing spectacles, with grey hair pinned back. Her round face held an expression of kindness and good humour. Anna guessed she was in her mid-sixties. Definitely not Indira who would be in her eighties. When they all sat down, Gita had a conversation with her in Gujarati. It was clear from their body language that Sharda-*ben* did not know the Rajahs.

Anna resigned herself to accepting defeat. After all that, they were not in the right place. She was about to say to Gita that they should leave, when they heard someone call from the front door. It was a man's voice.

Sharda-*ben* shouted a reply, and an elderly man came to join them. Aditi introduced him as her husband's grandfather, Shanker-*bhai*. Anna watched his face as he listened to Sharda-*ben*, his wife, explain who they were and why they had come to their home. He rubbed his chin. Plump and bespectacled like his wife, he was of medium height with a thick head of grey hair and bushy eyebrows. He sported a moustache that drooped on either side of his mouth. He took a seat and addressed Anna in English.

'I don't think there are any Rajahs in this village.' Looking into the distance, he pondered for a moment. 'But that name sounds familiar. I have heard it somewhere. Just can't remember where.'

Anna's heart skipped a beat. 'Could it be from Mumbai?' she ventured. 'There is a Rajah family there who told us they had distant cousins in this village. And we know that the cousins were from a fishing family.'

Shanker-*bhai* looked surprised. 'We also come from a fishing family. My father was a fisherman and we lived just down the road right next to the river. I think I know most of the fishing people from around here, but I've never heard of any Rajahs.' He mulled over the question. Anna could see he was trying hard to remember. Eventually, he shook his head. 'No. I don't know that name, not here and not in Mumbai.'

Anna turned to Gita with a question. 'What was the name of the grandmother? Mr Rajah's grandmother who had relatives here?'

Gita's answer was prompt. 'Mohini.'

Shanker-*bhai*'s face cleared up. It was as if the sun had come out from the clouds. 'Mohini? I know *that* name. Mohini was the matchmaker who arranged the marriage between my mother and father. They told me about her.'

'So you are related to Mohini?' Anna could hear the tremor in her voice.

'I don't think so. She was just a friend, I think. If we were related, I'm sure we would have met.'

Anna started to work things out in her head. The Rajahs in Zimbabwe had given her the address of their cousin Hemant Rajah in Mumbai. Hemant's wife had remembered that his grandmother Mohini came from a fishing family in Sonwadi. And now this man, whose father had been a fisherman in Sonwadi, remembered that someone called Mohini was the matchmaker for his parents. There just had to be a connection.

Hesitating, Anna asked the question that was burning a hole in her heart. 'Are your parents still with us?'

'My father died many years ago. But my mother is in good health. She lives here with us. Would you like to meet her?'

With a catch in her voice, she said, 'Yes. Very much.'

Shanker-*bhai* turned to speak to his wife. She nodded and gave Anna a smile. Shanker-*bhai* explained that his mother was having her afternoon nap.

'We will go check on her shortly. I'm sure she will be up soon.'

'Thank you.' Anna could hear her heartbeat pounding in her ears. She was desperate to know if she had finally found Indira. But she was afraid to ask the question that rested so heavily on her chest. With extreme effort, she leaned forward. 'Could I ask please . . . what is your mother's name?'

'She's known as Indu-*ben*, but her real name is Indira. Indira Jhinwar.'

For a moment, Anna felt nothing. It seemed as if all the air had been sucked from the room. The name Indira hung above their heads. Anna stared at Shanker-*bhai*. Then, with a sharp intake of breath, she clamped a hand over her mouth and sat back abruptly. Gita squeezed her other hand, her face a picture of concern.

'Is something wrong?' asked Shanker-*bhai*.

Anna gave him a rueful smile and apologised. 'No. Nothing's wrong. But can I just check: did you say your mother's name is Indira?'

Shanker-*bhai* was frowning. 'Yes, it is. But why . . . ?'

Anna put her hand to her chest. 'Before she married your father, where did she live?'

'She lived in Africa. Her father brought her to India to arrange her marriage.'

A low moan escaped her lips. 'Oh my God! I've found her,' she whispered.

Shanker-*bhai*'s frown deepened. 'I don't understand.'

Gita squeezed her hand again. 'Anna. I think you had better explain.'

Three pairs of eyes were looking at Anna with such intensity that she suddenly felt lost for words. She didn't know where to begin. Silently, she begged Gita to start.

Gita nodded. 'Anna is looking for her father's family. He was born in 1954 in Southern Rhodesia. After his birth, he was adopted, and he never knew who his real parents were. Anna has been searching for them and her investigations have brought her here, to your house.'

The Jhinwars looked confused. Aware that her story was going to be a shock to them, Anna's nerves were on edge. Filled with anxiety, she managed to keep herself calm and took over the story, speaking in a controlled voice.

'I live in London, but my parents are from Zimbabwe. I went to Zimbabwe and made some enquiries about my father's past and discovered that his mother's name was Indira Rajah. She had a baby in January 1954 when she was very young. Her father forced her to give the baby up, then brought her to India that same year. I believe the two of them went to the house of Mohini and Narayan Rajah in Mumbai. I don't know what happened to Indira after that, but I was told that her father returned to Africa without her.'

There was stunned silence in the room. When no one said anything, Anna continued. 'We came to Sonwadi in the hope of finding the relatives of the Rajah family or finding someone who might know something about Indira.' Anna paused again. 'From what we've heard, it sounds like we have found her; we have found who I have been looking for.'

Shanker-*bhai* gaped at her with his mouth open. His wife still looked confused. She was staring at Aditi for a translation, but Aditi was too stupefied to oblige. Anna stayed quiet to let the information sink in. It was a long time before Shanker-*bhai* broke the silence.

'Are you saying that you think my mother is your father's mother?' There was shock and disbelief in his voice. Anna pressed her lips together and gave a slow nod.

'And you think my mother had a baby before she came to India and that baby is your father?' He narrowed his eyes and spoke with a hard edge. 'That is impossible! My mother is not the person you are looking for.'

Anna bit her lip. The atmosphere in the room had become charged.

'I know this is hard to believe. And it's a shock.' Anna's voice quivered. She looked at Aditi who was now translating to Sharda-*ben*. In slow motion, Anna unfastened the gold chain round her neck and held it out in her palm.

'This is the only thing my father has from the time of his birth. It was left inside the blanket that was wrapped around him when he was abandoned as a baby. We believe it belonged to his birth mother.'

Everyone dropped their gaze on to her palm, but no one picked up the chain. Anna held it up with both hands leaving the pendant dangling. 'There is a name engraved on the pendant. Please, have a look.'

It was Aditi who took it from Anna and read the name. With a gasp, she passed it over to Shanker-*bhai*. He scrutinised the pendant, staring at it for a long minute. When he returned his gaze to Anna, she thought she saw a flicker of uncertainty in his eyes.

Keeping her voice low, she continued. 'Because of the inscription, my parents gave me Indira as my middle name. That is my link to the woman who gave birth to my father. My biological grandmother.'

Shanker-*bhai* let out a low growl. 'No. You are wrong. She is not your grandmother!'

Anna felt a pain in her throat. Panic tightened her chest. Reaching for her limbu-pani, she took a few gulps. He was upset and in a state of shock. She knew that. Her instinct was to apologise and walk away, leaving them all in peace. But she couldn't do that. This was too important. From deep within, she found the strength to go on.

'All his life, my father has felt alone and abandoned. All *my* life, I have known there was something missing. I need to fill in the gaps in our history. By some miracle, I have found Indira. I was so afraid it would be too late. But she is here, alive, surrounded by her children and grandchildren and even great-grandchildren. I can't believe I have found her.' She paused and looked deep into his eyes. 'Would it be so wrong to show her this necklace? If she says it's hers, then we will know for certain.'

Shanker-*bhai's* face darkened. 'I tell you, you have the wrong person.' His voice was low and stern.

Two sharp points of pain prickled behind Anna's eyes. She looked down and pressed her eyelids gently with her fingers. Her father's biological mother was resting upstairs. She was convinced of that. She had found Indira. But how was she going to get through to her? Anna knew she couldn't give up now.

The Jhinwars were talking among themselves. Aditi was translating for Sharda-*ben*, and there seemed to be an argument between the old couple. When Anna looked up, Sharda-*ben* had taken the necklace into her hands and was questioning her husband. It sounded as if she was remonstrating with him. His responses, which were loud to begin with, seemed to be getting weaker by the minute.

Eventually he looked at his watch and gave his wife a grudging nod. Closing her fist around the necklace, Sharda-*ben* stood up.

She gave Anna a searching look, then made her way back into the house. Without so much as a glance in her direction, Shanker-*bhai* followed his wife.

Anna's heart was pounding in her chest. She looked at Gita with a questioning frown. What was going on? Gita shrugged and returned the frown. Aditi took pity and explained. 'They have gone to show *Dadima* the necklace. If it is hers, maybe she will come down to meet you.'

Anna's anxiety went into overdrive. So much depended on the next few minutes. She was certain they were in the right place and the woman upstairs was her father's mother. But would she recognise the necklace? Would an eighty-year-old woman remember what had happened such a long time ago? Anna gripped Gita's hand and waited, her stomach in knots.

# Chapter 28

The sound of footsteps approaching the veranda made Anna and Gita flick their heads up in unison. With nervous expectation, they watched to see who would be coming through the back door. Hardly daring to breathe, Anna wondered if it would be Indira herself. But it was a new face. Anna exhaled slowly. A young girl in a grey *salwar kameez* stopped at the doorway and spoke to Aditi, speaking in a subservient manner.

'That's their housemaid,' whispered Gita.

Aditi answered the maid who then retreated inside. Almost immediately, the two boys came bounding out in excitement. They capered around their mother while she chided them gently.

'Looks like you have your hands full,' said Gita.

'Yes. But I have help so it's okay.' She persuaded the boys to return inside with the maid. They went quietly, giving Anna and Gita shy looks.

Aditi became serious. With furrowed brow, she addressed Anna. 'What you have told us is hard to believe. It doesn't seem possible for our *Dadima* to have that kind of past.'

Anna didn't know how to respond. Once again, Gita came to her aid. 'We understand how difficult this must be. But it is possible that your *Dadima* never spoke about her past because it was too painful for her.'

'Yes,' breathed Anna. 'Too painful. An experience like that would be traumatising for anyone, so for a young girl, it must have been devastating. Just to survive, she probably had to put it out of her mind.'

No one spoke for a while. Then Anna continued. 'What is she like, your *Dadima*?'

A slow smile came to Aditi's lips. 'She's a real character. She tells everyone she is eighty years young, not eighty years old. We are all very fond of her. The whole village. She used to teach English to children and adults from all around this area. Still does on and off. Her mind is as sharp as ever. She puts us all to shame with her memory.'

Anna breathed a quiet sigh of relief. The question of Indira's mental health condition had come up many times because of her age. Her mother, Dominic and Gita had reminded her that even if she found Indira, there was always the possibility that she would not remember anything about her past. But Anna had remained optimistic. Most of her elderly patients in London enjoyed good mental health.

'How many children does your *Dadima* have?' asked Gita.

'Three. Two sons and one daughter. Shanker-*dada* is her eldest.'

'Where are the others?'

'The daughter lives in Surat, a city not too far away. But the younger son is in America with his family.' She stopped and gave a short laugh. 'You know, we are five generations living together in this house. My sons have their father, grandfather, great-grandfather and great-great-grandmother all living under one roof.' Aditi grinned. 'That's quite an achievement, isn't it?'

They both agreed. Anna's mind was busy working out how that could be possible. If Aditi's husband was in his mid-twenties, his grandfather Shanker was probably in his mid-sixties. That was how old Anna thought he looked. If Indira had him when she was young, say twenty years of age, then it was quite feasible that in 2019, she would be around eighty years old.

Anna was starting to get nervous and anxious again. Her stomach was in knots thinking about what could be happening upstairs. At least fifteen minutes had gone by since the grandparents had left with her necklace. Why were they taking so long? They had not returned immediately, so Indira was almost certainly awake. Surely fifteen minutes was sufficient time to recognise her own chain and pendant? Why was she not coming down the stairs to see her right away?

As the minutes dragged on, Anna began to wonder if Indira was ever going to come down. Perhaps she did not want to rake up the past. If that was the case, she could easily say that the necklace did not belong to her. After keeping the secret from her family for so long, it would be distressing for her to explain what had happened before she arrived in India. The most distressing and painful part would be to admit that she had a baby when she was sixteen; a baby boy that she had left behind in Africa.

This train of thought made Anna feel sick. Her father's face flashed across her mind. He would be heartbroken if he heard that his birth mother was found but she was unwilling to acknowledge him as her son. It would destroy him. He would feel like he was being abandoned all over again. This was what Anna's mother had been fearful of all along. It was the reason she had been trying to stop Anna from going after the truth.

All of a sudden, she heard a flurry of footsteps approaching from inside. The sound of slippers slapping on the kitchen tiles grew louder then stopped abruptly. She looked up, and her stomach lurched. A ghost-like figure stood at the door, staring down at them, dressed all in white. Small and plump, she wore a white sari with a long-sleeved white blouse. Striking silvery hair framed a pale round face with silver-rimmed spectacles through which her eyes seemed enormous. They were wide open, darting from Anna to Gita and back again to Anna. Her lips formed a huge oval shape, as if she was saying a long silent oh!

'Who is Indira?' she asked in a tremulous voice.

Anna was struck dumb. This was Indira, her real-life biological grandmother. She could hardly believe her eyes. With a slow cathartic exhale, she raised her hand.

'Indira.' This time, the old woman whispered the name. Keeping her eyes fixed on Anna's, she took a few slow steps forwards. At her elbow were Shanker and his wife, both looking concerned. No one said a word.

Anna stood up but stayed where she was, unsure of what to do. For so long she had thought about finding Indira, but she'd never considered what would happen at the moment of the first meeting. She didn't know what to expect.

Indira dangled the necklace in one hand. 'Does this belong to you?' Her face was set into tense lines and her voice was hushed.

Anna puckered her brow. 'It belongs to my father.' She kept her voice low.

'Where did he get it from?' The question was urgent.

'It was left in the basket he was found in as a newborn baby.'

Indira gave a startled gasp. 'In a basket? Where was it left?'

'At Rukuvoko Church near Fort Victoria in Southern Rhodesia.'

Indira exhaled. 'What was the date when the basket was found?'

'Twenty-fifth of January 1954.'

Indira let out a low choking moan. She turned to face her son who was standing a few steps behind her. 'That is the correct date,' she murmured, holding out the necklace to him. 'I was wearing this on that day. My mother took it away from me and I never saw it again. I didn't know what happened to it. Until today.'

Shanker dropped his shoulders and sighed. Stepping forward, he took the proffered necklace. Anna willed him to look at her and admit that she was right. But it was clearly too difficult for him. He'd had a shock and he wasn't ready to accept the truth.

Indira came up close to Anna. Taking both her hands into hers, she gazed up at Anna's face with a searching expression. Anna returned the gaze. It was as if there was no one else in the room. It was just her and Indira. A tightness gripped her throat and her eyes filled with tears. Almost a head taller, Anna stared down at her grandmother with blurred vision and raw emotion. She tried and failed to hold back her tears.

Indira's expression softened and a tender maternal smile formed on her face. She put her hands on Anna's shoulders and drew her into a warm hug. Leaning forward, Anna clasped her hands round Indira's small frame and pressed her wet cheek against Indira's head. She breathed in a faint scent of coconut oil in her hair. They stayed like that for a long moment, Indira sighing and Anna letting her tears roll down her cheeks. Eventually Indira moved back and held Anna's face in her palms, her thumbs stroking away the tears.

'My sweet Indira,' she said in a soft voice. 'They named you after me. I'm glad.'

Anna didn't trust herself to speak. There was a lump as big as a golf ball in her throat. Indira moved to sit on the swing, gently pulling Anna down beside her. Only then did Anna notice that Gita had moved away and was standing with the others, watching the two of them, looking tearful herself.

'Sit down, everyone,' said Indira, gesturing with one hand while holding on to Anna's hand with the other.

Gita removed a pack of tissues from her handbag and gave it to Anna before taking a seat. Giving her a grateful smile, Anna wiped away her tears and blew her nose. Seeing Gita do the same, they smiled weakly at one another with a mixture of disbelief, joy and relief. They had found Indira.

'This is my friend, Gita,' said Anna, clearing her throat. 'Without her, I don't think I would have made it here.'

Indira's smile broadened until it crinkled up her face. Anna noticed that for an eighty-year-old woman, she had only a few wrinkles around her eyes and mouth. Her brown skin was smooth and silky. She had a broad forehead, prominent cheekbones and a straight nose. Anna realised with a little pang that Mathew had inherited his mother's skin tone and facial features.

'Thank you for coming to look for me.' Indira sounded breathless. 'Never in a million years did I think this would ever happen.' Turning her gaze to the necklace in her son's hand, she shook her head. 'I can't believe I'm seeing that again. It was given to me when I turned eleven. I loved it and wore it all the time.' She closed her eyes and puckered her eyebrows. Then she groaned as if she were in agony.

She opened her eyes. 'It broke my heart when they took my baby away. I didn't even get a chance to hold him.'

Anna squeezed her hand. 'Please don't distress yourself.'

Indira took a deep breath, calmed herself and nodded. 'I have never spoken about this because my father made me swear on my mother's life that I should remain silent on this.' She turned to face her son. 'Shanker, I'm so sorry. I know how difficult this must be for you. But I was badly hurt, and I couldn't tell anyone. Not even your father. But he knew. He didn't ask me any questions and gave me all the support I needed. The kindest man that ever lived, your father. Without him, I don't know what I would have done.'

Shanker's face was creased with deep sadness. Anna could see that he was heartbroken for his mother.

Indira straightened her shoulders. She lifted her chin and spoke in a calm and determined voice. 'I hid my secret in the deepest part of my mind. I had to do that, or I would never have survived. My pain, my family and my whole life had to be buried when I came to Sonwadi. It was very hard, and there were times when I couldn't bear to be alive. But because my husband was such a good man, I managed to hold things together.' She paused and gave a short laugh. 'Another thing that kept me going was my private diary. I wrote down all my thoughts and feelings there, and somehow, it helped.'

In the hush that followed, Anna could feel Indira's eyes on her. There were dozens of questions on her lips, but all she could ask was: 'Do you still have your diary?'

Indira smiled. 'No. After my Shanker was born, I had no need for it, so I got rid of it.'

She looked at her son with an expression of heartfelt tenderness. 'I made a promise to myself that whenever I showered you with love, I would think about my firstborn son at the same time. It's silly, I know, but it helped me.' She turned to Anna. 'I missed your father so much that it hurt. But eventually, I had to lock him away in my heart and focus on my family here.'

Shanker's face was filled with ineffable sadness. He gazed at Indira with tears threatening to spill out.

Indira sighed then swept her gaze over everyone present. 'I will tell all of you the whole story. I think it's time. But first . . .' Putting her hand on her heart, she turned to Anna. 'First you must tell me about your father. What is his name? What happened to him? How is he?'

Anna took a deep breath. Slowly and softly, she began to tell Indira the life story of her firstborn son who had been taken away from her at birth.

# Chapter 29

Anna and Gita were persuaded to stay the night with Indira and her family. There was too much to say and too many gaps to fill in. They needed more than a few hours to catch up on all that had happened in the lives of both Indira and Mathew. By 5 p.m., it was clear that it was too late to make the journey back to Mumbai. Indira insisted that they had dinner with them, then stay overnight.

Gita telephoned her brother to let him know that she would be back the next day. The maid brought out cups of chai and plates of savoury snacks including tikhi puri and ganthia. Anna accepted the chai but was too keyed up to eat anything. Indira urged her to continue with her update on Mathew's life.

They were all astounded to hear that he had been left in a basket as a newborn. Indira was visibly pained. She explained she had no idea he was going to be abandoned in that way. She had believed her baby was going to a loving family. When Anna told them Mathew had been adopted by a kind couple who gave him a good life, she folded her palms together, looked up to the ceiling and uttered a quiet prayer of gratitude.

She was desperately sad to learn that all his life, Mathew had felt that his birth mother had not wanted him. 'You must tell him that I would never have given him up. I was forced to do it. When the midwife carried him away, I was stricken with grief. My father was a cold-hearted man. My mother and I were powerless against him.'

Anna was appalled to hear about the cruelty inflicted on Indira by her father. All of them sat in stunned silence when Indira described the horrendous treatment that she'd had to endure during her pregnancy and delivery. Shanker was in tears and his wife patted his arm and made sympathetic clucking noises. In a low murmur, Aditi translated for her.

Indira told them everything. Everything except the one thing that was hammering inside Anna's head. Who was Mathew's father? Anna's nerves were on edge while she waited for Indira to say his name. But she was noticeably silent about him. She seemed to be deliberately holding back on mentioning him. Anna was desperate to know. Who was he? What was his name? Where was he? She guessed that everyone wanted to know. But no one felt able to ask.

Indira spoke about her experience in a calm matter-of-fact manner, as if she was describing something that had happened to someone else. Anna realised that she'd had years to accept her lot and put her sadness behind her. She explained how naive she'd been at sixteen, her shock at realising she was pregnant, the fear her father had instilled in her and her banishment to the bushlands to have her baby delivered. Describing how she felt when forced to leave her home forever, she talked about her feelings of loss and grief. She had been abandoned herself. It had taken her a long time to accept her fate.

Anna took a breath and summoned up her courage to ask the question on her lips. But just at that moment, Aditi's husband and father-in-law came home from work. It was 6.30 p.m. After the introductions, they disappeared into the house. Aditi followed, saying she was going to feed the children and join the men for their evening meal. The rest of them were to eat later.

Indira had fallen silent. She looked down at her hands and twisted the rings on her fingers. Clearly, she was wrestling with herself over what she should say. Eventually she faced her son and offered him a smile full of affection and regret.

'You know, Shanker? Your father was a wonderful man. He was my saviour. He never ever asked me about my past. Many times I wanted to tell him, but he said he didn't need to know. When he died twelve years ago, he still didn't know any details.' Her eyes grew soft and misty.

Shanker's face contorted, tears welling up in his eyes. He nodded his head in sympathy.

Indira turned to Anna. 'Shanker's father didn't want to know, but you and your father *need* to know. Your father deserves to know. So I will tell you.'

Anna's heart started racing, feeling the weight of anticipation. Indira's intense gaze held her attention as she continued.

'I was sixteen years old when we had a visitor from India. He came to stay with us for a few weeks. He was very handsome, like a film star. We all fell for his charms, especially me. We liked each other and spent a lot of time together. But we made a big mistake. A mistake that cost me dearly. I found out I was pregnant *after* he returned to India.'

Anna felt a painful flutter in her chest, and the silence in the room became heavy. Everyone seemed shell-shocked. She struggled to comprehend the meaning of Indira's words. Mathew's father had been someone who had visited them briefly, and Indira hardly knew him. It seemed incredible.

With a furrowed brow, she watched Indira's face. Her intense expression had changed to something soft and relaxed. She continued.

'After the initial shock of realising I was going to have a baby, I was happy. I had no thoughts at all about giving up my child. Naively, I believed everything would work out. I thought that I would marry the father of my baby and together we would bring up our child.' Pausing for a moment, she shook her head in sorrow. 'I was young and very innocent. I knew nothing about the way of the world. I actually thought everything would be fine and I would live happily with my baby and the man who had come to visit. But that was just a dream. My father was never going to let that happen.'

A wave of sympathy washed over Anna as she listened to Indira's story, feeling humbled by the strength and resilience this woman had shown despite her traumatic experiences. With huge respect, Anna listened to Indira explain how she had managed to stay strong and not let her nightmare break her. Looking calm and resolute, she spoke about the way she coped after her baby was taken away from her.

In a gentle and tentative voice, Anna asked: 'Can I ask . . . what happened to the visitor? The man who stayed with your family?'

Indira's expression changed, her features hardening and her eyes turning cold. She pressed her lips tightly together, taking a long moment before responding in a calm and stoic tone, 'He died in a car accident soon after I arrived in India.'

An audible gasp went round the group followed by stunned silence.

'I'm sorry,' whispered Anna, eventually. She cleared her throat nervously before going on. 'What was his name? My father will ask.'

Indira directed her gaze at her with narrowed eyes. 'No.' There was a finality in her voice. 'That road is closed. No one needs to know his name. He was never told about the baby, and he died a long time ago.'

Anna blinked, taken aback by her strong and definite response. It was clear that Indira was firmly resolved on the matter. But Anna felt compelled to press for an answer. She opened her mouth to ask, but from the corner of her eye, she noticed Gita shifting in her seat. Glancing up, she saw Gita look at her pointedly and give a small shake of the head. Anna understood. It was not a good idea to persist on the subject at that moment. Reluctantly, she put aside her question. She would raise it at another time.

Changing the topic, Anna enquired if Indira ever saw her parents again.

Indira's face clouded over. Shaking her head, she exhaled noisily. 'Never. My mother would have been too afraid to disobey my father's orders. But I did hope my brother Laxman would come looking for me when he grew up. I hoped in vain.' With a deep sigh of sadness, she continued. 'I gave up hope.' She closed her eyes. When she opened them, she smiled and blinked. 'But now, here *you* are. My granddaughter Indira.'

Her loving gaze roved over Anna's face. She raised her hand and brushed a strand of hair away from her face. Then, suddenly, her expression changed, her eyebrows furrowing, and she gasped. 'Your father . . .' Her voice cracked. 'Will he ever forgive me?'

Anna gave her a watery smile. 'There is nothing to forgive. You didn't want to leave him. He will understand.'

Watching the concern fade from Indira's face, Anna spoke slowly and gently, suggesting, 'I know this is a lot to take in. But when you are ready, I can video call him so you can see him and speak to him yourself.'

Indira fiddled with her rings on her fingers. Anna could tell she was carefully considering what she should do. Eventually, she faced Shanker and gave him a questioning look. She wanted him to help her decide. But he shook his head with regret, clearly unable to help. Indira turned to his wife, Sharda-*ben*. Nodding sagely, she made the decision for her. In a gentle voice, she said something that seemed to satisfy Indira.

Indira turned to Anna. 'Seeing you today has been one of the happiest days of my life. What you have told me about your father has filled me with so much joy. To know he was brought up by kind people is a huge relief. But I am agonised about his difficult start, and his lifelong feelings of being abandoned. My heart is overflowing with so many emotions right now, I can't think straight. I need time to process all that you have told me.'

'I understand,' said Anna simply, watching the concern fade from Indira's face.

Indira spoke slowly and gently, suggesting, 'I want to see him, talk to him and tell him so many things. But after all these years, I have to prepare myself first.'

Anna reached for her hand and held it between both of hers. Bringing her eyebrows together, she explained that her father would also be in shock when he heard that his mother had been found.

Indira nodded. 'You must tell him that I want to meet him in person, to hold him and tell him how much I love him. He must never think that he was not wanted.' Her face clouded over. 'Do you think he might refuse to see me?'

Anna squeezed her hand. 'When he hears what happened and realises how much you loved him, I know he will want to see you. He is a kind, gentle and sensitive man. He will understand the agony you went through. But he will also need time. He is bound to be extremely emotional when I tell him your story.'

Indira drew a deep shaky breath and nodded. It was going to be a powerful moment when Mathew heard that Indira was alive and well. He would be moved to tears to hear how desperate she had been to keep him, and how much she loved him. Anna knew she would need to be extremely sensitive to his roiling emotions when she gave him the news.

# Chapter 30

Dinner was lavish with a wide variety of dishes laid out on the dining table. A delicious aroma filled the room. Aditi placed a little of everything on their plates and invited them to help themselves to the rotlis piled on a serving plate in the middle.

Tempting as it was, Anna found she could not eat very much. Her thoughts were focused on all that she'd heard about Indira and the suffering she'd experienced around Mathew's birth. Images flashed through her mind of Indira going into labour in the Zimbabwean bushveld, having her baby delivered by a local midwife then watching him being taken away from her, never to be seen again. Anna had been to the town of Umzuma and seen the place with her own eyes, so she could vividly picture the scene. She could only imagine how agonising and heart-breaking it must have been for the sixteen-year-old Indira.

After dinner, Anna and Gita were shown to a bedroom facing the back of the house. It was dark outside, but a light glowed on a small courtyard. There appeared to be an outhouse at the end of the property. Beyond that, more houses were lit up by electric lights and lamps. From the open window, the smell of cooking wafted over, and Anna could see people having their evening meals in many of the homes.

'You didn't eat much,' said Gita. 'Was the food too rich for you?'

'The food was great. But my stomach is in knots. I'm excited I've found Indira, but nervous about how I'm going to tell my dad. I also really want to know more about the man who is my dad's biological father.'

'I understand your curiosity, but I'm not sure it's wise to push for that right now. It might be too soon.'

Anna sighed. 'I guess you're right. It's Indira's personal story and up to her to share if she wants to. It may be too painful for her to talk about. I need to respect that. But my dad is bound to ask when I call him.'

'Are you going to give him the news tonight?'

'Yes.' Anna glanced at her wristwatch. 'It's 8.15 p.m. here so it will be 4.45 p.m. in Harare. I'll phone in an hour or so. He'll be at my Uncle Peter's house.'

Just then, there was a knock on the door and Aditi entered with two bath towels. 'I left some clean nighties for you on the beds. I hope they are okay?'

'They're perfect,' said Anna. 'It's very good of you.'

'Not at all. And I have a message for you, Anna. *Dadima* would like to see you in her room. Shall I take you?'

Surprised and pleased, Anna followed Aditi down a short passageway to a room on the opposite side to theirs. After Aditi let her in, she closed the door and walked away, leaving Anna alone with Indira.

She was sitting in an armchair near a balcony that overlooked the front lawn and gate. The glass door was open, allowing the night air to breeze in. Anna noticed a faint smell of coconut oil in the bedroom. The spacious room had a mix of minimalist and cosy elements, the white walls adorned with only a few photos. On one side of the room, there was a double bed, a dressing table, and a bedside table. On the other side, a modern office desk was filled with piles of books, magazines, notepads, and loose sheets of paper. An open laptop occupied a prominent spot on the desk.

'Pull that swivel chair over and sit next to me,' said Indira with a smile. 'And yes. I *can* use a computer. My grandson bought that for me and taught me. I write short stories on Word. Some of them have even been published.'

'That's wonderful. I would love to read them.'

'Maybe one day. But come. I need to talk to you.' Anna watched as Indira got up, closed the balcony door, and returned to her seat.

As they sat across from each other, Indira gave Anna a steady look, her expression solemn. She cleared her throat.

'I've been struggling with something for the last few hours. When I told you about the visitor who came to stay with us, the man who was your father's father, I wasn't entirely honest. I'm sorry about that, but I couldn't speak the truth in front of everyone there. My son Shanker would be horrified. It would shake up the whole family and I just can't do that to them.'

Anna frowned, wondering what was coming next.

'If your father hears the truth about this man, it will upset him too. It would cause him a lot of pain. He has suffered enough, and I don't want to put him through further torment.'

Anna's frown deepened. Her chest felt tight. She knew she was not going to like what she was about to hear.

'All my life, I have hidden this secret from everyone. It is a heavy burden to carry. But I learnt how to cope by locking it away deep inside me.'

Indira paused and stared at her with narrowed eyes before going on. 'Now you are here, it has all come back to the surface. After careful consideration, I've decided to share my secret with you because I think you will be able to handle it. It's also very important for you to know the whole truth. You deserve to know about the man who caused so much damage. But you have to promise you will never repeat what I tell you.'

It was as if all the air had been sucked out of the room. Anna nodded and waited with bated breath.

Indira held Anna's gaze with a fierce intensity. 'Mathew's father was my uncle. Yes, my own uncle; my mother's younger brother. *He* was the visitor in our house.'

Anna knitted her brow, not sure if she had heard correctly. She sat still, not saying a word. Indira continued to speak.

'My uncle was young and handsome. He came from India for a short visit. He was extremely nice to me. I thought it was because I was his niece, but he took advantage of my innocence. Do you understand what I'm saying? He took advantage. He forced himself on me.'

Anna bit her lower lip as she let this staggering revelation sink in. Then she gasped, bringing her hand up to her mouth, her eyes wide with shock. 'He . . . he raped you?'

Indira nodded. 'I blamed myself for years. I thought it was my fault. But I know it wasn't. He was a grown man. I was only sixteen and very innocent. It was rape.'

Anna grabbed Indira's hand. 'Oh my God!'

They sat like that for a long time: Indira in sober silence, Anna in shocked horror. She pictured a very young Indira being sexually violated by her own uncle, in her own home, where she should have been safe from harm.

After a while, Indira went into more detail about how the man gained her trust then sexually abused her. As if that was not enough, it was she who was punished most cruelly by her father. Indira had suffered intolerable injustice. She'd been betrayed by two men in her own family, first by her uncle, then by her father. And what of the uncle? A paedophile! He had preyed on his own sister's daughter. Anna felt a surge of revulsion at the thought of what he had done. The sour taste of bile rose up in her throat.

'I hate to call him my uncle,' continued Indira. 'But that's who he was. He was never told I was pregnant with his child. When I heard he'd died in a car crash, I was happy and very relieved that there was no chance of me ever seeing him again. It happened soon after I was brought to India.'

Swallowing hard, Anna pondered over the fate of this man who had violated Indira. He had continued to live his life with no punishment and no idea he had wreaked such havoc. But then he died in a car accident. He'd met his end in a sudden and brutal fashion. *That* had been his punishment. Anna was glad he was dead. He didn't deserve to live after what he had done to Indira.

'You see why we have to keep this between us, don't you?' said Indira.

Anna gave a slow nod. Mathew should never know that his mother had been raped. And he should never find out that his biological father was his mother's uncle. It would be too painful for him. To tell him was unthinkable.

'My father must never know the truth. He would be tormented for the rest of his life.'

Indira squeezed Anna's hand. 'This is distressing for you too. But I had to tell you. You went through a lot to find me. You never gave up. It didn't feel right to keep this from you.'

Anna puckered her brows. 'I am shocked, but I'm glad you told me.' She breathed in and blew out her cheeks.

Indira patted her hand and turned to stare out of the glass doors. They sat like that, in silence, for a long time. Anna tried to process what she had just heard. Her grandfather had committed a despicable crime. He had caused immeasurable suffering for Indira and her whole family. Because of his actions, both Indira and Mathew had endured years of unnecessary pain and distress.

Looking at Indira now, calm, composed, accepting of her fate, Anna felt a deep admiration for this woman who had suffered so much and yet survived. Putting her horrific troubles behind her, she'd made a good life for herself. Her resilience, willpower and strength of character shone through. Against all odds, she had managed to carve out her own destiny in a place she knew nothing about with people she had never met before. She was an inspiration.

'You know,' said Anna. 'I grew up with a strong understanding of my mother's black Zimbabwean heritage. But because my father didn't know anything about his past, I was brought up with no knowledge about Indian culture. I was always curious about that. I wanted so much to know about the Indian way of life. Without that, I felt like an unfinished portrait of myself. A part of my history was missing and it affected my confidence and self-worth. All my life, I've suffered with self-doubt and low self-esteem. It felt like a hardship. But when I think about it, I have no right to complain about that. Real hardship is what you have been through.'

Indira shook her head. 'We all have our demons, Indira. What we have to do is slay them and move on. It's not easy, but it has to be done.' She inclined her head. 'You came in search of something: your Indian identity. Is it too soon to ask how you feel now that you've found it?'

Anna gave it some thought before responding. 'I feel proud and privileged to be part of this family. To have you as my grandmother. To finally meet the Indira I have been searching for is a dream come true. I can't describe how happy I am to be piecing together the jigsaw puzzle of my life.'

'I'm happy too,' she said, then smiled with a mischievous glint in her eye. 'You don't strike me as someone suffering with self-doubt and low esteem. I think you are a confident and determined young woman. You tracked me down, didn't you? You set about looking for me and never gave up.'

Anna gave a short laugh. 'Maybe this journey of discovery has toughened me up a little. Who knows? Right now, because I've found you, I feel on top of the world.'

'Good. You must stay strong and never doubt yourself. Will you do that, Indira?'

Anna laughed again. 'Everyone calls me Anna, not Indira. But I like that you call me that. May I call you *Dadima?*'

In response, Indira rose to her feet. She walked to her bedside table and returned with something in her fist. Reaching for Anna's hand, she placed her gold chain and pendant on her palm. Then she gathered her into her arms. Anna stood up and hugged her back, holding her tightly, feeling an overwhelming closeness to this woman who she had been wondering about all her life. When they finally parted, Anna left the room with a strong sense of purpose. She was going to make sure her father understood how special his birth mother was.

# Chapter 31

Mathew answered on the first ring.

'Hello?'

'Hi Dad. It's me.'

'Where are you? We haven't heard from you since you reached Mumbai.'

'I did text you when I arrived.'

'But you didn't call again. Your mother and I were worried.'

'I'm fine. My friend is with me.' Anna hesitated. She looked across at Gita sitting on her bed, wondering how she should go on. 'I . . . erm . . . I'm not in Mumbai right now. I'm in a small village called Sonwadi.'

'Where?'

Anna took a breath. 'I'm in a place called Sonwadi. Listen, Dad. I have something to tell you. Something important.'

'Oh?' Anna heard the concern in his voice.

'Nothing bad. Don't worry. It's good news.'

'What is it?'

Anna lowered her voice. 'I'm going to tell you. But first . . . are you sitting down?'

'Yes. What's going on?'

An unexpected anxiety settled in the pit of Anna's stomach. Suddenly she was tongue-tied. Gita leaned over and pressed her hand on Anna's arm in encouragement.

'Erm . . . When I left Harare, you were very angry with me. You didn't want me to come to India. You didn't believe I would find Indira, your biological mother.' She paused and spoke in a lowered tone. 'Guess what, Dad? I've found her. I've found Indira. She's alive and she's well.'

Anna heard a sharp intake of breath, but no words.

'I'm here at her house,' she continued, keeping her voice soft. 'I've met her, and we have talked. I have a lot to tell you. But before I say another word, you must know one thing. Indira *never* wanted to give you away. You were taken from her by force as soon as you were born.'

Mathew uttered a low moaning sound. Anna thought she heard a sob. She waited for him to speak. But he seemed dumbstruck. 'Dad?' she called. Still nothing. Just the sound of his loud breathing. Then her mother called out. 'Give me the phone!'

'Anna?' Theresa hollered down the line. 'You've upset your father again. What have you said to him?'

Anna sighed. 'I gave him good news, Mum. I've found Indira. I can't believe I'm saying this, but I'm staying with her right now in her house.'

'What?' Theresa's voice was a mixture of shock and disbelief.

As briefly as she could, Anna gave Theresa an update on how she had found Indira and what had happened at the time of Mathew's birth. With sensitivity, she gave the explanation that Indira had given their group on the veranda. Theresa listened without interrupting. She was speechless, even after Anna finished talking.

'You still there, Mum?'

'Yes.' Theresa was clearly in a state of shock. 'Anna? Are you sure you've found the right person?' she asked urgently.

'Yes, I'm sure. All the dates and facts match up so there is no doubt at all. And guess what? She has confirmed that the necklace is hers. The name on it is hers.'

'Oh my God!' Theresa sounded stunned.

In a gentle voice, Anna continued. 'She's really nice, Mum. She didn't abandon her baby. Will you tell Dad?'

Theresa didn't answer straight away. Then she asked Anna to hold on while she spoke softly to Mathew. After what seemed like hours, not minutes, Mathew was back on the line.

'Hello?' His voice trembled. 'How did you find her?'

Anna went through the same update again, keeping it brief. When she finished, he drew a deep shaky breath and let it out slowly. He stayed silent on the phone. She asked if he was all right. He tried to give her an answer, but his voice came out like a strangulated squeak.

'It's okay, Dad. You're allowed to be emotional. This is a big deal. I'm still processing it all myself.'

Eventually, he verbalised what was on his mind. 'Is my father with her?' His question was almost a whisper.

'No. He died years ago.' Anna paused. 'Dad? I don't think we should ask her about him. It's too painful for her. We will need to respect that, Dad. She's been through terrible traumas in her life. When you hear how much she suffered all those years ago, you will understand why we'll have to leave that in the past.'

Mathew was mute again. Anna went further. 'What I can tell you is that she has confirmed her maiden name was Rajah. Her younger brother Laxman lived all his life in Zimbabwe. You didn't believe his story, but it was all true. He really was trying to unburden himself of the truth about his sister. He must have suffered too.'

Anna paused, hoping Mathew would have some questions. But he was clearly too shocked to say much. She continued. 'Indira was taken by force to India. I went to the address I was given in Harare and tracked her down to this village.'

Anna waited to allow Mathew to take it in. After a moment, he coughed and cleared his throat. 'This is . . . I mean . . . is it the truth? Do you believe this is all true?'

'It *is* true! Indira recognised her necklace straight away. We have evidence. I wouldn't have said a word if I thought there was no truth in all this. It seems unreal and it will take a while for all this to sink in. But it's good news. The best. I'll give you the details another time. There's lots to tell. But at long last you know what happened. Indira was devastated when you were taken away. It broke her heart. She wanted to know all about you, Gran and Grandad Kotze and our life in London.' Anna paused.

'Anna?' His voice became shaky and a little unclear. 'Does she . . . does she want to meet me?'

'She does!' Anna spoke with quiet certainty. 'She wants to meet you very much.'

Mathew let out a strangled cry followed by an agonised sob. Anna knew he was an emotional wreck. He was speechless. After a few moments, she continued. 'Dad? When you've had time to reflect, and you feel ready to have contact, I will connect you by video call. Would that be okay?'

There was a deathly hush. Mathew made no sound, yet Anna knew that neurons were firing off in his brain. She tried to calm him. 'One step at a time, Dad. There is no need to rush.'

Mathew made a guttural sound deep in his throat. He gave a little cough. Then, in a quiet voice asked: 'What is she like?'

'She's lovely: kind and wise and beautiful. You're going to love her.'

Mathew didn't respond. Knowing the emotional turmoil he must be going through, she promised to call him again soon to tell him more about Indira. Her mother came back on the line to ask a few more questions. Anna promised to answer all their questions over the next few days.

That night, Anna lay awake contemplating Mathew's reaction upon hearing that his biological mother had been found. She imagined him tossing and turning in his bed, picturing his first meeting with Indira through a video call. She was determined to call him again, every day if necessary, to share more about the wonderful woman who was his mother. The more he heard about her, what she looked like, how she spoke and what she'd said about her past, the more he would understand.

As for Indira, Anna had no doubt that she was also feeling anxious about the first meeting with Mathew. But she was strong and resilient. After all she'd been through in her life, she was probably better able to handle and manage her emotions. Reflecting on Indira's past, Anna felt a deep sadness for the young Indira who had suffered greatly at the hands of her uncle and father. Instead of providing protection, both men had caused her unimaginable harm. Anna wished someone had been there at the time to keep Indira safe.

~

The next day, Anna and Gita prepared to leave after lunch. When it was time to say goodbye, Anna was surprised to see tears in Indira's eyes. Throughout their conversations, this was the first time Anna had witnessed Indira becoming teary.

'Thank you for coming to find me,' she said, her voice breaking. She blinked, and the tears rolled down her cheeks.

Anna drew her into a hug. 'I *needed* to find you. Without you, I didn't really know who I was. By finding you, I feel I have found myself too.'

Indira didn't want them to leave. She held on to Anna, urging her to stay longer with them. 'You should be here. Not in a hotel. This is where you belong; with us.'

Aditi agreed. 'We want to get to know you. Please come back and stay with us until you go back to London.'

Anna promised to return within a few days. She explained that she had some work to do in Mumbai. With Gita's help, she planned to visit a few charity agencies. Nick had already sent her an email with details of various organisations that he thought she could approach.

As they set off for Navsari and then onwards to Mumbai, Anna found it hard to believe that just the day before, she and Gita had arrived in the village in search of Indira. She felt like a different person now. It was as if she had arrived in Sonwadi with a broken heart and was now leaving with it mended. Against all odds, she had managed to find Indira. The mystery surrounding her father's birth had finally been solved. It had been a long hard road but at last, Anna could rest easy. She looked forward to spending more time with Indira.

# Chapter 32

At Mumbai Central Station, Gita and Anna parted ways. It was just past 7 p.m. when Anna reached the hotel. As she made her way up to the room, Anna thought she would have a shower and go straight to bed. She was physically and emotionally drained after the exciting events of the last two days.

The next morning, Anna had a lie-in and went down for breakfast just before 10 a.m. She wanted to give Nick a call but knew it would be too early in London. Mumbai time was four and a half hours ahead. Deciding to wait a few hours, Anna whiled away the time by exploring the 5-star hotel.

In addition to the various dining outlets, the hotel boasted facilities such as a leisure, business and fitness centre, swimming pool and spa. As she walked around, Anna noticed the polished and shiny tiled corridors and hallways. The reception area was huge with several comfortable-looking bars and lounges. The wall on one side was adorned with framed photographs of Indian patriots such as Mahatma Gandhi and Subhas Chandra Bose. On the opposite side, wide windows looked out to the sea. The whole area had an ambiance of relaxed elegance.

It was a beautiful hotel. But Anna knew the guests milling around the reception area were not representative of the local populace. To understand something of the real Indian culture, she needed to step out of the hotel and mingle with the crowds where she would be surrounded by Indians from all walks of life. She resolved to go for a walk later that afternoon.

Anna sat on a sofa at the back of the reception and picked up a magazine from the coffee table. It was a Bollywood publication with photographs and articles about the famous stars and celebrities of India. She was aware of how popular they were both in India and abroad and how idolised they were by their fans.

In London, out of curiosity, Anna sometimes flicked through the subtitled Indian films on Netflix. They gave her an insight into the culture and traditions of India, but she was only too aware of how little she understood. Anna was determined to educate herself. She hoped to absorb as much as she could while she was in the country.

At exactly 1 p.m., she gave Nick a call. He answered straight away, saying he was about to leave for work. He asked if she'd had a chance to contact the charity organisations he had shared with her.

'No,' she replied. 'I've been too busy tracking down my biological grandmother.' She had confided in him about her quest and explained how important it was for her to trace her roots.

'Any luck with that?' he asked. Anna gave him the incredible news about finding Indira.

'Hold on, hold on,' he said dramatically. 'My jaw has just dropped to the floor. You've actually found your father's birth mother?'

'Yes,' laughed Anna.

'That's awesome! How? Tell me everything.'

Anna gave him a detailed account of how she and Gita had located Indira in Sonwadi. He was suitably amazed and impressed. 'I am really happy for you. I know how much this means to you.'

'It means the world. I'm going to spend the rest of my time in India with her. But Nick, you gave me a long list of charities. Do you have an idea of which one I should contact first?'

Nick considered for a moment, then said: 'I have a friend who might be able to help you with that. He's a doctor who runs a clinic in the Dadar area close to where I usually stay. He knows a lot about support agencies for the city's street kids.'

'Street kids?'

'You know, the orphans and children of families who live on the streets. The doctor's name is Anil Deshmukh. He'll be very happy to talk to you when you say you're also a medic and you want to help. I'll let him know you might call on him and forward you his contact details right now.'

'Thanks, Nick. That's a great help.'

As soon as the text came through, Anna dialled the doctor's number and got through to his receptionist. When she explained who she was and her reason for wanting to meet him, she was advised that as there was no appointment system, she would need to turn up at any time before 6.p.m and wait for her turn to be seen.

Anna went to the hotel reception desk to check the location of Dadar and find out how best to get there. She was advised to take a taxi which would get her there within half an hour. Deciding to have some lunch before heading out, she stepped towards the lifts. Before she got there, her phone rang. It was Gita, saying she was on her way to see her.

She arrived with an invitation from her sister-in-law for Anna to join them for dinner that evening. They were keen to meet her. Equally keen, Anna readily accepted. But she explained her need to go to Dadar in the afternoon.

'That's no problem,' said Gita. 'You can come home after you finish your meeting. Would you like me to come with you?'

'I was hoping you'd say that. Thanks, Gita. Shall we go upstairs for some lunch first?'

Gita had a better idea. 'Why don't we go out for lunch? You haven't seen much of Mumbai, have you? You should try the city's famous street food. It's really good.'

Anna agreed with enthusiasm. A walk around Mumbai was just what she needed. They left immediately on foot for an area familiar to Gita, fifteen minutes away from the seafront. Walking past crowds of people, they rounded a corner and came to a stop on a street full of stalls selling snacky foods. In front of the stalls and on the streets were lone hawkers frying fresh delights on huge vats of boiling oil in the open air. Gita pointed out the various dishes such as pav bhaji, bhel puri, pani puri, ragda-pattice and various chaats.

Anna looked around in amazement at the street packed with crowds of people enjoying their fast-food lunch. The air was filled with noisy chatter and the pungent aroma of spicy food. People were standing and eating right beside the large frying vats, unafraid of being splashed or burned by the hot cooking oil. Anna noted that the customers were from all different economic classes: well-dressed businessmen and women, students in tee shirts and jeans, and others in tattered clothes looking like the homeless on the streets. They all milled around together.

Anna and Gita chose their dishes, paying no more than 50 pence for each plate. Anna couldn't believe how inexpensive everything was. This was delicious freshly made fast-food at bargain prices. Holding their small disposable plates and spoons, they ate exactly like the locals, standing to one side of a skilful man making their masala dosas on an enormous hot frying pan.

After they'd eaten, Anna suggested they return to the hotel and take a taxi to Dadar to see Dr Deshmukh. They freshened up in her room before heading out. Once again, Anna looked out at the heavy traffic and the throng of people rushing about. When the street children came begging at the windows of their taxi, Anna had to look away. She couldn't bear to see their pleading faces.

The drive to Dadar didn't seem that long and the clinic was located very easily. They took their seats with the waiting patients, who glanced up at them, then turned away. They sat quietly on long benches facing the reception desk, looking tired and listless. Anna had seen the same faces countless times in her own GP waiting room in London. When people were ill, their fatigue and lack of energy were clear to see.

The room itself was basic but clean and tidy, with a few health notices adorning the walls. It was the same in the doctor's room. When it was their turn, they stepped into a small square room with a desk, chair and examination bed. The doctor stood up immediately to greet them.

'Good afternoon,' he said formally, extending his hand to Anna. 'I'm Anil Deshmukh. I believe you are a GP from London?'

'Yes,' smiled Anna. 'And a friend of Nick Gopal. This is my friend Gita. Thank you for seeing us.'

The doctor returned her smile. He was a small middle-aged man, neat and tidy in appearance. He had dark skin, jet-black hair and a pencil-thin moustache.

'Sorry for the wait. What can I do for you?'

'I'm interested in helping orphans and destitute women if I can. I'm told you know a lot about the needs of the street children in Mumbai.'

Dr Deshmukh nodded. 'There are a lot of them. I try to help where I can.'

From the first day of her arrival in Mumbai, Anna had been concerned about families cooking, sleeping and begging on the streets. She'd wondered if the state provided any health services for them. She worried about the children who put their lives in danger by walking up to cars on busy roads begging for a few rupees. Dr

Deshmukh told her that not all those children were orphans. Many lived with their parents who sent them out to beg. Anna asked him what happened to them if they became ill.

'They come to clinics like this one to access free healthcare. This is funded by a charity and run by volunteers like me. There are many clinicians providing this service.'

'What about education?' Anna asked. 'Do the children go to school?'

'Not mainstream schools, but there are charities offering free education in small centres here and there. Homeless children can attend these classes regularly or just drop in when they can. In some places, there are bigger centres offering this kind of help. The problem is, not all the street children take advantage of this support. Sometimes it is their parents who don't let them attend because they need them to go out begging.'

'That's really sad.' Anna pursed her lips. 'I was wondering about the orphans. Are there any children's homes for them?'

'There are. But not enough.' The doctor wobbled his head with sorrow. 'It is a big problem all over India.'

Anna asked if it was possible for doctors from abroad to work as volunteers in the children's homes. The answer was an emphatic yes. Volunteers were always welcome in institutions that cared for orphans. With a warm smile, he gave Anna details of how she could apply to be a volunteer medic. He assured her that her clinical skills were in huge demand and all charities would be very grateful for her help. He advised her to visit an orphanage he knew well called Ushapuri Children's Home. Anna accepted the contact details from him and resolved to reach out to the home the next day. After thanking him, they hailed a taxi and headed out to Gita's brother's house.

'If you start volunteering for a charity, does it mean you will be staying longer in Mumbai?' asked Gita, looking hopeful.

'It means I will be returning to London but coming back as often as I can.' She laughed out loud at the pure joy on Gita's face.

~

At Gita's brother's house, Anna was welcomed with warm hospitality. Her brother Jayprakash, her sister-in-law and their four-year-old son were all at home waiting to meet her. They invited her to sit down on the one armchair they had in their front room while they sat on chairs around a small wooden table. In broken English, Jayprakash thanked her for looking after his sister in London. His wife beamed at Anna, then hurried away to bring in the meal she had prepared. Her son helped her set the table.

Anna couldn't be sure, but it looked like they were sitting in a multi-purpose room for eating, sleeping and entertaining. It was clearly a small home but a happy one. They chatted freely in Gujarati to one another, though Gita translated whenever necessary. The food was a mini feast with two vegetable curries, rice, rotli, papad and mango pickle. To drink, they had salty lassi and bottled water. Only five days in India and Anna was already becoming familiar with authentic Indian cuisine and loving it.

Jayprakash asked if she'd had a chance to see the Gateway of India, Chowpatty Beach and the Hanging Gardens.

'Not yet. I'm going to be busy the next few days visiting some charity agencies, but after that, I'd love to see more of Mumbai.'

'I can definitely take you sightseeing,' said Gita, with a smile beaming on her face. 'And I don't need to ask where you're going after that.'

Anna chuckled. 'Yes. I'm going to Sonwadi to get to know my *Dadima*.'

~

That evening, alone in her hotel room, Anna made a video call to her father on WhatsApp. With his bushy eyebrows knitted together, he appeared anxious. She could tell he was still reeling from the shock of hearing that his birth mother had been found.

'Are you sure she wants to meet me?' he asked.

'She does,' Anna assured him. 'Don't be nervous, Dad. She knows this is difficult for you. She'll put you at ease very quickly.'

Mathew looked troubled. 'But what if . . . what if she asks me why I didn't try to look for her?'

Anna took a breath. 'Do you feel guilty about that?' She watched his face contort with pain.

'I should have tried. I should have tried a long time ago.' His voice trembled with self-reproach.

Very gently, Anna asked him why he hadn't. 'Were you afraid she wouldn't want to know you?'

Mathew drew a long breath before speaking. 'That was one of the reasons. But I was also worried about causing trouble for her. If she had a family that didn't know about me, I didn't want to get in the way.'

That was so like her dad, thought Anna, putting himself last.

'I just thought it was best to accept things and get on with my life,' he continued. 'There was a lot of anger in me, so it wasn't easy. I hated my birth parents for years. I wished them all kinds of bad luck. But it was my adoptive parents who made me see that I was only punishing myself by holding on to such feelings.'

'They were good people.'

Mathew nodded. 'They were very good to me. That was another thing. I worried that it would hurt them if I went looking for my birth parents. It seemed best to put it out of my mind and never speak of it.'

'But you know, Dad. It's never good to bottle things up. Did you talk to Mum about it?'

'When we were first married, yes. But we agreed to leave it behind and move on.'

'Then why did you name me Anna Indira?'

'That was your mother's idea. She said it was important to honour the person who used to own the necklace, even if we didn't know who she was.'

Anna sighed. Hidden under her mother's tough exterior, there was a heart of gold. Like the proverbial dog whose bark was worse than his bite, she always spoke to Anna in a hectoring manner.

'You know,' she said. 'I used to think she didn't like me much because she always seemed annoyed with me. I blamed her for a lot of my insecurities.'

Mathew looked astonished. 'No, Anna. That's not right. She loves you so much.'

'I know she does. But when I was younger, I thought differently.'

Separated by thousands of miles, they faced one another on their computer screens. After years of not expressing their innermost feelings, they finally shared their deepest emotions and with that came understanding. If only her dad had opened up a little. Going forward, Anna was determined to ensure there was better communication between them. She was confident things were going to improve for them all.

# Epilogue

*London, May 2019*

Anna and Fiona were waiting for Nick to join them at The Wisteria pub. Sitting at the back in the courtyard, they enjoyed the warmth of the sun on their faces. Anna gazed at the beautiful cascade of wisteria blooms gushing forth from the pub wall. She was enthralled by the explosion of purple.

'Isn't it amazing?' she asked. 'The blossoms are even better than last year.'

Fiona craned her neck to look behind her. 'Yes, but never mind the blossoms. Where is your other half? I saw him at work this morning, and he said he'd be here by five.'

Anna laughed. 'We're not joined at the hip, you know.'

'Really? How many times have you seen him since you came back from India?'

'I *have* to see him regularly because I'm helping him with his charity work! And he's late because he's caught up in the six o'clock traffic.' Anna took a sip of her wine and smiled at her friend.

'Has he told you what our duties will be?' asked Fiona.

'No. All I know is that there will be a lot of wealthy people coming to his Bollywood Night Extravaganza who will hopefully donate big sums of money. It's for destitute families in developing countries.'

'I'm guessing that will include orphans and victims of domestic abuse in India.'

Anna nodded. Fiona was aware of Anna's plans to support those two causes. 'I've already applied to be a volunteer at an orphanage in Mumbai. My plan is to spend a few months of every year in India.'

Fiona raised her eyebrows. 'How does Nick feel about that?'

'Fine. He's going to join me there whenever he can.'

Fiona smiled. 'You and Nick were made for each other. I never understood what you saw in that Tom Ingles. So glad you gave him his marching orders.'

Anna sighed. 'Seems like a lifetime ago that we split up.'

Just then, she saw Nick coming through the door to join them. 'Here he is . . .' she said and beamed at him as he swung his long legs over to sit beside her.

'Hey,' he said, giving her a peck on the cheek. 'Sorry I'm late. The traffic was murder.' Smiling across at Fiona, he greeted her. 'Thanks for joining us for this event. It's going to be huge this time and we're hoping to raise big money on the night.'

'Happy to help.' Fiona gave him a broad smile. 'What do you want us to do?'

'Lots of things.' He looked at their glasses. 'But first, let me get a drink. I'm parched.'

Anna slid off the seat. 'I'll get it for you.'

Leaving them chatting, she went inside to order his favourite beer. She'd met him enough times at The Wisteria to know which one he preferred. Walking back with his beer, she saw Fiona throw her head back and laugh out loud at something he said.

Nick took a big gulp of beer and smacked his lips. He began to talk in more detail about the fundraising event. Nick wanted them to meet and greet the invited guests, usher them to their tables and look after their needs throughout the evening. With deep pockets, the invitees would include bankers, investors, business tycoons and celebrities. It was important to pamper them so that they felt more inclined to part with their money.

After a while, the conversation shifted to Anna's grandmother Indira.

'What about your father?' asked Fiona. 'Is he coming out of his shell a bit?'

'He is. He was very nervous in the beginning. I first connected them up via video call the day before I left India. It was at my grandmother's house. Individually, they told me they were ready to meet online. Dad wanted Mum to be present when they met, and my grandmother wanted me with her. Just me.'

Anna paused to remember the initial virtual meeting between her father and grandmother. 'You know, since that first conversation, my parents have been video-calling Indira at least once a week. Dad's even spoken to his brother. That was a bit tricky because it was a huge shock for Shanker-*bhai* to hear that he had an older brother. It took him a while to accept that.'

They all reflected on that for a moment.

'So when are they going to meet face-to-face?' asked Fiona.

'Next month. The three of us are flying out together: Mum, Dad and me. They will return after four weeks, but I'm going to stay longer. There's no pressure for me to get back because I'm only doing locum work now. No more permanent job.'

Fiona grimaced. 'Don't stay away too long, will you? I miss you when you're not here. And Nick? How are *you* going to manage without Anna?'

Nick's dimples appeared below twinkling eyes. 'I won't have to manage without her. I'm going to join her there for two weeks at the Ushapuri Children's Home.'

'You jammy so-and-so!' laughed Fiona. She turned to Anna and teased, 'I thought you said you weren't joined at the hip?'

～

Three weeks later, the incredible and unimaginable moment arrived. It was the most emotional day of Anna's life. The taxi picked them up in the morning from the guest house where they were staying, and as they got closer and closer to Sonwadi, Anna could sense her father's mounting nervous excitement. She was acutely aware of how important this day would be for him.

They all sat in silence, as if in awe, when they read the village sign at the side of the road written in both English and Gujarati: SONWADI. Just seeing the name made Anna's stomach lurch. All three of them filled the car with a collective nervous energy.

When they arrived at Indira's home, Mathew and Theresa stood at the gate while Anna paid the taxi fare. Turning around, she saw Aditi hurrying down from the house, her twins following closely behind.

'*Namaste*,' she greeted before she reached them. She opened the gate and stood aside. 'Please come in.' Smiling widely, she told Anna that her *Dadima* was inside, eagerly awaiting their arrival.

They were led into the front living room with windows open to the lawn. Indira was sitting on a cream leather sofa, facing the door. Anna entered first then stood to one side to allow her parents to come through. Indira stood up and fixed her eyes firmly on Mathew. He stood motionless, looking dazed. Theresa was by his side, gripping his upper arm.

'My son,' whispered Indira. She took two quick steps forward, then stopped. 'My son,' she said aloud. 'You are here at last.'

Anna saw her mother nudge Mathew towards Indira. He walked forward in slow motion, his face contorted into a mixture of anguish and elation. His arms were like stiff rods by his side. Indira opened her arms wide and covered the space between them in a sudden rush. With a beaming smile, she hugged him.

Mathew wrapped his arms around her shoulders and pressed his cheek on the top of her head. Gradually, his nervous tension faded. His shoulders dropped and his face relaxed. He closed his eyes and swayed gently, now looking calm and serene. Anna blinked away tears as she gazed at her father and grandmother locked in an embrace for what seemed like an eternity.

When finally they moved apart to look at one another, Indira said in a soft and gentle voice: 'I always loved you, son. Always. Welcome home.'

# ACKNOWLEDGEMENTS

Having an idea and turning it into a book is not as easy as it might seem. It is a challenging and solitary experience. But it is also extremely rewarding and satisfying when it's done. I am hugely grateful to a number of individuals who helped me through the long and demanding process of writing and having a novel published.

Firstly, I'd like to thank my agent Kemi Ogunsanwo from the Good Literary Agency, without whom I may never have become an author. It is because of her encouragement that I have reached for my dreams and aimed for the stars. Thank you, Kemi, for being there for me.

Special thanks go to my extraordinary editor, Victoria Oundjian at Lake Union Publishing. I owe her an enormous debt for her generous advice, keen insight and amazing vision throughout the writing of this novel. Her belief that I had something valuable to share kept me going through all the periods of self-doubt, setbacks and uncertainty familiar to any writer.

I am also grateful to my lovely development editor, Salma Begum. Her empathy with my characters was truly amazing. By helping me tighten and polish my manuscript, she has made my story come to life.

There are many others at Lake Union who have helped make this novel shine, such as Victoria Haslam, Sadie Mayne and Swati

Gamble. A big thank you to them all. Thanks also to my cultural sensitivity reader, Helen Gould. Her advice on how to portray the mixed-race experience was invaluable.

Constructive criticism from Rosie Canning and Carol Sampson from The Peartree Writers group ensured that I did not go overboard with my descriptions and dialogue. And my friends in Zimbabwe, Shobna Chakravati and Beejal Madhvi, made sure my protagonist went to the right places to look for her missing history. For details of the house in Sonwadi, my cousin Jayanti Kalidas gave me all the information I needed to picture my heroine's life in her new environment. I am immensely grateful to them all.

And finally, my family. The last few years have been a very busy time for us. But through it all, their constant support and encouragement has kept me going. To each of them, I say a special thank you.

Read on for an exclusive chapter from Vasundra Tailor's debut novel, *The Secret of Elephants*

# PROLOGUE

Her eyes burned with unshed tears. She fought to keep her emotions in check as she held him close, rocking gently on his tiny bed. He felt limp in her arms, tired after being poked and prodded in the doctor's surgery. The words kept rolling around in her head. *Epilepsy. My son has epilepsy.* Visions of him suffering debilitating seizures flared across her mind. It was too much to bear.

'Nirmala! What is the matter with you? Can't you hear me calling you?' She flinched at the acidity in her husband's voice and the boy woke up with a start.

'It's all right, my *dikra*,' she whispered. Clearing her throat, she turned to her husband: 'Ajay. The doctor says Varun has a very serious condition. He is having epileptic fits and needs special medicine. He might need it his whole life!'

She watched him frown as he took this in. Then he spluttered, 'What nonsense is this? The doctor is talking rubbish. Varun has never had a fit. He is just a lazy five-year-old good-for-nothing boy who doesn't want to talk. That's all.'

Nirmala reached for a single sheet of paper. Unfolding it, she read the three words written in neat block letters. 'The doctor called it Childhood Absence Epilepsy.' She looked at her husband pleadingly, hoping that for once he would listen and try to understand. 'You know how he stops what he is doing and goes into a trance. That is a type of epilepsy. We have to get his medicine today.' Trying to stay calm, she asked him for some money.

'You think rupees grow on trees?' His nostrils flared. 'How much do you think I earn stitching sari blouses for the snotty-nosed women of this town? You want rupees?' He leaned forward until his face was level with hers. 'Well, you know where you can get them from.' With eyes narrowed, he glared at her for a moment before whirling around and marching out of the room and house.

Varun trembled and buried his face in Nirmala's chest. She stroked his back and cooed softly in his ear. Not for the first time, she wondered what she had done in her previous life to deserve such an unreasonable husband. If only she had not rushed into marriage.

Stop that, Nirmala told herself. What was done was done and she had to make the best of things. She must not let him intimidate her. But that was easier said than done, especially when it came to matters of money. She remembered how quickly he had flown into a rage when she'd last asked for some. The topic always brought out the worst in him because they never seemed to have enough, even to feed their small family properly.

Varun felt hot and clammy in her arms. She wished the room was cooler and more comfortable, as it used to be when she was little. The ceiling fan had broken down years ago and it had never been fixed. She looked around the small, dark windowless room. On one side, it led to the kitchen, and on the other, it opened out to the front room. The only air and light that came into the house was from this room, which doubled up as Ajay's sewing room and their bedroom. The window and front door opened out to their small porch, which housed her treasured *jhula* swing. Nirmala decided to carry Varun outside.

'You love this *jhula*, don't you, my *dikra*?' she crooned as he lay on the cushions with his head on her lap. As always, she thanked her late father for having the *jhula* built all those years previously. Most people had these at the entrance of their homes, but hers was special, made of solid wood, suspended from the ceiling on four heavy chains. She used to love sitting there as a child, her beloved parents on either side of her.

The afternoon sun was scorching. The porch roof afforded a welcome shade at that time of day. February was meant to be a winter month, but here in the state of Gujarat, Nirmala felt that most days of the year were either hot or unbearably hot. She kicked off her slippers, removed the *odhani* from her neck, and re-tied her long brown hair into a knot further up the back of her head. Even in a thin cotton *salwar kameez*, she was sweating.

There were very few people in the street and Nirmala was glad of it. She was in no mood to return greetings from cheery neighbours or respond to hawkers and street vendors. She watched the few auto rickshaws and scooters buzzing by, leaving behind a trail of dust which tickled her nostrils. There was the usual steady stream of cows and calves strolling along without a care in the world, happy in the knowledge that no one would hurt them. They were a nuisance on the busy roads, where everything had to stop for them. But here in Golwad Street, they were a soothing sight.

Several women walked past carrying bags full of fresh vegetables from the market up the road. They looked at her enviously as she sat in the shade while they sweltered under the blazing sun, wearing brightly coloured saris with the ends tied neatly around their waists. A food seller pulled his stall on wheels in the opposite direction, no doubt on his way to trade at the market. The smell of spicy onion bhajiya and khaman dhokra came wafting through from his wagon, making her mouth water. She considered what she might cook for their evening meal. With a sigh, she knew it would have to be daal and rice again.

Varun twitched in his sleep. Nirmala looked at her beautiful little boy with his curly brown hair, smooth dark skin and perfect features. He was small for his age and thin. A quiet, sensitive child; full of curiosity about the world around him. But recently he had shown signs of something being not quite right. She had noticed that occasionally, right in the middle of a sentence, he would suddenly freeze and stare blankly into space. It was worrying how he would not respond for up to a minute, and afterwards, not even be aware that he had gone into a trance.

Nirmala was terrified that without proper care and treatment, this might develop into full-blown seizures. She could not bear the thought. Somehow, money would have to be found to pay for the treatment. If Ajay would not help, what was she going to do? Her heart began to race. Realising she was beginning to panic she took a deep breath. Think logically, she told herself, and consider what could be done.

She mulled over what Ajay was alluding to. She knew only too well what he meant. Whenever they were short of money, he would put pressure on her to go cap in hand to her father's rich sister, who lived across the road. But Nirmala knew she would get no help from her Aunt Jasumati. Only humiliation. The memory of Jasu-*foi*'s scathing attack flashed through her mind.

'Don't come to me for handouts, Nirmala. Tell that lazy husband of yours to get off his backside and do some proper work.'

That was the first and last time Nirmala asked her for help. She had too much pride and self-respect to ask again. But Ajay had no such feelings. He had gone to her himself several times, but always returned with hands empty and a face distorted with fury.

'You are a stubborn donkey. Go and get some money from your high and mighty Jasu-*foi*. For God's sake!' He always spat out Aunt Jasu's name as if it tasted bitter in his mouth.

Nirmala stroked Varun's hair absent-mindedly while they rocked back and forth. She looked up at the magnificent four-storey mansion standing opposite her house. It was a brick building, painted a soft sky blue, with balconies on every level stretching across the width of the mansion. Colourful ornate decorations embellished the front of the balconies. Once again, Nirmala marvelled at the words etched in an elegant font across the facades of the second- and third-floor balconies: SUPARNA MANSIONS 1952.

'When it was built, it was the tallest and most iconic building in Navsari,' her father had told her when she was a child swinging on the *jhula*. 'Your grandfather Harilal-*dada* was very proud of it, you know.'

'But why is it all broken now?' she had asked. He had never given her a proper answer. The building looked even worse now.

Why was her aunt letting it go like this? It was in an appalling, dilapidated condition, with paint peeling, walls crumbling and stonework looking dirty and decayed. There must be more than enough money to pay for the building's maintenance. The apartments on the top two floors where Jasu-*foi* lived with her family were testament to this. They were lavishly decked out with expensive furniture and fittings. There was also the regular income from the rent paid by all the tenants living below.

Nirmala remembered her father saying he had been very happy living there when his father Harilal had been alive. It was he who'd built the mansion that was now owned by Nirmala's aunt. Her father had often told her that he had been a kind and generous man who would have been a loving grandfather to her.

'Did you have a lot of money, Pappa?' Nirmala had asked.

'Yes, *beta*, but money isn't everything. It doesn't always make you happy. Remember that.'

As she gazed at the mansion, Nirmala could not help wishing she did have some money. A worm of resentment worked its way into her heart and she swallowed saliva that tasted warm and sour. Why couldn't she have a small share of the family fortune? Jasu-*foi* had plenty and could afford to be a little generous. But she was mean and unfeeling, very different from her one and only brother, Suresh, Nirmala's father.

The thought of her father made Nirmala smile. He had doted on her, always bringing home special treats when she was little. Her mother's gentle chiding came to mind.

'Suresh! You must stop spoiling her.'

Nirmala wished she could spoil her own child from time to time. Looking up at the mansion, she pictured her father playing happily with his siblings in lavish surroundings. Why had he turned his back on such a life of luxury and privilege? All she knew was that he'd argued with his mother just before his wedding and walked out of the house forever.

Varun stirred and reached up to touch her cheek. 'I'm thirsty, Mumma.'

She kissed his hand briefly before getting up to fetch a cup of water from the kitchen. He sat up and drank it all in one go. Nirmala was relieved to see that his face was no longer flushed, and he seemed altogether better than before.

'I saved some jalebi for you.' She laughed when she saw his face light up. Her friend Hema had dropped by the day before with a bag full of sweetmeats for them. Nirmala gave Varun the bag and watched him pick out his favourites: yellow jalebi, pink coconut barfi, green halva and orange laddus. He took small bites with relish.

Her thoughts returned to the problem at hand, and she wondered if she might borrow money from Hema yet again. She knew her friend would never deny her a loan, as they had grown up together and felt more like sisters. They'd helped each other out countless times. She remembered how, when they were little, Hema's family had battled with money worries. But now the tables had turned and Hema was earning a good salary as a schoolteacher.

Nevertheless, Nirmala did not like to ask her. Reluctantly, she looked down at her mother's diamond-encrusted gold ring on her finger. Perhaps she should pawn it again. It always fetched a lot of ready cash. But could she really risk losing this precious memory of her parents? Nirmala felt sick at the very idea.

Another thought flashed through her mind, unbidden, which made her catch her breath. *I will always be there for you.* That's what he had said: her dearest love. Not a day went by without her remembering how it used to be. But no. Nirmala pushed all thoughts of him away. She would not allow herself to go down that painful road again.

'Mumma, shall I leave the last ones for Pappa?'

'No, *dikra*. This is all yours.' She watched him hesitate, before dipping into the bag for more. Her beautiful and generous son. He deserved so much more. It broke her heart to see him go without. Tears were beginning to prickle behind her eyes. She fought them away and forced herself to be strong. I will get through this, she told herself firmly.

A sudden thump on the porch startled her out of her despair. Ajay was leaning against the door, staring at them grim-faced.

'You're back.' Nirmala forced a smile on her face.

For a moment, he stood silent and motionless; statue-like. Then he walked forward and thrust a wad of notes into her hand.

'I got this from people who are owing me. Don't ask me for any more.' Bending down to look his son in the eye, he frowned and said in a stern voice, 'You must get better quickly. Rupees don't grow on trees, you know.' Then, making no attempt to soften his words, he walked away to his sewing machine.

Nirmala gave Varun a reassuring smile. She counted out the rupees in her hand and felt immense relief. He could start his treatment today. But even as she enjoyed this happy thought, she felt a nagging tug in her stomach. With all their expenses, how were they going to afford the long-term costs? She looked up at the mansion again and whispered to herself, Why did you give it all up, Pappa? Why is Jasu-*foi* so selfish? What happened between you and your mother?

# ABOUT THE AUTHOR

*Photo © 2020 Jodine Rianna Williams*

Vasundra Tailor, bestselling author of the novel *The Secret of Elephants*, was born in India and raised in Zimbabwe when it was called Rhodesia. She is a qualified pharmacist who completed her Masters in Pharmaceutical Microbiology at the University of Strathclyde. After a long career in the NHS, she is now indulging in her passion for reading and writing novels. In 2019 she received the Mo Siewcharran Fiction Competition runner-up prize for her first novel, and in 2023 she was awarded Student of the Year from The Writers Bureau. Based in London, Vasundra loves meeting people from diverse backgrounds and learning about their individual journeys in life.

You can follow Vasundra on Instagram and Twitter @vasundrajay.

# Follow the Author on Amazon

If you enjoyed this book, follow Vasundra Tailor on Amazon to be notified when the author releases a new book!
To do this, please follow these instructions:

## Desktop:

1) Search for the author's name on Amazon or in the Amazon App.
2) Click on the author's name to arrive on their Amazon page.
3) Click the 'Follow' button.

## Mobile and Tablet:

1) Search for the author's name on Amazon or in the Amazon App.
2) Click on one of the author's books.
3) Click on the author's name to arrive on their Amazon page.
4) Click the 'Follow' button.

## Kindle eReader and Kindle App:

If you enjoyed this book on a Kindle eReader or in the Kindle App, you will find the author 'Follow' button after the last page.